THE ALIEN FELT THE FIRST TENUOUS PULSING OF ANTICIPATION.

He lay quietly, watching the small square lights of windows against the snow, thanking the Unexplainable that matters had been so devised that he would not have to venture out into the miserable cold.

Presently an alarming thought struck him. These humans moved with uncommon speed for intelligent creatures. Even without devices, it was distinctly possible that they could be gone before nightfall. He could take no chance, of course. He spun more dials and pressed a single button, and lay back again comfortably, warmly, to watch the disabling of the colonists' ship. . . .

SOLDIER BOY

MICHAEL SHAARA

A TIMESCAPE BOOK
PUBLISHED BY POCKET BOOKS NEW YORK

Another *Original* publication of TIMESCAPE BOOKS

A Timescape Book published by
POCKET BOOKS, a Simon & Schuster division of
GULF & WESTERN CORPORATION
1230 Avenue of the Americas, New York, N.Y. 10020

ISBN: 0-671-83342-1

First Timescape Books printing March, 1982

10 9 8 7 6 5 4 3 2 1

ACKNOWLEDGMENTS

"Soldier Boy," Copyright 1953 by Galaxy Publishing Corp. From *Galaxy Science Fiction*, July 1953.

"Grenville's Planet," Copyright 1952 by Fantasy House, Inc. From *The Magazine of Fantasy and Science Fiction*, October 1952.

"Opening Up Slowly," Copyright © 1973 by Redbook Publishing Co. From *Redbook*, August 1973.

"The Book," Copyright 1953 by Galaxy Publishing Corp. From *Galaxy Science Fiction*, November 1953.

"Come to My Party," Copyright © 1956 by Dude. From *Dude Magazine*, August 1956.

"Time Payment," Copyright 1954 by Fantasy House, Inc. From *The Magazine of Fantasy and Science Fiction*, June 1954.

"Citizen Jell," Copyright © 1959 by Galaxy Publishing Corp. From *Galaxy Science Fiction*, August 1959.

"Wainer," Copyright 1954 by Galaxy Publishing Corp. From *Galaxy Science Fiction*, April 1954.

"All the Way Back," Copyright 1952 by Street & Smith Publications, Inc. From *Astounding Science Fiction*, July 1952.

"2066: Election Day," Copyright © 1956 by Street & Smith Publications, Inc. From *Astounding Science Fiction*, December 1956.

"Border Incident," Copyright © 1976 by Mississippi Review. From *Mississippi Review*, Volume V, November 1976.

"The Peeping Tom Patrol," Copyright © 1958 by Playboy. From *Playboy*, September 1958.

"The Orphans of the Void," Copyright 1952 by Galaxy Publishing Corp. From *Galaxy Science Fiction*, June 1952.

"Death of a Hunter," Copyright © 1957 by King-Size Publications. From *Fantastic Universe*, October 1957.

CONTENTS

INTRODUCTION

THIS PAST WEEKEND I WENT OUT TO A LUNCHEON with a flock of writers in the Colorado Writer's club, and they were chatting away about technical matters, naturally, and one asked me, after hearing my normal dream, "Don't you ever think of the *reader?*" And I said I didn't, and he didn't believe it, and so I tried to explain. I've written for a long time and it has always been fun to do, because every time I'm ready to write the story, the story is out there waiting to be told, to be *seen,* and there are ahead such moments as those with Chamberlain on the hill at Little Round Top, or with McClain going into the ring with Dover Brown, or with Nielson killing Maas, or in the mind of a robot seeing the maker coming, and all those worlds are real, and when I read I can sometimes go back, and writing to me has always meant just that: going for a while into another, real world. So when asked, "Do you think of the reader?" I can't say I do, or ever did. But when the reader comes by, and talks, and has *been also in that world,* has gone up the hill with Armistead, held the boy close in "The Dark Angel," if it's all been real to *him,* then that's the moment of link with the reader, who has seen and felt the same thing, and so we have much in common, that reader and I, and that, after the writing, has always been the best moment in living as a writer: to know that somebody else has seen what you see, felt what you felt, in those other worlds, or maybe *that other world,* beyond this one out there, this incomprehensible mess I live in—maybe that's the whole point: create your own world. Which I often did. Welcome.

SOLDIER BOY

In the northland, deep, and in a great cave, by an ever-burning fire the Warrior sleeps. For this is the resting time, the time of peace, and so shall it be for a thousand years. And yet we shall summon him again, my children, when we are sore in need, and out of the north he will come, and again and again, each time we call, out of the dark and the cold, with the fire in his hands, he will come.
—*Scandinavian legend*

THROUGHOUT THE NIGHT THICK CLOUDS HAD been piling in the north; in the morning it was misty and cold. By eight o'clock a wet, heavy, snow-smelling breeze had begun to set in, and because the crops were all down and the winter planting done, the colonists brewed hot coffee and remained inside. The wind blew steadily, icily, from the north. It was well below freezing when, sometime after nine, an army ship landed in a field near the settlement.

There was still time. There were some last brief moments in which the colonists could act and feel as they had always done. They therefore grumbled in annoyance. They wanted no soldiers here. The few who had convenient windows stared out with distaste and a mild curiosity, but no one went out to greet them.

After a while a rather tall, frail-looking man came out of the ship and stood upon the hard ground looking toward the village. He remained there, waiting stiffly, his face turned from the wind. It was a silly thing to do. He was obviously not coming in, either out of pride or just plain orneriness.

"Well, I never," a nice lady said.

"What's he just *standing* there for?" another lady said.

And all of them thought: Well, God knows what's in the

13

mind of a soldier, and right away many people concluded that he must be drunk. The seed of peace was deeply planted in these people, in the children and the women, very, very deep. And because they had been taught, oh, so carefully, to hate war, they had also been taught, quite incidentally, to despise soldiers.

The lone man kept standing in the freezing wind.

Eventually, because even a soldier can look small and cold and pathetic, Bob Rossel had to get up out of a nice, warm bed and go out in that miserable cold to meet him.

The soldier saluted. Like most soldiers, he was not too neat and not too clean, and the salute was sloppy. Although he was bigger than Rossel he did not seem bigger. And, because of the cold, there were tears gathering in the ends of his eyes.

"Captain Dylan, sir." His voice was low and did not carry. "I have a message from Fleet Headquarters. Are you in charge here?"

Rossel, a small sober man, grunted. "Nobody's in charge here. If you want a spokesman I guess I'll do. What's up?"

The captain regarded him briefly out of pale-blue, expressionless eyes. Then he pulled an envelope from an inside pocket, handed it to Rossel. It was a thick, official-looking thing and Rossel hefted it idly. He was about to ask again what was it all about when the airlock of the hovering ship swung open creakily. A beefy, black-haired young man appeared unsteadily in the doorway, called to Dylan.

"C'n I go now, Jim?"

Dylan turned and nodded.

"Be back for you tonight," the young man called, and then, grinning, he yelled, "Catch," and tossed down a bottle. The captain caught it and put it unconcernedly into his pocket while Rossel stared in disgust. A moment later the airlock closed and the ship prepared to lift.

"Was he *drunk?*" Rossel began angrily. "Was that a bottle of *liquor?*"

The soldier was looking at him calmly, coldly. He indicated the envelope in Rossel's hand. "You'd better read that and get moving. We haven't much time."

He turned and walked toward the buildings and Rossel had to follow. As Rossel drew near the walls the watchers could see his lips moving but could not hear him. Just then the ship lifted and they turned to watch that and followed it upward, red spark-tailed, into the gray, spongy clouds and the cold.

14

After a while the ship went out of sight, and nobody ever saw it again.

The first contact man had ever had with an intelligent alien race occurred out on the perimeter in a small quiet place a long way from home. Late in the year 2360—the exact date remains unknown—an Alien force attacked and destroyed the colony at Lupus V. The wreckage and the dead were found by a mailship which flashed off screaming for the army.

When the army came it found this: Of the seventy registered colonists, thirty-one were dead. The rest, including some women and children, were missing. All technical equipment, all radios, guns, machines, even books, were also missing. The buildings had been burned; so had the bodies. Apparently the Aliens had a heat ray. What else they had, nobody knew. After a few days of walking around in the ash, one soldier finally stumbled on something.

For security reasons, there was a detonator in one of the main buildings. In case of enemy attack, Security had provided a bomb to be buried in the center of each colony, because it was important to blow a whole village to hell and gone rather than let a hostile Alien learn vital facts about human technology and body chemistry. There was a bomb at Lupus V too, and though it had been detonated it had not blown. The detonating wire had been cut.

In the heart of the camp, hidden from view under twelve inches of earth, the wire had been dug up and cut.

The army could not understand it and had no time to try. After five hundred years of peace and anti-war conditioning the army was small, weak, and without respect. Therefore the army did nothing but spread the news, and man began to fall back.

In a thickening, hastening stream he came back from the hard-won stars, blowing up his homes behind him, stunned and cursing. Most of the colonists got out in time. A few, the farthest and loneliest, died in fire before the army ships could reach them. And the men in those ships, drinkers and gamblers and veterans of nothing, the dregs of a society that had grown beyond them, were for a long while the only defense earth had.

This was the message Captain Dylan had brought, come out from earth with a bottle on his hip.

* * *

An obscenely cheerful expression upon his gaunt, not too well shaven face, Captain Dylan perched himself upon the edge of a table and listened, one long booted leg swinging idly. One by one the colonists were beginning to understand. War is huge and comes with great suddenness and always without reason, and there is inevitably a wait between acts, between the news and the motion, the fear and the rage.

Dylan waited. These people were taking it well, much better than those in the cities had taken it. But then, these were pioneers. Dylan grinned. Pioneers. Before you settle a planet you boil it and bake it and purge it of all possible disease. Then you step down gingerly and inflate your plastic houses, which harden and become warm and impregnable; and send your machines out to plant and harvest; and set up automatic factories to transmute dirt into coffee; and, without ever having lifted a finger, you have braved the wilderness, hewed a home out of the living rock, and become a pioneer. Dylan grinned again. But at least this was better than the wailing of the cities.

This Dylan thought, although he was himself no fighter, no man at all by any standards. This he thought because he was a soldier and an outcast; to every drunken man the fall of the sober is a happy thing. He stirred restlessly.

By this time the colonists had begun to realize that there wasn't much to say, and a tall, handsome woman was murmuring distractedly, "Lupus, Lupus—doesn't that mean wolves or something?"

Dylan began to wish they would get moving, these pioneers. It was very possible that the Aliens would be here soon, and there was no need for discussion. There was only one thing to do and that was to clear the hell out, quickly and without argument. They began to see it.

But when the fear had died down the resentment came. A number of women began to cluster around Dylan and complain, working up their anger. Dylan said nothing. Then the man Rossel pushed forward and confronted him, speaking with a vast annoyance.

"See here, soldier, this is our planet. I mean to say, this is our *home*. We demand some protection from the fleet. By God, we've been paying the freight for you boys all these years, and it's high time you earned your keep. We demand . . ."

It went on and on, while Dylan looked at the clock and waited. He hoped that he could end this quickly. A big gloomy man was in front of him now and giving him that name of ancient contempt, "soldier boy." The gloomy man wanted to know where the fleet was.

"There is no fleet. There are a few hundred half-shot old tubs that were obsolete before you were born. There are four or five new jobs for the brass and the government. That's all the fleet there is."

Dylan wanted to go on about that, to remind them that nobody had wanted the army, that the fleet had grown smaller and smaller . . . but this was not the time. It was ten-thirty already, and the damned aliens might be coming in right now for all he knew, and all they did was talk. He had realized a long time ago that no peace-loving nation in the history of earth had ever kept itself strong, and although peace was a noble dream, it was ended now and it was time to move.

"We'd better get going," he finally said, and there was quiet. "Lieutenant Bossio has gone on to your sister colony at Planet Three of this system. He'll return to pick me up by nightfall, and I'm instructed to have you gone by then."

For a long moment they waited, and then one man abruptly walked off and the rest followed quickly; in a moment they were all gone. One or two stopped long enough to complain about the fleet, and the big gloomy man said he wanted guns, that's all, and there wouldn't nobody get him off his planet. When he left, Dylan breathed with relief and went out to check the bomb, grateful for the action.

Most of it had to be done in the open. He found a metal bar in the radio shack and began chopping at the frozen ground, following the wire. It was the first thing he had done with his hands in weeks, and it felt fine.

Dylan had been called up out of a bar—he and Bossio —and told what had happened, and in three weeks now they had cleared four colonies. This would be the last, and the tension here was beginning to get to him. After thirty years of hanging around and playing like the town drunk, a man could not be expected to rush out and plug the breach, just like that. It would take time.

He rested, sweating, took a pull from the bottle on his hip.

Before they sent him out on this trip they had made him a captain. Well, that was nice. After thirty years he was a captain. For thirty years he had bummed all over the west end of space, had scraped his way along the outer edges of mankind, had waited and dozed and patrolled and got

17

drunk, waiting always for something to happen. There were a lot of ways to pass the time while you waited for something to happen, and he had done them all.

Once he had even studied military tactics.

He could not help smiling at that, even now. Damn it, he'd been green. But he'd been only nineteen when his father died—of a hernia, of a crazy fool thing like a hernia that killed him just because he'd worked too long on a heavy planet—and in those days the anti-war conditioning out on the Rim was not very strong. They talked a lot about guardians of the frontier, and they got him and some other kids and a broken-down doctor. And . . . now he was a captain.

He bent his back savagely, digging at the ground. You wait and you wait and the edge goes off. This thing he had waited for all those damn days was upon him now, and there was nothing he could do but say the hell with it and go home. Somewhere along the line, in some dark corner of the bars or the jails, in one of the million soul-murdering insults which are reserved especially for peacetime soldiers, he had lost the core of himself, and it didn't particularly matter. That was the point: It made no particular difference if he never got it back. He owed nobody. He was tugging at the wire and trying to think of something pleasant from the old days when the wire came loose in his hands.

Although he had been, in his cynical way, expecting it, for a moment it threw him and he just stared. The end was clean and bright. The wire had just been cut.

Dylan sat for a long while by the radio shack, holding the ends in his hands. He reached almost automatically for the bottle on his hip, and then, for the first time he could remember, let it go. This was real; there was no time for that.

When Rossel came up, Dylan was still sitting. Rossel was so excited he did not notice the wire.

"Listen, soldier, how many people can your ship take?"

Dylan looked at him vaguely. "She sleeps two and won't take off with more'n ten. Why?"

His eyes bright and worried, Rossel leaned heavily against the shack. "We're overloaded. There are sixty of us, and our ship will only take forty. We came out in groups; we never thought . . ."

Dylan dropped his eyes, swearing silently. "You're sure? No baggage, no iron rations; you couldn't get ten more on?"

"Not a chance. She's only a little ship with one deck— she's all we could afford."

Dylan whistled. He had begun to feel lightheaded. "It 'pears that somebody's gonna find out firsthand what them aliens look like."

It was the wrong thing to say and he knew it. "All right," he said quickly, still staring at the clear-sliced wire, "we'll do what we can. Maybe the colony on Three has room. I'll call Bossio and ask."

The colonist had begun to look quite pitifully at the buildings around him and the scurrying people.

"Aren't there any fleet ships within radio distance?"

Dylan shook his head. "The fleet's spread out kind of thin nowadays." Because the other was leaning on him he felt a great irritation, but he said as kindly as he could, "We'll get 'em all out. One way or another, we won't leave anybody."

It was then that Rossel saw the wire. Thickly, he asked what had happened.

Dylan showed him the two clean ends. "Somebody dug it up, cut it, then buried it again and packed it down real nice."

"The damn fool!" Rossel exploded.

"Who?"

"Why, one of . . . of us, of course. I know nobody ever liked sitting on a live bomb like this, but I never . . ."

"You think one of your people did it?"

Rossel stared at him. "Isn't that obvious?"

"Why?"

"Well, they probably thought it was too dangerous, and silly too, like most government rules. Or maybe one of the kids . . ."

It was then that Dylan told him about the wire on Lupus V. Rossel was silent. Involuntarily he glanced at the sky, then he said shakily, "Maybe an animal?"

Dylan shook his head. "No animal did that. Wouldn't have buried it, or found it in the first place. Heck of a co-incidence, don't you think? The wire at Lupus was cut just before an alien attack, and now this one is cut too—newly cut."

The colonist put one hand to his mouth, his eyes wide and white.

"So something," said Dylan, "knew enough about this camp to know that a bomb was buried here and also to know why it was here. And that something didn't want

19

the camp destroyed and so came right into the center of the camp, traced the wire, dug it up, and cut it. And then walked right out again."

"Listen," said Rossel, "I'd better go ask."

He started away but Dylan caught his arm.

"Tell them to arm," he said, "and try not to scare hell out of them. I'll be with you as soon as I've spliced this wire."

Rossel nodded and went off, running. Dylan knelt with the metal in his hands.

He began to feel that, by God, he was getting cold. He realized that he'd better go inside soon, but the wire had to be spliced. That was perhaps the most important thing he could do now, splice the wire.

All right, he asked himself for the thousandth time, who cut it? How? Telepathy? Could they somehow control one of us?

No. If they controlled one, then they could control all, and then there would be no need for an attack. But you don't know, you don't really know.

Were they small? Little animals?

Unlikely. Biology said that really intelligent life required a sizable brain, and you would have to expect an alien to be at least as large as a dog. And every form of life on this planet had been screened long before a colony had been allowed in. If any new animals had suddenly shown up, Rossel would certainly know about it.

He would ask Rossel. He would damn sure have to ask Rossel.

He finished splicing the wire and tucked it into the ground. Then he straightened up and, before he went into the radio shack, pulled out his pistol. He checked it, primed it, and tried to remember the last time he had fired it. He never had—he never had fired a gun.

The snow began falling near noon. There was nothing anybody could do but stand in the silence and watch it come down in a white rushing wall, and watch the trees and the hills drown in the whiteness, until there was nothing on the planet but the buildings and a few warm lights and the snow.

By one o'clock the visibility was down to zero and Dylan decided to try to contact Bossio again and tell him to hurry. But Bossio still didn't answer. Dylan stared long and thoughtfully out the window through the snow at the gray shrouded shapes of bushes and trees which were beginning to become horrifying. It must be that Bossio was still drunk —maybe sleeping it off before making planetfall on Three. Dylan held no grudge. Bossio was a kid and alone. It took a special kind of guts to take a ship out into space alone, when Things could be waiting. . . .

A young girl, pink and lovely in a thick fur jacket, came into the shack and told him breathlessly that her father, Mr. Rush, would like to know if he wanted sentries posted. Dylan hadn't thought about it but he said yes right away, beginning to feel both pleased and irritated at the same time, because now they were coming to him.

He pushed out into the cold and went to find Rossel. With the snow it was bad enough, but if they were still here when the sun went down they wouldn't have a chance. Most of the men were out stripping down their ship, and that would take a while. He wondered why Rossel hadn't yet put a call through to Three, asking about room on the ship there. The only answer he could find was that Rossel knew that there was no room and wanted to put off the answer as long as possible. And, in a way, you could not blame him.

Rossel was in his cabin with the big, gloomy man—who turned out to be Rush, the one who had asked about sentries. Rush was methodically cleaning an old hunting rifle. Rossel was surprisingly full of hope.

"Listen, there's a mail ship due in, been due since yesterday. We might get the rest of the folks out on that."

Dylan shrugged. "Don't count on it."

"But they have a contract!"

The soldier grinned.

The big man, Rush, was paying no attention. Quite suddenly he said, "Who cut that wire, Cap?"

Dylan swung slowly to look at him. "As far as I can figure, an alien cut it."

Rush shook his head. "No. Ain't been no aliens near this camp, and no peculiar animals either. We got a planet-wide radar, and ain't no unidentified ships come near, not since we first landed more'n a year ago." He lifted the rifle and peered through the bore. "Uh-uh. One of us did it."

The man had been thinking. And he knew the planet.

"Telepathy?" asked Dylan.

"Might be."

"Can't see it. You people live too close; you'd notice right away if one of you wasn't . . . himself. And if they've got one, why not all?"

Rush calmly—at least outwardly calmly—lit his pipe. There was a strength in this man that Dylan had missed before.

"Don't know," he said gruffly. "But there are aliens, mister. And until I know different I'm keepin' an eye on my neighbor."

He gave Rossel a sour look and Rossel stared back, uncomprehending.

Then Rossel jumped. "My God!"

Dylan moved to quiet him. "Look, is there any animal at all that ever comes near here that's as large as a dog?"

After a pause Rush answered. "Yep, there's one. The viggle. It's like a reg'lar monkey but with four legs. Biology cleared 'em before we landed. We shoot one now and then when they get pesky." He rose slowly, the rifle held under his arm. "I b'lieve we might just as well go post them sentries."

Dylan wanted to go on with this, but there was nothing much else to say. Rossel went with them as far as the radio shack, with a strained expression on his face, to put through that call to Three.

When he was gone Rush asked Dylan, "Where you want them sentries? I got Walt Halloran and Web Eggers and six others lined up."

Dylan stopped and looked around grimly at the circling wall of snow. "You know the site better than I do. Post 'em in a ring, on rises, within calling distance. Have 'em check with each other every five minutes. I'll go help your people at the ship."

The gloomy man nodded and fluffed up his collar. "Nice day for huntin'," he said, and then he was gone, with the snow quickly covering his footprints.

The Alien lay wrapped in a thick electric cocoon, buried in a wide warm room beneath the base of a tree. The tree served him as antennae; curiously he gazed into a small view-screen and watched the humans come. He saw them fan out, eight of them, and sink down in the snow. He saw that they were armed.

He pulsed thoughtfully, extending a part of himself to absorb a spiced lizard. Since the morning, when the new ship had come, he had been watching steadily, and now it was apparent that the humans were aware of their danger. Undoubtedly they were preparing to leave.

That was unfortunate. The attack was not scheduled until late that night, and he could not, of course, press the assault by day. But *flexibility,* he reminded himself sternly, *is the first principle of absorption,* and therefore he moved to alter his plans. A projection reached out to dial several knobs on a large box before him, and the hour of assault was moved forward to dusk. A glance at the chronometer told him that it was already well into the night on Planet Three and that the attack there had probably begun.

The Alien felt the first tenuous pulsing of anticipation. He lay quietly, watching the small square lights of windows against the snow, thanking the Unexplainable that matters had been so devised that he would not have to venture out into that miserable cold.

Presently an alarming thought struck him. These humans moved with uncommon speed for intelligent creatures. Even without devices, it was distinctly possible that they could be gone before nightfall. He could take no chance, of course. He spun more dials and pressed a single button, and lay back again comfortably, warmly, to watch the disabling of the colonists' ship.

When Three did not answer, Rossel was nervously gazing at the snow, thinking of other things, and he called again. Several moments later the realization of what was happening struck him like a blow. Three had never once failed to answer. All they had to do when they heard the signal buzz was go into the radio shack and say hello. That was all they had to do. He called again and again, but nobody answered. There was no static and no interference and he didn't hear a thing. He checked frenziedly through his own apparatus and tried again, but the air was as dead as deep space. He raced out to tell Dylan.

Dylan accepted it. He had known none of the people on Three, and what he felt now was a much greater urgency to be out of here. He said hopeful things to Rossel and then went out to the ship and joined the men in lightening her. About the ship, at least, he knew something and he was able to tell them what partitions and frames could go and what would have to stay or the ship would never get off the planet. But even stripped down, it couldn't take them all. When he knew that, he realized that he himself would have to stay here, for it was only then that he thought of Bossio.

Three was dead. Bossio had gone down there some time ago, and if Three was dead and Bossio had not called, then the fact was that Bossio was gone too. For a long, long moment Dylan stood rooted in the snow. More than the fact that he would have to stay here was the unspoken, unalterable, heart-numbing knowledge that Bossio was dead —the one thing that Dylan could not accept. Bossio was the only friend he had. In all this dog-eared, aimless, ape-run universe Bossio was all his friendship and his trust.

He left the ship blindly and went back to the settlement. Now the people were quiet and really frightened, and some of the women were beginning to cry. He noticed now that they had begun to look at him with hope as he passed, and in his own grief, humanly, he swore.

Bossio—a big-grinning kid with no parents, no enemies, no grudges—Bossio was already dead because he had come out here and tried to help these people. People who had kicked or ignored him all the days of his life. And, in a short while, Dylan would also stay behind and die to save the life of somebody he never knew and who, twenty-four hours earlier, would have been ashamed to be found in his company. Now, when it was far, far too late, they were coming to the army for help.

But in the end, damn it, he could not hate these people. All they had ever wanted was peace, and even though they had never understood that the universe is unknowable and that you must always have big shoulders, still they had always sought only for peace. If peace leads to no conflict at all and then decay, well, that was something that had to be learned. So he could not hate these people.

But he could not help them either. He turned from their eyes and went into the radio shack. It had begun to dawn on the women that they might be leaving without their husbands or sons, and he did not want to see the fierce struggle that he was sure would take place. He sat alone and tried, for the last time, to call Bossio.

After a while an old woman found him and offered him coffee. It was a very decent thing to do, to think of him at a time like this, and he was so suddenly grateful he could only nod. The woman said that he must be cold in that thin army thing and that she had brought along a mackinaw for him. She poured the coffee and left him alone.

They were thinking of him now, he knew, because they were thinking of everyone who had to stay. Throw the dog a bone. Dammit, don't be like that, he told himself. He had not had anything to eat all day, and the coffee was warm and strong. He decided he might be of some help at the ship.

24

It was stripped down now, and they were loading. He was startled to see a great group of them standing in the snow, removing their clothes. Then he understood. The clothes of forty people would change the weight by enough to get a few more aboard. There was no fighting. Some of the women were almost hysterical and a few had refused to go and were still in their cabins, but the process was orderly. Children went automatically, as did the youngest husbands and all the women. The elders were shuffling around in the snow, waving their arms to keep themselves warm. Some of them were laughing to keep their spirits up.

In the end, the ship took forty-six people.

Rossel was one of the ones that would not be going. Dylan saw him standing by the airlock holding his wife in his arms, his face buried in her soft brown hair. A sense of great sympathy, totally unexpected, rose up in Dylan, and a little of the lostness of thirty years went slipping away. These were his people. It was a thing he had never understood before, because he had never once been among men in great trouble. He waited and watched, learning, trying to digest this while there was still time. Then the semi-naked colonists were inside and the airlock closed. But when the ship tried to lift, there was a sharp burning smell—she couldn't get off the ground.

Rush was sitting hunched over in the snow, his rifle across his knees. He was coated a thick white, and if he hadn't spoken Dylan would have stumbled over him. Dylan took out his pistol and sat down.

"What happened?" Rush asked.

"Lining burned out. She's being repaired."

"Coincidence?"

Dylan shook his head.

"How long'll it take to fix?"

"Four—five hours."

"It'll be night by then." Rush paused. "I wonder."

"Seems like they want to wait till dark."

"That's what I was figurin'. Could be they ain't got much of a force."

Dylan shrugged. "Also could mean they see better at night. Also could mean they move slow. Also could mean they want the least number of casualties."

Rush was quiet, and the snow fell softly on his face, on his eyebrows, where it had begun to gather. At length he said, "You got any idea how they got to the ship?"

Dylan shook his head again. "Nobody saw anything—but

they were all pretty busy. Your theory about it maybe being one of us is beginning to look pretty good."

The colonist took off his gloves, lit a cigarette. The flame was strong and piercing and Dylan moved to check him, but stopped. It didn't make much difference. The aliens knew where they were.

And this is right where we're gonna be, he thought.

"You know," he said suddenly, speaking mostly to himself, "I been in the army thirty years, and this is the first time I was ever in a fight. Once in a while we used to chase smugglers—never caught any, their ships were new—used to cut out after unlicensed ships, used to do all kinds of piddling things like that. But I never shot at anybody."

Rush was looking off into the woods. "Maybe the mail ship will come in."

Dylan nodded.

"They got a franchise, dammit. They got to deliver as long as they's a colony here."

When Dylan didn't answer, he said almost appealingly, "Some of those guys would walk barefoot through hell for a buck."

"Maybe," Dylan said. After all, why not let him hope? There were four long hours left.

Now he began to look down into himself, curiously, because he himself was utterly without hope and yet he was no longer really afraid. It was a surprising thing when you looked at it coldly, and he guessed that, after all, it was because of the thirty years. A part of him had waited for this. Some crazy part of him was ready—even after all this time—even excited about being in a fight. Well, what the hell, he marveled. And then he realized that the rest of him was awakening too, and he saw that this job was really his . . . that he had always been, in truth, a soldier.

Dylan sat, finding himself in the snow. Once long ago he had read about some fool who didn't want to die in bed, old and feeble. This character wanted to reach the height of his powers and then explode in a grand way—"in Technicolor," the man had said. Explode in Technicolor. It was meant to be funny, of course, but he had always remembered it, and he realized now that that was a small part of what he was feeling. The rest of it was that he was a soldier.

Barbarian, said a small voice, *primitive.* But he couldn't listen.

26

"Say, Cap," Rush was saying, "it's getting a mite chilly. I understand you got a bottle."

"Sure," he said cheerfully, "near forgot it." He pulled it out and gave it to Rush. The colonist drank appreciatively, saying to Dylan half seriously, half humorously, "One for the road."

Beneath them the planet revolved and the night came on. They waited, speaking briefly, while the unseen sun went down. And faintly, dimly, through the snow they heard at last the muffled beating of a ship. It passed overhead and they were sighting their guns before they recognized it. It was the mail ship.

They listened while she settled in a field by the camp, and Rush was pounding Dylan's arm. "She will take us all," Rush was shouting, "she'll take us all," and Dylan too was grinning, and then he saw a thing.

Small and shadowy, white-coated and almost invisible, the thing had come out of the woods and was moving toward them, bobbing and shuffling in the silent snow.

Dylan fired instinctively, because the thing had four arms and was coming right at him. He fired again. This time he hit it and the thing fell, but almost immediately it was up and lurching rapidly back into the trees. It was gone before Dylan could fire again.

They both lay flat in the snow, half buried. From the camp there were now no sounds at all.

"Did you get a good look?"

Rush grunted, relaxing. "Should've saved your fire, son. Looked like one o' them monkeys."

But there was something wrong. There was something that Dylan had heard in the quickness of the moment which he could not remember but which was very wrong.

"Listen," he said, suddenly placing it. "Dammit, that was no monkey."

"Easy—"

"I hit it. I hit it cold. It made a *noise*."

Rush was staring at him.

"Didn't you hear?" Dylan cried.

"No. Your gun was by my ear."

And then Dylan was up and running, hunched over, across the snow to where the thing had fallen. He had seen a piece of it break off when the bolt struck, and now in the snow he picked up a paw and brought it back to Rush. He saw right away there was no blood. The skin was real and furry, all right, but there was no blood. Because the bone

27

was steel and the muscles were springs and the thing had been a robot.

The Alien rose up from his cot, whistling with annoyance. When that ship had come in his attention had been distracted from one of the robots, and of course the miserable thing had gone blundering right out into the humans. He thought for a while that the humans would overlook it— the seeing was poor and they undoubtedly would still think of it as animal, even with its firing ports open—but then he checked the robot and saw that a piece was missing and knew that the humans had found it. Well, he thought unhappily, flowing into his suit, no chance now to disable that other ship. The humans would never let another animal near.

And therefore—for he was, above all, a flexible being— he would proceed to another plan. The settlement would have to be detonated. And for that he would have to leave his own shelter and go out in that miserable cold and lie down in one of his bunkers which was much farther away. No need to risk blowing himself up with his own bombs; but still, that awful cold.

He dismissed his regrets and buckled his suit into place. It carried him up the stairs and bore him out into the snow. After one whiff of the cold he snapped his view-plate shut and immediately, as he had expected, it began to film with snow. Well, no matter, he would guide the unit by coordinates and it would find the bunker itself. No need for caution now. The plan was nearly ended.

In spite of his recent setback, the Alien lay back and allowed himself the satisfaction of a full tremble. The plan had worked very nearly to perfection, as of course it should, and he delighted in the contemplation of it.

When the humans were first detected, in the region of Bootes, much thought had gone into the proper method of learning their technology without being discovered themselves. There was little purpose in destroying the humans without first learning from them. Life was really a remarkable thing—one never knew what critical secrets a starborne race possessed. Hence the robots. And it was an extraordinary plan, an elegant plan. The Alien trembled again.

The humans were moving outward toward the rim; their base was apparently somewhere beyond Centaurus. Therefore a ring of defense was thrown up on most of the habit-

28

able worlds toward which the humans were coming—oh, a delightful plan—and the humans came down one by one and never realized that there was any defense at all.

With a cleverness which was almost excruciating, the Aliens had carefully selected a number of animals native to each world, and then constructed robot duplicates. So simple then to place the robots down on a world with a single Director, then wait . . . for the humans to inhabit. Naturally the humans screened all the animals and scouted a planet pretty thoroughly before they set up a colony. Naturally their snares and their hunters caught no robots and never found the deep-buried Alien Director.

Then the humans relaxed and began to make homes, never realizing that in among the animals which gamboled playfully in the trees there was one which did not gambol, but watched. Never once noticing the moneylike animals, or the small thing like a rabbit which was a camera eye, or the thing like a rat, which took chemical samples, or the thing like a lizard which cut wires.

The Alien rumbled on through the snow, trembling so much now with ecstasy and anticipation that the suit which bore him almost lost its balance. He very nearly fell over before he stopped trembling, and then he contained himself. In a little while, a very little while, there would be time enough for trembling.

"They could've been here till the sun went out," Rush said, "and we never would've known."

"I wonder how much they've found out," Dylan said.

Rush was holding the paw.

"Pretty near everything, I guess. This stuff don't stop at monkeys. Could be any size, any kind. . . . Look, let's get down into camp and tell 'em."

Dylan rose slowly to a kneeling position, peering dazedly out into the far white trees. His mind was turning over and over, around and around, like a roulette wheel. But at the center of his mind there was one thought, and it was rising up slowly now, through the waste and waiting of the years. He felt a vague surprise.

"Gettin' kind of dark," he said.

Rush swore. "Let's go. Let's get out of here." He tugged once at Dylan's arm and started off on his knees.

Dylan said, "Wait."

Rush stopped. Through the snow he tried to see Dylan's eyes. The soldier was still looking into the woods.

Dylan's voice was halting and almost inaudible. "They know everything about us. We don't know anything about them. They're probably sittin' out there right now, a swarm of 'em there behind those trees, waitin' for it to get real nice and dark."

He paused. "If I could get just one."

It was totally unexpected, to Dylan as well as Rush. The time for this sort of thing was past, the age was done, and for a long while neither of them fully understood.

"C'mon," Rush said with exasperation.

Dylan shook his head, marveling at himself. "I'll be with you in a little while."

Rush came near and looked questioningly into his face.

"Listen," Dylan said hurriedly, "we only need *one*. If we could just get one back to a lab we'd at least have some clue to what they are. This way we don't know anything. We can't just cut and run." He struggled with the unfamiliar, time-lost words. "We got to make a stand."

He turned from Rush and lay forward on his belly in the snow. He could feel his heart beating against the soft white cushion beneath him. There was no time to look at this calmly, and he was glad of that. He spent some time being very much afraid of the unknown things beyond the trees, but even then he realized that this was the one thing in his life he had to do.

It is not a matter of dying, he thought, but of *doing*. Sooner or later a man must do a thing which justifies his life, or the life is not worth living. The long, cold line of his existence had reached this point, here and now in the snow at this moment. He would go on from here as a man . . . or not at all.

Rush had sat down beside him, beginning to understand, watching without words. He was an old man. Like all earthmen, he had never fought with his hands. He had not fought the land or the tides or the weather or any of the million bitter sicknesses which man had grown up fighting, and he was beginning to realize that somewhere along the line he had been betrayed. Now, with a dead paw of the enemy in his hand, he did not feel like a man. And he was ready to fight now, but it was much too late and he saw with a vast leaden shame that he did not know how, could not even begin.

"Can I help?" he said.

Dylan shook his head. "Go back and let them know

about the robots, and if the ship is ready to leave before I get back, well—then good luck."

He started to slither forward on his belly, but Rush reached out and grabbed him, holding with one hand to peace and gentleness and the soft days which were ending.

"Listen," he said, "you don't owe anybody."

Dylan stared at him with surprise. "I know," he said, and then he slipped up over the mound before him and headed for the trees.

Now what he needed was luck. Just good, plain old luck. He didn't know where they were or how many there were or what kinds there were, and the chances were good that one of them was watching him right now. Well, then, he needed some luck. He inched forward slowly, carefully, watching the oncoming line of trees. The snow was falling on him in big, leafy flakes and that was fine, because the blackness of his suit was much too distinct, and the more white he was, the better. Even so, it was becoming quite dark by now, and he thought he had a chance. He reached the first tree.

Silently he slipped off his heavy cap. The visor got in his way, and above all he must be able to see. He let the snow thicken on his hair before he raised himself on his elbows and looked outward.

There was nothing but the snow and the dead quiet and the stark white boles of the trees. He slid past the first trunk to the next, moving forward on his elbows with his pistol in his right hand. His elbow struck a rock and it hurt and his face was freezing. Once he rubbed snow from his eyebrows. Then he came through the trees and lay down before a slight rise, thinking.

Better to go around than over. But if anything is watching, it is most likely watching from above.

Therefore go around and come back up from behind. Yes.

His nose had begun to run. With great care he crawled among some large rocks, hoping against hope that he would not sneeze. Why had nothing seen him? Was something following him now? He turned to look behind him, but it was darker now and becoming difficult to see. But he would have to look behind him more often.

He was moving down a gorge. There were large trees above him and he needed their shelter, but he could not risk slipping down the sides of the gorge. And far off, weakly, out of the gray cold ahead, he heard a noise.

31

He lay down in the snow, listening. With a slow, thick shuffle, a thing was moving through the trees before him. In a moment he saw that it was not coming toward him. He lifted his head but saw nothing. Much more slowly, now, he crawled again. The thing was moving down the left side of the gorge ahead, coming away from the rise he had circled. It was moving without caution, and he worried that if he did not hurry he would lose it. But for the life of him he couldn't stand up.

The soldier went forward on his hands and knees. When his clothes hung down, the freezing cold entered his throat and shocked his body, which was sweating. He shifted his gun to his gloved hand and blew on the bare fingers of his right, still crawling. When he reached the other end of the gorge he stood upright against a rock wall and looked in the direction of the shuffling thing.

He saw it just as it turned. It was a great black lump on a platform. The platform had legs, and the thing was plodding methodically upon a path which would bring it past him. It had come down from the rise and was rounding the gorge when Dylan saw it. It did not see him.

If he had not ducked quickly and brought up his gun, the monkey would not have seen him either, but there was no time for regret. The monkey was several yards to the right of the lump on the platform when he heard it start running; he had to look up this time, and saw it leaping toward him over the snow.

All right, he said to himself. His first shot took the monkey in the head, where the eyes were. As the thing crashed over, there was a hiss and a stench and flame seared into his shoulder and the side of his face. He lurched to the side, trying to see, his gun at arm's length as the lump on the platform spun toward him. He fired four times. Three bolts went home in the lump; the fourth tore a leg off the platform and the whole thing fell over.

Dylan crawled painfully behind a rock, his left arm useless. The silence had come back again and he waited, but neither of the Alien things moved. Nothing else moved in the woods around him. He turned his face up to the falling snow and let it come soothingly upon the awful wound in his side.

After a while he looked out at the monkey. It had risen to a sitting position but was frozen in the motion of rising. It had ceased to function when he hit the lump. Out of the numbness and the pain he felt a great gladness rising.

32

The guide. He had killed the guide.

He would not be cautious any more. Maybe some of the other robots were self-directing and dangerous, but they could be handled. He went to the lump, stared at it without feeling. A black, doughy bulge was swelling out through one of the holes.

It was too big to carry, but he would have to take something back. He went over and took the monkey by a stiff jutting arm and began dragging it back toward the village.

Now he began to stumble. It was dark and he was very tired. But the steel he had been forging in his breast was complete, and the days which were coming would be days full of living. He would walk with big shoulders and he would not bother to question, because man was not born to live out his days at home, by the fire.

It was a very big thing that Dylan had learned and he could not express it, but he knew it all the same, knew it beyond understanding. And so he went home to his people.

One by one, increasing, in the wee black corner of space which man had taken for his own, other men were learning. And the snow fell and the planets whirled; and when it was spring where Dylan had fought, men were already leaping back out to the stars.

GRENVILLE'S PLANET

WISHER DID NOT SEE THE BRIGHTNESS BECAUSE he was back aft alone. In the still ship he sat quietly, relaxed. He was not bored. It was just that he had no interest. After fourteen years in the Mapping Command even the strangest of new worlds was routine to him and what little imagination he had was beginning to center upon a small farm he had seen on the southern plains of Vega VII.

The brightness that Wisher did not see grew with the passing moments. A pale young man named Grenville, who was Wisher's crewman, watched it for a long while absently. When the gleam took on brilliance and a blue-white, dazzling blaze Grenville was startled. He stared at the screen for a long moment, then carefully checked the distance. Still a few light minutes away, the planet was already uncommonly bright.

Pleasantly excited, Grenville watched the planet grow. Slowly the moons came out. Four winked on and ringed the bright world like pearls in a vast necklace. Grenville gazed in awe. The blueness and the brightness flowed in together; it was the most beautiful thing that Grenville had ever seen.

Excited, he buzzed for Wisher. Wisher did not come.

Grenville took the ship in close and now it occurred to him to wonder. The glare was incredible. That a planet should shine like that, like an enormous facet of polished glass, was incredible. Now, as he watched, the light began to form vaguely into the folds of clouds. The blue grew richer and deeper. Long before he hit the first cloud layer, Grenville knew what it was. He pounded the buzzer. Wisher finally came.

When he saw the water in the screen he stopped in his tracks.

37

"Well I'll be damned!" he breathed.

Except for a few scuds of clouds it was blue. The entire world was blue. There was the white of the clouds and the icecaps, but the rest was all blue and the rest was water.

Grenville began to grin. A world of *water!*

"Now how's *that* for a freak?" he chuckled. "One in a million, right, Sam? I bet you never saw anything like that."

Wisher shook his head, still staring. Then he moved quickly to the controls and set out to make a check. They circled the planet with the slow, spiraling motion of the Mapping Command, bouncing radar off the dark side. When they came back into the daylight they were sure. There was no land on the planet.

Grenville, as usual, began to chatter.

"Well, naturally," he said, "it was bound to happen sooner or later. Considering Earth, which has a land area covering only one fourth—"

"Yep." Wisher nodded.

"—and when you consider the odds, chances are that there are quite a number of planets with scarcely any land area at all."

Wisher had moved back to the screen.

"Let's go down," he said.

Grenville, startled, stared at him.

"Where?"

"Down low. I want to see what's living in that ocean."

Because each new world was a wholly *new* world and because experience therefore meant nothing, Wisher had decided a long while ago to follow the regs without question. For without the regs, the Mapping Command was a death trap. Nowhere in space was the need for rules so great as out on the frontier where there were no rules at all. The regs were complex, efficient, and all-embracing; it was to the regs that the men of the Mapping Command owed their lives and the rest of mankind owed the conquest of space.

But inevitably, unalterably, there were things which the regs could not have foreseen. And Wisher knew that too, but he did not think about it.

According to plan, then, they dropped down into the stratosphere, went further down below the main cloud region, and leveled off at a thousand feet. Below them, mile after rolling, billowy mile, the sea flowed out to the great bare circle of the horizon.

With the screen at full magnification, they probed the water.

It was surprising, in all that expanse of sea, to observe so little. No schools of fish of any kind, no floating masses of seaweed, nothing but a small fleet shape here and there and an occasional group of tiny plant organisms.

Wisher dropped only a hundred or so feet lower. In a world where evolution had been confined underwater it would be best to keep at a distance. On the other worlds to which he had come Wisher had seen some vast and incredible things. Eight hundred feet up, he thought, is a good safe distance.

It was from that height, then, that they saw the island.

It was small, too small to be seen from a distance, was barely five miles in length and less than two miles wide. A little brown cigar it was, sitting alone in the varying green-blue wash of the ocean.

Grenville began to grin. Abruptly he laughed out loud. Grenville was not the kind of man who is easily awed, and the sight of that one bare speck, that single stubby persistent butt of rock alone in a world of water, was infinitely comical to him.

"Wait'll we show the boys *this*," he chuckled to Wisher. "Break out the camera. My God, what a picture *this* will make!"

Grenville was filled with pride. This planet, after all, was *his* assignment. It was his to report on, his discovery—he gasped. They might even name it after *him*.

He flushed, his heart beat rapidly. It had happened before. There were a number of odd planets named after men in the Mapping Command. When the tourists came they would be coming to Grenville's Planet, one of the most spectacular wonders of the Universe.

While the young man was thus rejoicing, Wisher had brought the ship around and was swinging slowly in over the island. It was covered with some kind of brownish-green, stringy vegetation. Wisher was tempted to go down and check for animal life, but decided to see first if there were any more islands.

Still at a height of 800 feet, they spiraled the planet. They did not see the second island, radar picked it out for them.

This one was bigger than the first and there was another island quite near to the south. Both were narrow and elongated in the cigarlike shape of the first, were perhaps twenty miles in length, and were encrusted with the same brown-green vegetation. They were small enough to have been hidden from sight during the first check by a few scattered clouds.

The discovery of them was anticlimactic and disappointing. Grenville would have been happier if there was no land at all. But he regained some of his earlier enthusiasm when he remembered that the tourists would still come and that now at least they would be able to land.

There was nothing at all on the night side. Coming back out into the daylight, Wisher cautiously decided to land.

"Peculiar," said Wisher, peering at the dunes of the beach.

"What is?" Grenville eyed him through the fish bowls of their helmets.

"I don't know." Wisher turned slowly, gazed around at the shaggy, weedy vegetation. "It doesn't feel right."

Grenville fell silent. There was nothing on the island that could hurt them, they were quite sure of that. The check had revealed the presence of a great number of small, four-footed animals, but only one type was larger than a dog, and that one was slow and noisy.

"Have to be careful about snakes," Wisher said absently, recalling the regs on snakes and insects. Funny thing, that. There were very few insects.

Both men were standing in close to the ship. It was the rule, of course. You never left the ship until you were absolutely sure. Wisher, for some vague reason he could not define, was not sure.

"How's the air check?"

Grenville was just then reading the meters. After a moment he said: "Good."

Wisher relaxed, threw open his helmet, and breathed in deeply. The clean fresh air flowed into him, exhilarating. He unscrewed his helmet entirely, looking around.

The ship had come down on the up end of the beach, a good distance from the sea, and was standing now in a soft, reddish sand. It was bordered on the north by the open sea and to the south was the scrawny growth they had seen from above. It was not a jungle—the plants were too straight and stiff for that—and the height of the tallest was less than ten feet. But it was the very straightness of the things, the eerie regularity of them, which grated in Wisher's mind.

But, breathing in the cool sea air of the island, Wisher began to feel more confident. They had their rifles, they had the ship and the alarm system. There was nothing here that could harm them.

Grenville brought out some folding chairs from the ship. They sat and chatted pleasantly until the twilight came.

Just before twilight two of the moons came out.

"Moons," said Wisher suddenly.

"What?"

"I was just thinking," Wisher explained.

"What about the moons?"

"I wasn't thinking exactly about them, I was thinking about the tide. Four good-sized moons in conjunction could raise one heck of a tide."

Grenville settled back, closing his eyes.

"So?"

"So that's probably where the land went."

Grenville was too busy dreaming about his fame as discoverer of Grenville's Planet to be concerned with tides and moons.

"Let the techs worry about that," he said without interest.

But Wisher kept thinking.

The tide could very well be the cause. When the four moons got together and started to pull they would raise a tremendous mass of water, a grinding power that would slice away the continent edges like no erosive force in history. Given a billion years in which to work—but Wisher suddenly remembered a peculiar thing about the island.

If tides had planed down the continents of this planet, then these islands had no right being here, certainly not as sand and loose rock. Just one tide like the ones those moons could raise would be enough to cut the islands completely away. Well, maybe, he thought, the tides are very far apart, centuries even.

He glanced apprehensively at the sky. The two moons visible were reassuringly far apart.

He turned from the moons to gaze at the sea. And then he remembered the first thought he had had about this planet—that uncomfortable feeling that the first sight of land had dispelled. He thought of it now again.

Evolution.

A billion years beneath the sea, with no land to take the first developing mammals. What was going on, right now as he watched, beneath the placid rolling surface of the sea?

41

It was a disturbing thought. When they went back to the ship for the night Wisher did not need the regs to tell him to seal the airlock and set the alarm screens.

The alarm that came in the middle of the night and nearly scared Wisher to death turned out to be only an animal. It was one of the large ones, a weird, bristling thing with a lean and powerful body. It got away before they were up to see it, but it left its photographic image.

In spite of himself, Wisher had trouble getting back to sleep, and in the morning was silently in favor of leaving for the one last star they would map before returning to base. But the regs called for life specimens to be brought back from all livable worlds whenever possible, whenever there was no "slight manifestation of danger." Well, here it was certainly possible. They would have to stay long enough to take a quick sampling of plants and animals and of marine life too.

Grenville was just as anxious to get back as Wisher was, but for different reasons. Grenville, figured Grenville, was now a famous man.

Early in the morning, then, they lifted ship and once more spiraled the planet. Once the mapping radar had recorded the size and shape and location of the islands, they went in low again and made a complete check for life forms.

They found, as before, very little. There were the bristling things, and—as Wisher has suspected—a great quantity of snakes and lizards. There were very few observable fish. There were no birds.

When they were done they returned to the original island. Grenville, by this time, had a name for it. Since there was another island near it, lying to the south, Grenville called that one South Grenville. The first was, of course, North Grenville. Grenville chuckled over that for a long while.

"Don't go too near the water."

"All right, mama," Grenville chirped, grinning. "I'll work the edge of the vegetation."

"Leave the rifle, take the pistol. It's handier."

Grenville nodded and left, dragging the specimen sack. Wisher, muttering, turned toward the water.

It is unnatural, he thought, for a vast warm ocean to be so empty of life. Because the ocean, really, is where life

42

begins. He had visions in his mind of any number of vicious, incredible, slimy things that were alive and native to that sea, and who were responsible for the unnatural sterility of the water. When he approached the waves he was very cautious.

The first thing he noticed, with a shock, was that there were no shellfish.

Not any. Not crabs or snails or even the tiniest of sea beings. Nothing. The beach was a bare, dead plot of sand.

He stood a few yards from the waves, motionless. He was almost positive, now, that there was danger here. The shores of every warm sea he had ever seen, from Earth on out to Deneb, had been absolutely choked with life and the remnants of life. There were always shells and fish scales, and snails, worms, insects; bits of jellyfish, tentacles, minutiae of a hundred million kinds, cluttering and crowding every square inch of the beach and the sea. And yet here, now, there was nothing. Just sand and water.

It took a great deal of courage for Wisher to approach those waves, although the water here was shallow. He took a quick water sample and hurried back to the ship.

Minutes later he was perched in the shadow of her side, staring out broodingly over the ocean. The water was Earth water as far as his instruments could tell. There was nothing wrong with it. But there was nothing much living in it.

When Grenville came back with the floral specimens Wisher quietly mentioned the lack of shellfish.

"Well, hell," said Grenville, scratching his head painfully, "maybe they just don't like it here."

And maybe they've got reason, Wisher said to himself. But aloud he said: "The computer finished constructing the orbits of those moons."

"So?"

"So the moons conjunct every 112 years. They raise a tide of 600 feet."

Grenville did not follow.

"The tide," said Wisher, smiling queerly, "is at least 400 feet higher than any of the islands."

When Grenville stared, still puzzled, Wisher grunted and kicked at the sand.

"Now where in hell do you suppose the animals came from?"

"They should be drowned," said Grenville slowly.

"Right. And would be, unless they're amphibian, which

43

they're not. Or unless a new batch evolves every hundred years."

"Um." Grenville sat down to think about it.

"Don't make sense," he said after a while.

Having thoroughly confounded Grenville, Wisher turned away and paced slowly in the sand. The sand, he thought distractedly, that's another thing. Why in heck is this island here at all?

Artificial.

The word popped unbidden into his brain.

That would be it. That would have to be it.

The island was artificial, was—restored. Put here by whoever or whatever lived under the sea.

Grenville was ready to go. He stood nervously eyeing the waves, his fingers clamped tightly on the pistol at his belt, waiting for Wisher to give the word.

Wisher leaned against the spaceship, conveniently near the airlock. He regretted disturbing Grenville.

"We can't leave yet," he said calmly. "We haven't any proof. And besides, there hasn't been any 'manifestation of danger.' "

"We have proof enough for me," Grenville said quickly.

Wisher nodded absently.

"It's easy to understand. Evolution kept right on going, adapting and changing just as it does everywhere else in the Universe. Only here, when the mammals began coming up onto the land, they had no room to expand. And they were all being washed away every hundred years, as the tides rose and fell and the continents wore down below tide level.

"But evolution never stopped. It continued beneath the sea. Eventually it came up with an intelligent race.

"God knows what they are, or how far they've progressed. They must be pretty highly evolved, or they couldn't have done something like this"—he broke off, realizing that the building of the islands was no clue. The ancient Egyptians on Earth had built the pyramids, certainly a much harder job. There was no way of telling how far evolved this race was. Or what the island was for.

Zoo?

No. He shook that out of the confusion of his mind. If the things in the sea wanted a zoo they would naturally build it below the surface of the water, where they themselves could travel with ease and where the animals could be kept in airtight compartments. And if this was a zoo, then by now there should have been visitors.

That was one more perplexing thing. Why had nothing come? It was unbelievable that an island like this should be left completely alone, that nothing had noticed the coming of their ship.

And here his thought broke again. They would not be just fish, these things. They would need . . . hands. Or tentacles. He pictured something like a genius squid, and the hair of his body stiffened.

He turned back to Grenville.

"Did you get the animal specimens?"

Grenville shook his head. "No. Just plants. And a small lizard."

Wisher's face, lined with the inbred caution of many years, now at last betrayed his agitation. "We'll have to get one of those things that set off the alarm last night. But to heck with the rest. We'll let HQ worry about that." He stepped quickly into the airlock, dragging the bag of specimens. "I'll pack up," he said, "you go get that thing."

Grenville turned automatically and struck off down the beach.

He never came back.

At the end of the third hour after Grenville had gone, Wisher went to the arms locker and pulled out a heavy rifle. He cursed the fact that he had no small scout sled. He could not take the ship. She was too big and unwieldy for low, slow flying and he could not risk cracking her up.

He was breaking the regs, of course. Since Grenville had not come back he must be considered dead and it was up to Wisher to leave alone. A special force would come back for Grenville, or for what was left of him. Wisher knew all that. He thought about it while he was loading the rifle. He thought about the vow he had made never to break the regs and he went right on loading the rifle. He told himself that he would take no chances and if he didn't find Grenville right away he would come back and leave, but he knew all along that he was breaking the regs. At the same time he knew that there was nothing else to do. This was the one reg he had never faced before and it was the one reg he would always break. For Grenville or for anyone else. For a skinny young fool like Grenville, or for anyone else.

Before he left he took the routine precautions concerning the ship. He set the alarm screens to blast anything that moved within two hundred feet of her. If Grenville came back before him it would be all right because the alarm was set to deactivate when it registered the sound pattern of either his or Grenville's voice. If Grenville came back and didn't see him, he would know that the alarm was on.

And if no one came back at all, the ship would blow by itself.

The beach was wide and curved on out of sight. Grenville's deep heel prints were easy to follow.

Stiffly, in the wind, the stalks of the brown vegetation scratched and rustled. Wisher walked along Grenville's track. He wanted to call, but stopped himself. No noise. He must make no noise.

This is the end of it, he kept saying to himself. When I get out of this I will go home.

The heel prints turned abruptly into the alien forest. Wisher walked some distance farther on, to a relatively clear space. He turned, stepping carefully, started to circle the spot where Grenville had gone in. The wood around him was soggy, sterile. He saw nothing move. But a sharp, shattering blast came suddenly to him in the still air.

The explosion blossomed and Wisher jerked spasmodically. The ship. Something was at the ship. He fought down a horrible impulse to run, stood quiet, gun poised, knowing that the ship could take care of itself. And then he stepped slowly forward. And fell.

He fell through a soft light mat of brushes into a hole. There was a crunching snap and he felt metal rip into his legs, tearing and cracking the bones. He went in up to his shoulders. He knew in a flash, with a blast of glacial fear, what it was. *Animal trap.*

He reached for his rifle. But the rifle was beyond him. A foot past his hand, it lay on the floor of the wood near him. His legs, his legs . . . he felt the awful pain as he tried to move.

It blazed through his mind and woke him. Out of his belt he dragged his pistol, and in a sea of pain, held upright by the trap, he waited. He was not afraid. He had broken the regs, and this had happened, and he had expected it. He waited.

Nothing came.

Why, why?

This had happened to Grenville, he knew. Why?

It had happened to him now, and for a moment he could not understand why he did not seem to care, but was just . . . curious. Then he looked down into the hole and saw the hot redness of his own blood, and as he watched it bubble he realized that he was dying.

He had very little time. He was hopeful. Maybe something would come and at least he would see what they were. He wanted awfully for something to come. In the red mist which was his mind he debated with himself whether or not to shoot it if it came, and over and over he asked himself why, why? Before something came, unfortunately, he died.

The traps had been dug in the night. From out the sea they had come to dig in the preserve—for a preserve was what the island was, was all that it could have been—and then had returned to the sea to wait.

For the ship had been seen from the very beginning, and its purpose understood. The best brains of the sea had gathered and planned, the enormous, mantalike people whose name was unpronounceable but whose technology was not far behind Earth's met in consultation and immediately understood. It was necessary to capture the ship. Therefore the Earthmen must be separated from it, and it was for this reason that Wisher had died.

But now, to the astonishment of the things, the ship was still alive. It stood silent and alone in the whiteness of the beach, ticking and sparking within itself, and near it, on the bloodied sand, were the remains of the one that had come too close. The others had fled in terror.

Time was of no importance to the clever, squidlike beings. They had won already, could wait and consider. Thus the day grew late and became afternoon, and the waves— the aseptic, sterile waves which were proof in themselves of the greatest of all oceanic civilizations—crumbled whitely on the beach. The things exulted. The conquest of space was in their hands.

Within the ship, of course, there was ticking, and a small red hand moved toward zero.

In a little while the ship would blow, and with it would go the island, and a great chunk of the sea. But the beings could not know. It was an alien fact they faced and an alien fact was unknowable. Just as Wisher could not have known the nature of the planet, these things could not now foresee the nature of the ship and the wheel had come full circle. Second by second, with the utter, mechanical loyalty of the machine, the small red hand crept onward.

The waves near the beach were frothy and white.

A crowd was forming.

OPENING UP SLOWLY

HARRY BEGAN THE NIGHT BY GOING TO A DRIVE-in movie to see *Romeo and Juliet*. He had never read it or wanted to see it, but he had been working very hard and his wife wanted to see it and so he went—the little boy asleep in the back seat—and watched it with a kind of strangeness in his brain. All this about love he did not quite understand and had no real faith in, especially since young Juliet was only about fourteen years old; nevertheless he found that when Romeo killed himself, it was a powerful moment, and something very strange and hard to talk about happened inside his mind, and he sat there for a long moment in silence with his young wife, Martha, who was crying over the ending. Then she reached out for him and held him for a moment, and he felt the tears on her face, and over her shoulder he saw the little boy, not even a year old, placidly asleep, and Harry did not know what to say.

After a moment his wife said, "Did you like it?"

"I don't know." Harry started the car. "I guess so."

"It's one of the finest . . . I've ever seen."

"I'm sorry you're crying."

"Don't be sorry," she said. She touched him on the arm. She was deeply moved and he knew it and was glad of it.

"I don't know what to say." He shook his head. "Would you kill yourself if I died?"

She said nothing.

"It just seems strange and for the very young," he said. "I thought it was out of date."

"I guess so," she said.

"I mean, love doesn't happen like that anymore. Not

51

now. You don't meet a girl and suddenly fall all in love like that, so that in two or three days you can die for her."

Martha said, "I suppose you don't."

And now he reached out himself and touched her once quickly, touching her leg while he drove, although he was a shy man who did not often show affection or even really know how to show it well except by something on his face in a wordless moment. And he said, "I love you, you know," which was a rare thing for him to say, and she leaned toward him immediately; but then he said, embarrassed, "But it's not like that for us, is it? I mean, it didn't happen in one day. It took a long time, and we slowly opened up, and even now I don't think you would die if I died."

She kissed him on the cheek. "We're happy," she said.

So it doesn't matter, he thought. And yet it did. He did not know why. There was the question in his brain of why he was so moved; and because for all his life he had been shy and wary about giving himself, and even now in marriage was opening up only slowly, day by day, he knew that he did not understand the ways in which other people loved. There in the back seat was his son, less than a year old, his first baby, and Harry did not yet know what he felt. He not only did not know how he felt, he also did not know how he was supposed to feel. In the long, dark back of his brain he was still alone.

Before they reached home the baby woke up. He sat up on the back seat and looked forward silently, innocently, with huge dark eyes and a slow, warm smile.

Harry drove into the yard and pulled up at the door while Martha picked up the baby and got out, and then he put the car away for the night. The day was done. Time now for bed, and early in the morning it would be time to work hard again. Harry sat alone behind the wheel, feeling very strange. Once more he saw the figure of Romeo on the body of Juliet, and Juliet still alive, Juliet only fourteen; again he saw Romeo kill himself, and now it touched him even more than when he had first seen it, in a way he still could not get used to or understand. Damn good movie, he thought. Ought to see it again. Old Shakespeare. Fine man.

He got out of the car and went into the house. The boy was sitting up in the playpen by the radiator, still smiling happily, delighted at being awake with Daddy here because

Daddy was not here often. Harry sat down near the playpen, not yet ready for sleep, staring at the baby's face. It was really a very soft and friendly and handsome face, not what it had been when first born—so stiff and hairy and red-faced. He had turned away from it on that day with a certain fear. He remembered that suddenly, and so he sat and stared at the child's face, and although it was time for bed and it had been just another long day in a hard world, he did not feel like going to sleep. There was something to think about, so he sat there.

Martha had gone automatically to make him coffee. She knew him, knew he was often a strange and silent man, hard to get on with by talking to, and so she made the coffee silently. It was a cold night, and the room was cold, although there was a radiator turned on near the playpen. That had led to the baby's first word, Harry suddenly remembered, looking at the small face, the wide eyes. The baby had touched the radiator and then had cried in pain. When Harry had told him that the radiator was too hot, trying to warn him even if he didn't understand language, the boy had stood there with tears in his eyes and had pointed toward the radiator and said the first word of his life, the first Harry had ever heard him say. He had pointed and said, "Hot!" just like that, and Harry had been amazed. Impressed and amazed, and now for some reason Harry, sitting there alone and staring at the boy, felt an odd stiffness in his chest. He thought for a moment something might be wrong with him. He found it hard to look at the boy's face. He turned away.

Martha came in with coffee and set it on the table near the playpen, and the baby reached for it.

"No, don't do that," Martha said. "Hot!" she said.

The baby nodded. "Hot!" he said. Harry looked up again and found his eyes blurring. He did not know what was happening. He thought again of a dying Romeo, a man in love. But Harry was not that way himself, not open all the way; he never had been and never would be, so why cry now? But he looked up at the baby again, and the baby stared back at him and then smiled, and when Harry reached out automatically for the coffee the baby reached suddenly out, warning him, and repeated earnestly, "Hot! Hot!" For a long moment Harry could not believe it; he just sat there, staring, and the boy stared back at him. And then Harry felt it truly for the first time in his life—the

53

incredible shock. It was total and permanent, and it came out of the back of his brain like sudden sunlight and enormous warmth. He sat staring at the little body, the tiny smile. He felt himself coming apart everywhere. He sat without moving. He could not speak or touch the boy. Martha came to him, and he reached out and touched her.

THE BOOK

BEAUCLAIRE WAS GIVEN HIS FIRST SHIP AT
Sirius. He was called up before the Commandant in the
slow heat of the afternoon and stood shuffling with awkward delight upon the shaggy carpet. He was twenty-five
years old and two months out of the Academy. It was a
wonderful day.

The Commandant told Beauclaire to sit down, and sat
looking at him for a long while. The Commandant was an
old man with a face of many lines. He was old, was hot,
was tired. He was also very irritated. He had reached that
point of oldness when talking to a young man is an irritation because they are so bright and certain and don't know
anything and there is nothing you can do about it.

"All right," the Commandant said, "there are a few
things I have to tell you. Do you know where you are going?"

"No, sir," Beauclaire said cheerfully.

"All right," the Commandant said again, "I'll tell you.
You are going to the Hole in Cygnus. You've heard of it,
I hope? Good. Then you know that the Hole is a large
dust cloud—estimated diameter, ten light-years. We have
never gone into the Hole, for a number of reasons. It's too
thick for light speeds, it's too big, and Mapping Command
ships are being spread thin. Also, until now, we never
thought there was anything in the Hole worth looking at.
So we have never gone into the Hole. Your ship will be the
first."

"Yes, *sir*," Beauclaire said, eyes shining.

"A few weeks ago," the Commandant said, "one of our
amateurs had a lens on the Hole, just looking. He saw a
glow. He reported to us; we checked and saw the same
thing. There is a faint light coming out of the Hole—

obviously, a sun, a star inside the cloud, just far enough in to be almost invisible. God knows how long it's been there, but we do know that there's never been a record of a light in the Hole. Apparently this star orbited in some time ago and is now on its way out. It is just approaching the edge of the cloud. Do you follow me?"

"Yes, sir," Beauclaire said.

"Your job is this: You will investigate that sun for livable planets and alien life. If you find anything—which is highly unlikely—you are to decipher the language and come right back. A Psych team will go out and determine the effects of a starless sky upon the alien culture—obviously, these people will never have seen the stars."

The Commandant leaned forward, intent now for the first time.

"Now, this is an important job. There were no other linguists available, so we passed over a lot of good men to pick you. Make no mistake about your qualifications. You are nothing spectacular. But the ship will be yours from now on, permanently. Have you got that?"

The young man nodded, grinning from ear to ear.

"There is something else," the Commandant said, and abruptly he paused.

He gazed silently at Beauclaire—at the crisp gray uniform, the baby-slick cheek—and he thought fleetingly and bitterly of the Hole in Cygnus which he, an old man, would never see. Then he told himself sternly to leave off self-pity. The important thing was coming up and he would have to say it well.

"Listen," he said. The tone of his voice was very strong and Beauclaire blinked. "You are replacing one of our oldest men. One of our best men. His name is Billy Wyatt. He—he has been with us a long time." The Commandant paused again, his fingers toying with the blotter on his desk. "They have told you a lot of stuff at the Academy, which is all very important. But I want you to understand something else: This Mapping Command is a weary business—few men last for any length of time, and those that do aren't much good in the end. You know that. Well, I want you to be very careful when you talk to Billy Wyatt; and I want you to listen to him, because he's been around longer than anybody. We're relieving him, yes, because he is breaking down. He's no good for us anymore; he has no more nerve. He's lost the feeling a man has to have to do his job right."

58

The Commandant got up slowly and walked around in front of Beauclaire, looking into his eyes.

"When you relieve Wyatt, treat him with respect. He's been farther and seen more than any man you will ever meet. I want no cracks and no pity for that man. Because, listen, boy, sooner or later the same thing will happen to you. Why? Because it's too big"—the Commandant gestured helplessly with spread hands—"it's all just too damn big. Space is never so big that it can't get bigger. If you fly long enough, it will finally get too big to make any sense, and you'll start thinking. You'll start thinking that it doesn't make sense. On that day we'll bring you back and put you into an office somewhere. If we leave you alone, you lose ships and get good men killed—there's nothing we can do when space gets too big. That is what happened to Wyatt. That is what will happen, eventually, to you. Do you understand?"

The young man nodded uncertainly.

"And that," the Commandant said sadly, "is the lesson for today. Take your ship. Wyatt will go with you on this one trip, to break you in. Pay attention to what he has to say—it will mean something. There's one other crewman, a man named Cooper. You'll be flying with him now. Keep your ears open and your mouth shut, except for questions. And don't take any chances. That's all."

Beauclaire saluted and rose to go.

"When you see Wyatt," the Commandant said, "tell him I won't be able to make it down before you leave. Too busy. Got papers to sign. Got more damn papers than the chief has ulcers."

The young man waited.

"That, God help you, is all," said the Commandant.

Wyatt saw the letter when the young man was still a long way off. The white caught his eye, and he watched idly for a moment. And then he saw the fresh green gear on the man's back and the look on his face as he came up the ladder, and Wyatt stopped breathing.

He stood for a moment blinking in the sun. *Me?* he thought ... *me?*

Beauclaire reached the platform and threw down his gear, thinking that this was one hell of a way to begin a career.

Wyatt nodded to him, but didn't say anything. He accepted the letter, opened it, and read it. He was a short

59

man, thick and dark and very powerful. The lines of his face did not change as he read the letter.

"Well," he said when he was done, "thank you."

There was a long wait, and Wyatt said at last: "Is the Commandant coming down?"

"No, sir. He said he was tied up. He said to give you his best."

"That's nice," Wyatt said.

After that neither of them spoke. Wyatt showed the new man to his room and wished him good luck. Then he went back to his cabin and sat down to think.

After twenty-eight years in the Mapping Command, he had become necessarily immune to surprise; he could understand this at once, but it would be some time before he would react. *Well, well,* he said to himself; but he did not feel it.

Vaguely, flicking cigarettes onto the floor, he wondered *why.* The letter had not given a reason. He had probably flunked a physical. Or a mental. One or the other, each good enough reason. He was forty-seven years old, and this was a rough business. Still, he felt strong and cautious, and he knew he was not afraid. He felt good for a long while yet . . . but obviously he was not.

Well, then, he thought, *where now?*

He considered that with interest. There was no particular place for him to go. Really no place. He had come into the business easily and naturally, knowing what he wanted —which was simply to move and listen and see. When he was young, it had been adventure alone that drew him; now it was something else he could not define, but a thing he knew he needed badly. He had to see, to watch . . . and *understand.*

It was ending, the long time was ending. It didn't matter what was wrong with him. The point was that he was through. The point was that he was going home, to nowhere in particular.

When evening came, he was still in his room. Eventually he'd been able to accept it all and examine it clearly, and had decided that there was nothing to do. If there was anything out in space which he had not yet found, he would not be likely to need it.

He left off sitting, and went up to the control room.

Cooper was waiting for him. Cooper was a tall, bearded, scrawny man with a great temper and a great heart and

60

a small capacity for liquor. He was sitting all alone in the room when Wyatt entered.

Except for the pearl-green glow of dashlights from the panel, the room was dark. Cooper was lying far back in the pilot's seat, his feet propped up on the panel. One shoe was off and he was carefully pressing buttons with his huge bare toes. The first thing Wyatt saw when he entered was the foot glowing luridly in the green light of the panel. Deep within the ship he could hear the hum of the dynamos starting and stopping.

Wyatt grinned. From the play of Coop's toes, and the attitude, and the limp, forgotten pole of an arm which hung down loosely from the chair, it was obvious that Coop was drunk. In port he was usually drunk. He was a lean, likable man with very few cares and no manners at all, which was typical of men in that Command.

"What say, Billy?" Coop mumbled from deep in the seat. Wyatt sat down. "Where you been?"

"In the port. Been drinkin' in the goddamn port. Hot!"

"Bring back any?"

Coop waved an arm floppily in no particular direction. "Look around."

The flasks lay in a heap by the door. Wyatt took one and sat down again. The room was warm and green and silent. The two men had been together long enough to be able to sit without speaking, and in the green glow they waited, thinking. The first pull Wyatt took was long and numbing; he closed his eyes.

Coop did not move at all. Not even his toes. When Wyatt had begun to think he was asleep, he said suddenly: "Heard about the replacement."

Wyatt looked at him.

"Found out this afternoon," Coop said, "from the goddamn Commandant."

Wyatt closed his eyes again.

"Where you goin'?" Coop asked.

Wyatt shrugged. "Plush job."

"You got any plans?"

Wyatt shook his head.

Coop swore moodily. "Never let you alone," he muttered. "Miserable bastards." He rose up suddenly in the chair, pointing a long matchstick finger into Wyatt's face. "Listen, Billy," he said with determination, "you was a good man, you know that? You was one hell of a good goddamn man."

Wyatt took another long pull and nodded, smiling.

"You said it," he said.

"I sailed with some good men, some *good* men," Coop insisted, stabbing shakily but emphatically with his finger, "but you don't take nothin' from nobody."

"Here's to me, I'm true blue." Wyatt grinned.

Coop sank back in the chair, satisfied. "I just wanted you should know. You been a good man."

"Betcher sweet life," Wyatt said.

"So they throw you out. *Me* they keep. *You* they throw out. They got no brains."

Wyatt lay back, letting the liquor take hold, receding without pain into a quiet world. The ship was good to feel around him, dark and throbbing like a living womb. *Just like a womb,* he thought. *It's a lot like a womb.*

"Listen," Coop said thickly, rising from his chair. "I think I'll quit this racket. What the hell I wanna stay in this racket for?"

Wyatt looked up, startled. When Coop was drunk, he was never a little drunk. He was always far gone, and he could be very mean. Wyatt saw now that he was down deep and sinking; that the replacement was a big thing to him, bigger than Wyatt had expected. In this team Wyatt had been the leader, and it had seldom occurred to him that Coop really needed him. He had never really thought about it. But now he let himself realize that, alone, Coop could be very bad. Unless this new man was worth anything and learned quickly, Coop would very likely get himself killed.

Now, more than ever, this replacement thing was ridiculous; but for Coop's sake, Wyatt said quickly: "Drop that, man. You'll be on this ship in the boneyard. You even look like this ship—you got a bright red bow."

When the tall man was dark and silent, Wyatt said gently, "Coop. Easy. We leave at midnight. Want me to take her up?"

"Naw." Coop turned away abruptly, shaking his head. "T'hell with you. Go die." He sank back deeply in the seat, his gaunt face reflecting the green glow from the panel. His next words were sad, and, to Wyatt, very touching.

"Hell, Billy," Coop said wearily, "this ain' no fun."

Wyatt let him take the ship up alone. There was no reason to argue about it. Coop was drunk; his mind was unreachable.

At midnight the ship bucked and heaved and leaped up into the sky. Wyatt hung tenuously to a stanchion by a port, watched the night lights recede and the stars begin blooming. In a few moments the last clouds were past, and they were out in the long night, and the million million speckled points of glittering blue and red and silver burned once more with the mighty light which was, to Wyatt, all that was real or had ever meant living. In the great glare and the black he stood, as always, waiting for something to happen, for the huge lonely beauty to resolve itself to a pattern and descend and be understood.

It did not. It was just space, an area in which things existed, in which mechanized substance moved. Wondering, waiting, Wyatt regarded the Universe. The stars looked icily back.

At last, almost completely broken, Wyatt went to bed.

Beauclaire's first days passed very quickly. He spent them in combing the ship, seeking her out in her deepest layers, watching and touching and loving. The ship was to him like a woman; the first few days were his honeymoon. Because there is no lonelier job that a man can have, it was nearly always this way with men in the Command.

Wyatt and Cooper left him pretty much alone. They did not come looking for him, and the few times that he did see them he could not help but feel their surprise and resentment. Wyatt was always polite. Cooper was not. Neither seemed to have anything to say to Beauclaire, and he was wise enough to stay by himself. Most of Beauclaire's life until now had been spent among books and dust and dead, ancient languages. He was by nature a solitary man, and therefore it was not difficult for him to be alone.

On a morning some weeks after the trip began, Wyatt came looking for him. His eyes twinkling, Wyatt fished him up, grease-coated and embarrassed, out of a shaft between the main dynamos. Together they went up toward the astrogation dome. And under the great dome, beneath the massive crystal sheet on the other side of which there was nothing for ever and ever, Beauclaire saw a beauty which he was to remember as long as he lived.

They were nearing the Hole in Cygnus. On the side which faces the center of the Galaxy the Hole is almost flat, from top to bottom, like a wall. They were moving in on the flat side now, floating along some distance from the

63

wall, which was so huge and incredible that Beauclaire was struck dumb.

It began above him, light-years high. It came down in a black, folding, rushing silence, fell away beneath him for millions upon millions of miles, passed down beyond sight so far away, so unbelievably far away and so vast, that there could be nothing as big as this, and if he had not seen the stars still blazing on either side he would have had to believe that the wall was just outside the glass, so close he could touch it. From all over the wall a haze reflected faintly, so that the wall stood out in ridges and folds from the great black of space. Beauclaire looked up and then down, and then stood and gazed.

After a while, Wyatt pointed silently down. Beauclaire looked in among the folds and saw it, the tiny yellow gleam toward which they were moving. It was so small against the massive cloud that he lost it easily.

Each time he took his eyes away he lost it, and had to search for it again.

"It's not too far in," Wyatt said at last, breaking the silence. "We'll move down the cloud to the nearest point, then we'll slow down and move in. Should take a couple of days."

Beauclaire nodded.

"Thought you'd like to see," Wyatt said.

"Thanks." Beauclaire was sincerely grateful. And then, unable to contain himself, he shook his head with wonder. "My God!" he said.

Wyatt smiled. "It's a big show."

Later, much later, Beauclaire began to remember what the Commandant had said about Wyatt. But he could not understand it at all. Sure, something like the Hole was incomprehensible. It did not make any sense—but so what? A thing as beautiful as that, Beauclaire thought, did not *have* to make sense.

They reached the sun slowly. The gas was not thick by any Earthly standards—approximately one atom to every cubic mile of space—but for a starship, any matter at all is too much. At normal speeds the ship would hit the gas like a wall. So they came in slowly, swung in and around the large yellow sun.

They saw one planet almost immediately. While moving in toward that one they scanned for others, found none at all.

Space around them was absolutely strange; there was nothing in the sky but a faint haze. They were in the cloud now, and of course could see no star. There was nothing but the huge sun and the green gleaming dot of that one planet and the endless haze.

From a good distance out Wyatt and Cooper ran through the standard tests while Beauclaire watched with grave delight. They checked for radio signals, found none. The spectrum of the planet revealed strong oxygen and water-vapor lines, surprisingly little nitrogen. The temperature, while somewhat cool, was in the livable range.

It was a habitable planet.

"Jackpot!" Coop said cheerfully. "All that oxygen, bound to be some kind of life."

Wyatt said nothing. He was sitting in the pilot chair, his huge hands on the controls, nursing the ship around into the long slow spiral which would take them down. He was thinking of many other things, many other landings. He was remembering the acid ocean at Lupus and the rotting disease of Altair, all the dark, vicious, unknowable things he had approached, unsuspecting, down the years.

. . . So many years that now he suddenly realized it was too long, too long.

Cooper, grinning unconsciously as he scanned with the telescope, did not notice Wyatt's sudden freeze.

It was over all at once. Wyatt's knuckles had gradually whitened as he gripped the panel. Sweat had formed on his face and run down into his eyes, and he blinked, and realized with a strange numbness that he was soaking wet all over. In that moment his hands froze and gripped the panel, and he could not move them.

It was a hell of a thing to happen on a man's last trip, he thought. He would like to have taken her down just this once. He sat looking at his hands. Gradually, calmly, carefully, with a cold will and a welling sadness, he broke his hands away from the panel.

"Coop," he said, "take over."

Coop glanced over and saw. Wyatt's face was white and glistening; his hands in front of him were wooden and strange.

"Sure," Coop said, after a very long moment. "Sure."

Wyatt backed off, and Coop slid into the seat.

"They got me just in time," Wyatt said, looking at his stiff, still fingers. He looked up and ran into Beauclaire's

65

wide eyes and turned away from the open pity. Coop was bending over the panel, swallowing heavily.

"Well," Wyatt said. He was beginning to cry. He walked slowly from the room, his hands held before him like old gray things that had died.

The ship circled automatically throughout the night, while its crew slept or tried to. In the morning they were all forcefully cheerful and began to work up an interest.

There were people on the planet. Because the people lived in villages and had no cities and no apparent science, Coop let the ship land.

It was unreal. For a long while none of them could get over the feeling of unreality, Wyatt least of all. He stayed in the ship and got briefly drunk, and then came out as carefully efficient as ever. Coop was gay and brittle. Only Beauclaire saw the planet with any degree of clarity. And all the while the people looked back.

From the very beginning it was peculiar.

The people saw the ship passing overhead, yet curiously they did not run. They gathered in groups and watched. When the ship landed, a small band of them came out of the circling woods and hills and ringed the ship, and a few came up and touched it calmly, ran fingers over smooth steel sides.

The people were human.

There was not, so far as Beauclaire could tell, a single significant difference. It was not really extraordinary— similar conditions will generally breed similar races—but there was something about these men and women which was hard and powerful, and in a way almost grand.

They were magnificently built, rounded and bronzed. Their women especially were remarkably beautiful. They were wearing woven clothes of various colors, in simple savage fashions; but there was nothing at all savage about them. They did not shout or seem nervous or move around very much, and nowhere among them was there any sign of a weapon. Furthermore, they did not seem to be particularly curious. The ring about the ship did not increase. Although several new people wandered in from time to time, others were leaving, unconcerned. The only ones among them who seemed at all excited were the children.

Beauclaire stood by the view-screen, watching. Eventually Coop joined him, looking without interest until he saw the women. There was one particular girl with shaded

66

brown eyes and a body of gentle hills. Coop grinned widely and turned up the magnification until the screen showed nothing but the girl. He was gazing with appreciation and making side comments to Beauclaire when Wyatt came in.

"Looka *that*, Billy." Coop roared with delight, pointing. "Man, we have come home!"

Wyatt smiled very tightly, changed the magnification quickly to cover the whole throng around them.

"No trouble?"

"Nope," Coop said. "Air's good, too. Thin, but practically pure oxygen. Who's first to go out?"

"Me," Wyatt said, for obvious reasons. He would not be missed.

No one argued with him. Coop was smiling as Wyatt armed himself. Then he warned Wyatt to leave that cute little brown-eyed doll alone.

Wyatt went out.

The air was clear and cool. There was a faint breeze stirring the leaves around him, and Wyatt listened momentarily to the far bell-calls of birds. This would be the last time he would ever go out like this, to walk upon an unknown world. He waited for some time by the airlock before he went forward.

The ring of people did not move as he approached, his hand upraised in what the Mapping Command had come to rely on as the universal gesture of peace. He paused before a tall, monolithic old man in a single sheath of green cloth.

"Hello," he said aloud, and bowed his head slowly.

From the ship, through the wide-angle sights of a gun, Beauclaire watched breathlessly as Wyatt went through the pantomime of greeting.

None of the tall people moved, except the old man, who folded his arms and looked openly amused. When the pantomime was done, Wyatt bowed again. The old man broke into a broad grin, looked amiably around at the circle of people, and then quite suddenly bowed to Wyatt. One by one, the people, grinning, bowed.

Wyatt turned and waved at the ship, and Beauclaire stood away from his gun, smiling.

It was a very fine way to begin.

In the morning Wyatt went out alone, to walk in the sun among the trees, and he found the girl he had seen from the ship. She was sitting alone by a stream, her feet cooling and splashing in the clear water.

Wyatt sat down beside her. She looked up, unsurprised, out of eyes that were rich and grained like small pieces of beautiful wood. Then she bowed, from the waist. Wyatt grinned and bowed back.

Unceremoniously he took off his boots and let his feet plunk down into the water. It was shockingly cold, and he whistled. The girl smiled at him. To his surprise, she began to hum softly. It was a pretty tune that he was able to follow, and after a moment he picked up the harmony and hummed along with her. She laughed, and he laughed with her, feeling very young.

Me Billy, he thought of saying, and laughed again. He was content just to sit without saying anything. Even her body, which was magnificent, did not move him to anything but a quiet admiration, and he regarded himself with wonder.

The girl picked up one of his boots and examined it critically, clucking with interest. Her lovely eyes widened as she played with the buckle. Wyatt showed her how the snaps worked and she was delighted and clapped her hands.

Wyatt brought other things out of his pockets and she examined them all, one after the other. The picture of him on his ID card was the only one which seemed to puzzle her. She handled it and looked at it, and then at him, and shook her head. Eventually she frowned and gave it definitely back to him. He got the impression that she thought it was very bad art. He chuckled.

The afternoon passed quickly, and the sun began to go down. They hummed some more and sang songs to each other which neither understood and both enjoyed, and it did not occur to Wyatt until much later how little curiosity they had felt. They did not speak at all. She had no interest in his language or his name, and, strangely, he felt all through the afternoon that talking was unnecessary. It was a very rare day spent between two people who were not curious and did not want anything from each other. The only words they said to each other were good-bye.

Wyatt, lost inside himself, plodding, went back to the ship.

In the first week Beauclaire spent his every waking hour learning the language of the planet. From the very beginning he had felt an unsettling, peculiar manner about these people. Their behavior was decidedly unusual. Although they did not differ in any appreciable way from human beings, they did not act very much like human beings in that they were almost wholly lacking a sense of awe, a sense of wonder. Only the children seemed surprised that the ship had landed, and only the children hung around and inspected it. Almost all the others went off about their regular business—which seemed to be farming—and when Beauclaire tried learning the language, he found very few of the people willing to spend time enough to teach him.

But they were always more or less polite, and by making a pest of himself he began to succeed. On another day when Wyatt came back from the brown-eyed girl, Beauclaire reported some progress.

"It's a beautiful language," he said as Wyatt came in. "Amazingly well developed. It's something like our Latin —same type of construction, but much softer and more flexible. I've been trying to read their book."

Wyatt sat down thoughtfully and lit a cigarette.

"Book?" he said.

"Yes. They have a lot of books, but *everybody* has this one particular book—they keep it in a place of honor in their houses. I've tried to ask them what it is—I think it's a bible of some kind—but they just won't bother to tell me."

Wyatt shrugged, his mind drifting away.

"I just don't understand them," Beauclaire said plaintively, glad to have someone to talk to. "I don't get them at all. They're quick, they're bright, but they haven't the damnedest bit of curiosity about *anything,* not even each other. My God, they don't even gossip!"

Wyatt, contented, puffed quietly. "Do you think not seeing the stars has something to do with it? Ought to have slowed down the development of physics and math."

Beauclaire shook his head. "No. It's very strange. There's something else. Have you noticed the way the ground seems to be sharp and jagged almost everywhere you look, sort of chewed up as if there was a war? Yet these people swear that they've never had a war within living memory, and they don't keep any history so a man could really find out."

When Wyatt didn't say anything, he went on: "And I can't see the connection about no stars. Not with these people. I don't care if you can't see the roof of the house you live in, you still have to have a certain amount of curiosity in order to stay alive. But these people just don't give a damn. The ship landed. You remember that? Out of the sky come gods like thunder—"

Wyatt smiled. At another time, at any time in the past, he would have been very much interested in this sort of thing. But now he was not. He felt himself—remote, sort of—and he, like these people, did not particularly give a damn.

But the problem bothered Beauclaire, who was new and fresh and looking for reasons, and it also bothered Cooper.

"Damn!" Coop grumbled as he came stalking into the room. "Here you are, Billy. I'm bored stiff. Been all over this whole crummy place lookin' for you. Where you been?" He folded himself into a chair, scratched his black hair broodingly with long, sharp fingers. "Game o' cards?"

"Not just now, Coop," Wyatt said, lying back and resting.

Coop grunted. "Nothin' to do, nothin' to do." He swiveled his eyes to Beauclaire. "How you comin', son? How soon we leave this place? Like Sunday afternoon all the time."

Beauclaire was always ready to talk about the problem. He outlined it now to Cooper again, and Wyatt, listening, grew very tired. There is just this one continent, Beauclaire said, and just one nation, and everyone spoke the same tongue. There was no government, no police, no law that he could find. There was not even, as far as he could tell, a system of marriage. You couldn't even call it a society, really, but dammit, it existed—and Beauclaire could not find a single trace of rape or murder or violence of any kind. The people here, he said, just didn't give a damn.

"You said it," Coop boomed. "I think they're all whacky."

"But happy," Wyatt said suddenly. "You can see that they're happy."

"Sure, they're happy," Coop chortled. "They're nuts. They got funny looks in their eyes. Happiest guys I know are screwy as—"

The sound which cut him off, which grew and blossomed and eventually explained everything, had begun a few seconds ago, too softly to be heard. Now suddenly, from a slight rushing noise, it burst into an enormous, thundering scream.

They leaped up together, horrified, and an overwhelming, gigantic blast threw them to the floor.

* * *

70

The ground rocked, the ship fluttered and settled crazily. In that one long second the monstrous noise of a world collapsing grew in the air and filled the room, filled the men and everything with one incredible, crushing, grinding shock.

When it was over there was another rushing sound, farther away, and another, and two more tremendous explosions; and though all in all the noise lasted for perhaps five seconds, it was the greatest any of them had ever heard, and the world beneath them continued to flutter, wounded and trembling, for several minutes.

Wyatt was first out of the ship, shaking his head as he ran to get back his hearing. To the west, over a long slight rise of green and yellow trees, a vast black cloud of smoke, several miles long and very high, was rising and boiling. As he stared and tried to steady his feet upon the shaking ground, he was able to gather himself enough to realize what this was.

Meteors.

He had heard meteors before, long before, on a world of Aldebaran. Now he could smell the same sharp burning disaster and feel the wind rushing wildly back to the west, where the meteors had struck and hurled the air away.

In that moment Wyatt thought of the girl, and although she meant nothing to him at all—none of these people meant anything in the least to him—he began running as fast as he could toward the west.

Behind him, white-faced and bewildered, came Beauclaire and Cooper.

When Wyatt reached the top of the rise, the great cloud covered the whole valley before him. Fires were burning in the crushed forest to his right, and from the lay of the cloud he could tell that the village of the people was not there anymore.

He ran down into the smoke, circling toward the woods and the stream where he had passed an afternoon with the girl. For a while he lost himself in the smoke, stumbling over rocks and fallen trees.

Gradually the smoke lifted, and he began running into some of the people. Now he wished that he could speak the language.

They were all wandering quietly away from the site of their village, none of them looking back. Wyatt could see a great many dead as he moved, but he had no time to stop, no time to wonder. It was twilight now, and the sun was

71

gone. He thanked God that he had a flashlight with him; long after night came, he was searching in the raw gash where the first meteor had fallen.

He found the girl, dazed and bleeding, in a cleft between two rocks. He knelt and took her in his arms. Gently, gratefully, through the night and the fires and past the broken and the dead, he carried her back to the ship.

It had all become frighteningly clear to Beauclaire. He talked with the people and began to understand.

The meteors had been falling since the beginning of time, so the people said. Perhaps it was the fault of the great dust-cloud through which this planet was moving; perhaps it was that this had not always been a one-planet system—a number of other planets, broken and shredded by unknown gravitational forces, would provide enough meteors for a very long time. And the air of the planet being thin, there was no real protection as there was on Earth. So year after year the meteors fell. In unpredictable places, at unknowable times, the meteors fell, like stones from the sling of God. They had been falling since the beginning of time. So the people, the unconcerned people, said.

And here was Beauclaire's clue. Terrified and shaken as he was, Beauclaire was the kind of man who saw reason in everything. He followed this one to the end.

In the meantime, Wyatt nursed the girl. She had not been badly hurt and recovered quickly. But her family and friends were mostly dead now, and so she had no reason to leave the ship.

Gradually Wyatt learned the language. The girl's name was ridiculous when spoken in English, so he called her Donna, which was something like her real name. She was, like all her people, unconcerned about the meteors and her dead. She was extraordinarily cheerful. Her features were classic, her cheeks slim and smiling, her teeth perfect. In the joy and whiteness of her Wyatt saw each day what he had seen and known in his mind on the day the meteors fell. Love to him was something new. He was not sure whether or not he was in love, and he did not care. He realized that he needed this girl and was at home with her, could rest with her and talk with her, and watch her walk and understand what beauty was; and in the ship in those days a great peace began to settle over him.

When the girl was well again, Beauclaire was in the middle of translating the book—the biblelike book which all the people seemed to treasure so much. As his work progressed, a striking change began to come over him. He spent much time alone under the sky, watching the soft haze through which, very soon, the stars would begin to shine.

He tried to explain what he felt to Wyatt, but Wyatt had no time.

"But, Billy," Beauclaire said fervently, "do you see what these people go through? Do you see how they live?"

Wyatt nodded, but his eyes were on the girl as she sat listening dreamily to a recording of ancient music.

"They live every day waiting," Beauclaire said. "They have no idea what the meteors are. They don't know that there is anything else in the Universe but their planet and their sun. They think that's all there is. They don't know why they're here—but when the meteors keep falling like that, they have only one conclusion."

Wyatt turned from the girl, smiling absently. None of this could touch him. He had seen the order and beauty of space, the incredible perfection of the Universe, so often and so deeply that, like Beauclaire, he could not help but believe in a Purpose, a grand final meaning. When his father had died of an insect bite at Oberon he had believed in a purpose for that and had looked for it. When his first crewmate fell into the acid ocean of Alcestis and the second died of a horrible rot, Wyatt had seen purpose, purpose; and each time another man died, for no apparent reason, on windless, evil, useless worlds, the meaning of things had become clearer and clearer, and now in the end Wyatt was approaching the truth, which was perhaps that none of it mattered at all.

It especially did not matter now. So many things had happened that he had lost the capacity to pay attention. He was not young anymore; he wanted to rest, and upon the bosom of this girl he had all the reason for anything and everything he needed.

But Beauclaire was incoherent. It seemed to him that here on this planet a great wrong was being done, and the more he thought of it the more angry and confused he became. He went off by himself and looked at the terrible wound on the face of the planet, at all the sweet, lovely, fragrant things which would never be again, and he ended by cursing the nature of things, as Wyatt had done so many years before. And then he went on with the translation of the book. He came upon the final passage, still cursing inwardly, and reread it again and again. When the sun was rising on a brilliant new morning, he went back to the ship.

"They had a man here once," he said to Wyatt, "who was as good a writer as there ever was. He wrote a book which these people use as their bible. It's like our bible sometimes, but mostly it's just the opposite. It preaches that a man shouldn't worship anything. Would you like to hear some of it?"

Wyatt had been pinned down and he had to listen, feeling sorry for Beauclaire, who had such a long way to go. His thoughts were on Donna, who had gone out alone to walk in the woods and say good-bye to her world. Soon he would go out and bring her back to the ship, and she would probably cry a little, but she would come. She would come with him always, wherever he went.

"I have translated this the best way I could," Beauclaire said thickly, "but remember this. This man could write. He was Shakespeare and Voltaire and all the rest all at once. He could make you *feel*. I couldn't do a decent translation if I tried forever, but please listen and try to get what he means. I've put it in the style of Ecclesiastes because it's something like that."

"All right," Wyatt said.

Beauclaire waited for a long moment, feeling this deeply. When he read, his voice was warm and strong, and something of his emotion came through. As Wyatt listened, he found his attention attracted, and then he felt the last traces of his sadness and weariness fall away.

He nodded, smiling.

These are the words Beauclaire had gathered from the Book:

Rise up smiling and walk with me. Rise up in the armor of thy body and what shall pass shall make thee unafraid. Walk among the yellow hills, for they belong to thee. Walk upon grass and let thy feet descend into soft soil; in the end when all has failed thee the soil shall comfort thee, the soil shall receive thee, and in thy dark bed thou shalt find such peace as is thy portion.

In thine armor, hear my voice. In thine armor, hear.

74

Whatsoever thou doest, thy friend and thy brother and thy woman shall betray thee. Whatsoever thou dost plant, the weeds and the seasons shall spite thee. Wheresoever thou goest, the heavens shall fall upon thee. Though the nations shall come unto thee in friendship thou art curst. Know that the Gods ignore thee. Know that thou art Life, and that pain shall forever come into thee, though thy years be without end and thy days without sleep, even and forever. And knowing this, in thine armor, thou shalt rise up.

Red and full and glowing is thy heart; a steel is forging within thy breast. And what can hurt thee now? In thy granite mansion, what can hurt thee ever? Thou shalt only die. Therefore seek not redemption nor forgiveness for thy sins, for know that thou hast never sinned.

Let the Gods come unto *thee*.

When it was finished, Wyatt sat very still.

Beauclaire was looking at him intently.

Wyatt nodded. "I see," he said.

"They don't ask for anything," Beauclaire said. "No immortality, no forgiveness, no happiness. They take what comes and don't—wonder."

Wyatt smiled, rising. He looked at Beauclaire for a long while, trying to think of something to say. But there was nothing to say. If the young man could believe this, here and now, he would save himself a long, long, painful journey. But Wyatt could not talk about it—not just yet.

He reached out and clapped Beauclaire gently upon the shoulder. Then he left the ship and walked out toward the yellow hills, toward the girl and the love that was waiting.

What will they do, Beauclaire asked himself, *when the stars come out? When there are other places to go, will these people, too, begin to seek?*

They would. With sadness he knew that they would. For there is a chord in man which is plucked by the stars, which will rise upward and outward into infinity, as long as there is one man anywhere and one lonely place to which he has not been. And therefore what does the meaning matter? We are built in this way, and so shall we live.

Beauclaire looked up into the sky.

Dimly, faintly, like God's eye peeking through the silvery haze, a single star had begun to shine.

COME TO MY PARTY

WHEN THE BELL RANG, MORGAN DID SOMEthing he had not done in years. He knelt briefly in his corner and crossed himself. Then he went out to meet his man.

The night was different but his style was unchanged. He moved in crouching with his hands low, ready to hook. The colored boy chopped him twice with the left and backed away, but Morgan caught him once with the hook, hard, just under the heart, and the colored boy grunted and went away. He was very fast. He came back from the side with a low right and put the left in Morgan's eyes.

Morgan went after him with the hook and missed, spinning himself halfway around and off balance, and the colored boy hit him in the kidneys. Morgan did not feel it. The boy couldn't hit. But he was very fast. Morgan went in again, hooking for the body. He would have to slow this one down before shooting for the head. He missed again and the colored boy caught him a good one on the ear. Morgan nodded and shuffled on in. The colored boy backed away, keeping the left in Morgan's eyes.

There was a big crowd and it was very noisy in the Garden, but Morgan did not hear it. He was conscious only of the colored boy and of the mortal need to hit him. He went forward half lunging, hooking for the body. He was hit once over the left eye. The colored boy backed off and made faces at him. They were terrible warning faces, but Morgan did not hear the crowd laugh. He was dimly aware of a deep feeling of contempt. They called this one Cyclone Billy Jones. A television fighter. A clown.

Morgan went in viciously with the overhand right. It landed on the boy's neck. The boy came inside, butting and clinching. Morgan was waiting and dug him with the hook over the heart and the boy tore loose and went away. But at a distance he was grinning and saying something.

"You comin' to mah party?" he said.

Morgan put the left low and went after him. Cyclone Billy Jones danced away.

"Vict'ry party. You comin' to mah party?"

He changed step suddenly and caught Morgan coming in. The punch exploded in white light on Morgan's nose. He hooked blindly at nothing. He was hit several times around the eyes. He heard the colored boy say: "Mah place, jus' after the fight. You comin', Mistuh Morgan?"

He looks better than I expected, Laura thought. You can see he's all right. But after what Shipp did to him last month it's incredible to see him even walking. Still, he's undoubtedly all right. His eyes are clear. And look at him go in. Always forward. Always being hit. Excelsior. Onward and upward with Smoky Joe Morgan. But at least he's all right.

She sat deep in her chair, white-faced and small and looking cold, her face half buried in the soft fur of her coat. She was very confused. She was relieved to see him all right and at the same time annoyed with herself for being relieved, and she was amazed to see him looking exactly the same. The beating Shipp had given him had been one of the most brutal she'd ever seen, but it had made no change in him. He had not let it make a change. My God, she thought, thinking suddenly of the future, what will happen to him . . .

She stopped thinking and crouched in her chair. The colored boy danced above her and Joe Morgan came rushing forward and missed and fell into the ropes. She saw his face very close and felt his sweat fall on her. She flinched. The face hung above her, black-bearded and murderous, white teeth sharp in the dark jaws, the eyes black gleaming slits and the black hair wet and streaked across the pale forehead. He did not see her. The colored boy hit him from behind and there was screaming around her and Joe Morgan spun away. She sat up in her seat. The man with her patted her on the arm. She looked up and saw that he understood and smiled back nervously and put her hand on his.

"Do you want to go?" he said.

"No."

"We have better things to do," he said. He smiled.

She looked at him.

"Possibly," she said.

He nodded cheerfully and turned back to the fight. Laura's heart was still beating wildly. She looked up at Joe Morgan and shivered. In that second when he had come toward her, had hung raging above her with that awful murdering face, she had felt as if he was coming to get her. In that one horrible moment she still belonged to him and the rage was for her and he was coming after her. She took hold of herself. She said to herself that she ought not to have sat so close. You will never be able to let him come toward you, she thought, without flinching. She watched Morgan until the round ended. She had been married to him for four years, but except for the fight with Shipp she had not seen him since the divorce six months ago.

"Well," Warren said cheerfully, "he's over the hill. No question about it."

Laura looked up at him. Handsome. A delicate face, fragile almost, but very handsome. We have better things to do. Perhaps.

"He looks fairly healthy," Laura said.

"Oh, he's still very strong. They don't lose that. But the legs are gone. He can't catch him. Washed up at his age. Tough racket." He looked thoughtfully out at Morgan, who sat quietly rocklike in his corner with his manager bending over him. "Must have had over a hundred fights," Warren said. "How many times was he knocked out?"

"Twice."

"Shipp once. Who did the other?"

"Robinson."

"Ah, yes. But that was only a TKO. He was still on his feet."

"You should have seen him," Laura said.

"Yes, but you know the kind of knockout I mean. He's got to go down. I mean really down. Like Shipp did to him last month. *There* was a knockout. Amazing he took it so long. Very tough lad, Morgan. Always did like him. And only two knockouts. Remarkable, considering his style. He must take one hell of a punch."

"Quite often," Laura said.

Warren chuckled.

"True, true. But he's still healthy." He paused and lighted a cigarette. He thought about asking her jocularly if she was worried, but the round began and he decided to drop it. There was still too much sympathy in her for Morgan and he thought the wisest thing from here on in would be to say nothing. Never knock a competitor. But watching her now, the wide soft eyes gazing anxiously at Morgan, he felt deeply irritated. Dammit, he thought, Morgan has the advantage, regardless of what the *real* facts are. A fighter on the way down. To a woman like Laura that would be very touching. Well, all right, it was a tough business, but after all you have to grow up sometime. Many a good fighter has gone through it and come out all right. There was Mickey Walker being knocked out by some bum in Yakima, and he got up from that and took up painting and never fought again. And then there was Ad Wolgast knocked punchy by Joe Rivers, still training for the rematch twenty years after Rivers was dead. Morgan might go that way. Looking at Morgan tonight, you wondered how far he would really go. Because in his day that son of a gun could fight. Really brawl. It was his bad luck to come along while Robinson was champ, old Sugar, one of the two or three best in the last fifty years—well, the hell with that. Luckily Morgan was not punchy yet and this joker Jones couldn't hurt him, so sympathy would be held to a minimum. But in the future he ought to keep Laura away from fights. Any fights.

He reached down and took her hand.

"Listen, baby," he said softly, "where do you want to go when this is over?"

But she was not listening to him. She was watching Morgan chase the dancing, laughing colored boy around the ring.

"Why doesn't he come in and *fight*," she said angrily. "All that bouncing is silly."

Warren frowned.

"If he came in and fought, honey pie, he'd get his ears blown off."

"Cyclone Billy Jones," Laura said scornfully. "He's a television fighter."

"But my dear"—Warren grinned—"so, in his way, is Morgan."

"Jeez," Gerdy said unhappily, "he was wide open."

"I couldn't get to him," Morgan said.

"Well, look, you see what he's doin'? He's got a move he makes ev'ry time he comes in. He hits you, then he moves away from your right. Sideways. You see? What you do is wait for him, then left hook him as he goes sideways—"

82

"I saw it," Morgan said.

"Well, jeez—"

"What you think I been tryin' to do?"

"Oh," Gerdy said. "Okay." Holy Christ, he thought, to be beat by a clown like this. Six months ago we'd've creamed him.

He glanced unhappily across the ring to where Vito Parilli, the Cyclone's flashily dressed manager, stood watching Morgan with sad, cold eyes. Gerdy thought enviously of all the money Parilli would make with this Cyclone character. Jeez, he thought, that's always the way. Them as has gets.

"I'll get him," Morgan said. He was tapping his gloves together nervously.

"Well, for crissakes duck a little. He's pilin' up points."

"He can't hurt me. He couldn't hurt your mother."

"But all them points. You got to watch it."

"If he holds still. What round is it?"

"Five. Hey. You wife's here."

Morgan stopped tapping his gloves together. He did not turn his head.

"Ex-wife."

"So okay," Gerdy said. "Thought you'd like to know."

"The hell with her," Morgan said.

"Okay, okay," Gerdy said.

The bell rang. Morgan rose and set himself and moved out to the center of the ring and the colored boy hit him three times with the jab and moved away. You son of a bitch, Morgan thought, come in and fight. This is a *fight*. This is you and me. Come in, you son of a bitch, and I'll kill you. Come in. Come in.

And the colored boy came in and hit him and went away again and Morgan missed wildly. He swore at himself. The opening was there and he had seen it, but he was too late. There were openings all over the place, it was unbelievable how many things the kid did wrong, but Morgan could not hit him. It was goading him. He was beginning to swing desperately. The kid danced in front of him grinning broadly, talking the whole while as he had been talking all during the fight. Morgan did not hear him. He held his left hand down by his hip, ready to hook, and the right hand high, tight, shaky, and the kid came in and hit him.

And went away too slow.

It was the fifth round. The kid was twenty-four years old,

but he had been dancing and moving throughout the fight and Morgan had hit him three or four times in the belly. So that although he did not show it, he was a shade slower, just a hair, which was just slow enough, so that when he moved sideways this time Morgan brought up the left and hung him with it, caught him clearly and beautifully, and felt the punch hit and explode and go through, and the kid's head twisted and he went down.

Morgan came alive. He went back to his corner and waited for the kid to get up. He was sure the kid would get up and what worried him was that it was late in the round and there might not be enough time. But if he could go in now he could take him finally and for good with both hands, now finally, the right, too, to finish it. If there was time. He waited. He saw the kid coming up shakily, the eyes still glazed, and when the glove left the canvas he rushed forward to end it. But the referee got in his way and held him and the kid was sitting down, and he realized that while the kid was on the floor the round had ended.

He went to his corner and sat down. Gerdy worked over him excitedly but he did not hear him or the screaming crowd. He was thinking that if he was lucky the kid would still be dazed in the next round and he would get him then for sure. A little luck, he thought, a little luck. I got him then, dammit, but it had to be at the end of the round. And he had to go down with it. If he had stayed up there was still time to get in and really hurt him, but he had to go down. Well, let him run now. I'll get him now. He knows it.

From the back of his mind a thought came suddenly, a picture of her. *She* saw that too. She's here. He started to turn to look for her but the bell rang.

He forgot her and went out for the colored boy. But the Cyclone was already up and dancing away. And his eyes were clear and there was nothing shaky about him, and he put the left in Morgan's face and said, grinning: "You worry me, man, you worry me. But you come to mah party *anyhow*."

From there on it was downhill. The colored boy never came close again. He stayed outside and kept hitting at the eyes and there was nothing Morgan could do. His left eye was closed and he had lost every round but one. The Cyclone couldn't put him down and it was brutal. But the crowd loved it. The Cyclone was putting on a real show.

He was bobbing up and down and making frightening faces and talking loud enough for the ringsiders to hear. He would draw back his right and fake with it dangerously, warningly, and then pop Morgan delicately with the left. Several times he changed styles, fighting Morgan left-handed. Once he put his right behind his back. And Morgan took it and came on, still hoping, pawing clumsily with the left, hooking to the body, half blinded and leg weary, but still charging his man. Because the night was still different.

It went on that way through the last round. Had Morgan begun to bleed the referee would have stopped it, but Morgan did not cut easily and he had never once been dazed, so there was no reason to stop it and besides it was a good show. Late in the last round, Morgan's legs began to give out from under him and he could not charge anymore. He stopped several times and beckoned the colored boy to come in and fight and the colored boy buzzed in once delicately and flitted away again. Once the colored boy took a close look at Morgan and then set his feet solidly as if he was really going to punch this time, but Morgan came at him with joy in his good eye and the colored boy changed his mind and went away again. He was still going away when the fight ended.

Morgan went back to his corner. He did not think anything, feel anything. He heard the decision, saw the colored boy laughing into the television cameras, describing the terrible things he would do to the champ. Morgan's right arm began to twitch. Gerdy caught him by the arm and tried to move him. He did not move. The radio man was coming at him with the mike but looked at his face thoughtfully and said something into the mike and went away. Morgan looked out over the crowd and faces looked back at him. He looked down into the faces and they were grinning at him. But there was one face suddenly very soft and beautiful and strangely twisted, large lovely eyes gazing at him filled with pity. It took him a moment to recognize Laura. She turned from him quickly and went up the aisle in the crowd. There was a tall, blond man at her side. Morgan felt sick all the way down, cold in the belly. This time when Gerdy pulled him he moved, went through the ropes and down the aisle. He began to remember that the night was different, the night was different.

In the dressing room he sat on the table and Gerdy stood across the room from him and watched him warily. Gerdy

itched to get out. He had many things to do and many
people to see, and there was nothing left here but trouble.
He had seen Morgan lose before and he had never taken it
well, but there had never been anything like tonight, not
even that time with Shipp, because even a knockout would
be better than this, and looking at Morgan, he thought
gloomily, I better get out of here. They none of them ever
lose a fight. Either he caught me a lucky one or I was sick
that night or I just couldn't seem to get started, it must be
my trainer or something like that. But Morgan now did not
say anything—he just sat on the table with the robe half
fallen from his shoulders, staring down at the gloves out of
puffed eyes, so Gerdy, very cautiously, said: "The crum.
The lousy crum. He dint fight no fight. He run all the way,
Joe. You call that a fight? Get a guy in a bar, in a real
fight, he runs away then, does he win it? Jesus! What they
gettin' nowadays. Now listen, Joe, don't you worry about
it, we get another crack at him."

He waited anxiously for Morgan to say something about
that because both of them knew there would be no other
fight with Cyclone Billy Jones. Vito Parilli had a boy on
the way up. He would not take a chance on having his boy
get caught with that left hook again. But Morgan did not
say anything.

"Listen, Joe, you gonna get dressed? You catch your
death."

"You in a hurry?" Morgan said.

"No, Joe, honest. But you better—"

"If you're in a hurry get out."

"Well, jeez, Joe"—Gerdy drew himself up huffily—"if
you feel that way—"

He was interrupted by a rap on the door. Grateful for
the release, he opened it. He saw a small frail man named
Sickhead Dugan, one of the Cyclone's handlers. The small
man was nervous and remained outside the room.

"Hiya, Gerdy," he said quickly, "lissen, Gerdy, I don't
want no trouble on'y Cyclone he said I should come. He
sent me, it wasn't my idea."

"What idea?"

"Well, see, Cyclone"—the small man backed away—"he
wants I should invite, you should invite Joe t'his vict'ry
party. See ya."

He went quickly away.

"I'll tell him you called," Gerdy yelled after him indig-
nantly, "ya lousy—" He turned and peered cautiously at

Morgan, keeping the door open. Gerdy was not sure if he had heard. Jeez, he thought distastefully, I hope he ain't hurt.

"Well, listen, Joe, I got to run. You sure you don't need me?"

Morgan did not look up and did not say anything.

"Well, okay. You take care a that eye. I'll see you."

Gerdy waited jumpily for Morgan to say something. After a moment he shrugged virtuously, having done his duty, and left, closing the door behind him.

Morgan was alone.

He was completely alone. He stared at the room, at the dirty tile floor, the chipped gray lockers. There was noise in the corridor outside and he sat for a long time listening to it and waiting dumbly for the feeling inside him to go away. But it did not go away, it was in his belly, running hot and cold like the slow bleeding of a hemorrhage. He tried to think his way out of it but the thinking led nowhere, it led into tomorrow, which was nowhere, wide and gray and nowhere, and then it turned and came back to her and her face, the beauty of the face and the pity in the eyes. The pity more than anything. Her pitying him beaten— only that was not it, he was *not* beaten, not even close to beaten, this one tonight had danced all around him, but it had not been a fight, not a real fight, and he felt strong and ready still, his arms tensed and thick, packed with the unexploded, unexpended readiness, still waiting for the *fight*—the man to man, the way it should have been strictly between you and me and the way it used to be back in the old days without the rules and the referees, back there when you fought for real for a dirty piece of bread, no rules then and no referees, and without the rules on his side . . . I would have killed him. . . .

Well, now, he thought suddenly, don't blame the rules. This is no time to start complaining about the rules. They said all along and you said it too that a man should face it and never lie about it, if he's licked he should admit it and let it go and not make alibis. . . .

But *she* saw it. All that dancing and laughing and me swinging like a gate. Probably never see me again and so to remember me that way, a clown, me a clown too as well as him . . . but all right, all right, forget about *that*. If you keep thinking about that . . . but, oh, the clown, the lousy clown, there was no need for the laughing too. . . .

He pushed his gloves together hard and held them that

way for a moment. They were new and glistening, almost unused. It was now very quiet outside and he could hear pails and mops in the halls, and the sweat had dried on him and he felt cold. But even now in the stillness he could not believe that it was over; he flexed his arms, feeling the strength still there, and looked dazedly around the room.

There had to be something left, something more to do. He could not quit with this still in his arms, the cold bleeding still in his belly. He looked ahead clearly and saw the way it was. Something had to be done to stop the bleeding, he did not know what, but it had to be done. A man could end decently if they gave him any kind of chance at all, and he still had a chance, somewhere a chance, because he was not beaten, not really beaten, and no matter about the rules and the woman and all of the rest, a man should never quit until he is really beaten ...

His arm was twitching again. He rose and patted cold water on his eye and began to dress. He was halfway through dressing when he realized what it was he had left to do.

He had been invited to a party.

He could hear the party from a long way off. He came slowly down the hallway and stopped outside the door. In the streets it had been raining heavily and he was wet. He took his hands out of his pockets and wiped his face. Now, for the first time in his life before going to a fight, he stopped and made a plan.

He had first of all to get near the kid—just get near him. He knew that there were many people there and also many of Parilli's hoods, and even if they let him in, he saw almost no chance of them letting him get close. Not on a bet. But maybe if he was calm and quiet and did not show anything. Maybe if he acted groggy and asked for a drink. There was always a chance. He thought briefly of waiting until later, when there would be fewer people. But he could not wait, not possibly. This way the fight was not yet over —there was this one more round and waiting would let it spoil. He rang the bell.

The man who opened the door was fat and drunk and he stepped back in surprise and Morgan was in the room.

"Well, Jesus K. Rist!" the fat man bawled. "Lookit here!"

Morgan stood stiffly and put his hands in his pockets and tried to grin. Heads turned toward him but the party went right on, and he saw three of Parilli's big boys get up and come at him. He stood perfectly still. It was like hunting deer. Make no quick motion. He looked past the three men and saw Cyclone across the room. He was leaning on the bar with a drink in his hand, talking to a girl in a silver dress. He had not looked up.

"All right, waddya want?" the fat man said. His eyes had focused and he was looking down warily. The three men came up moving all together almost in step, like soldiers.

"I been invited," Morgan said.

"You better move on," one of the three boys said.

"But I been invited," Morgan said. He grinned. "Ask Cyclone."

The three boys edged in on him slowly and they were all bigger than he was and he could not see past them anymore. They were looking at his clothes all wet with the rain.

"He's drunk—throw him the hell out."

"No he ain't."

"He don't look very big outside the ring."

"Get goin', boy."

"I ain't lookin' for trouble," Morgan said.

"You damn right."

"Hey, listen," the fat man said. "He *did* invite him. I heard him. I thought he was kiddin'."

"He owes me a drink."

"But he was kiddin'."

"The hell he was," Morgan said. He grinned again friendlily. The three boys were uncertain. Morgan took the moment.

"Come on, you guys, lay off me. On'y want a drink. Go ask Parilli."

When he mentioned Parilli's name he moved for the first time. He slipped through them gently, still grinning, and began walking slowly across the room toward the Cyclone.

"Hey, wait a second," one of them said, but nobody moved and he walked on slowly, smiling, across the room and around a long couch. He felt beautifully cold and clear and there was a high wide whistling going on in his head, like the wind on a high mountain. He could smell the cigar smoke and the liquor and feel the soft carpet beneath his feet, but he was not conscious of his wet clothes or of any part of his body, and the noises of the room were dim and the lights were all sharp and glittering.

He was getting close. Now it began to show on his face.

Out of the corner of his eye he saw Parilli. Parilli saw him too, and the little man stood up quickly and shouted something. Morgan heard a movement toward him, but it was too late. The Cyclone looked up

"You run away from me," Morgan said. "Lemme see you run now."

The Cyclone blinked, puzzled. The girl backed off. The Cyclone saw it coming and put his left up.

Morgan hit him with both hands in the belly. The kid tried to slip away and fell back across the bar. There was a sound of glass breaking. Morgan kept hitting him low, in and out, not risking a shot at the head until the hands came down and the boy leaned forward grunting, spitting, and then Morgan hit him once with everything, now and for keeps, aiming, and felt the jaw break and his bare hand crack as the punch hit and went through. And then he was grabbed from behind, not hit but grabbed, which was a mistake, because he whirled down low and happily, exultantly, and hit for the groin, getting two that way and making light between them, and he lunged to get out.

But one tackled him and he went down. He came back up to his knees and gouged at the eyes of the man holding him. He looked up and saw legs and a blackjack and dodged a kick at his face, hitting again at the groin, but the back of his head exploded and he could not see anything. Then they were all over him and hurting him and holding him down. He could not move and he felt them tear into his belly and there was a foot grinding down on his right hand. The fight went out of him suddenly. It was very dark and quiet.

After a while he began to hear. He was numb all over and he could not see. He felt himself being picked up under the shoulder. He could not move. He could hear them swearing.

"Kill him! Kill the son of a bitch!"

"Get him out first. Too many goddamn women—"

"Take him down in the alley and work on him, really work—"

"Shut up."

Somebody slapped his face.

"Morgan? You hear me?"

He recognized the voice. Parilli.

"You goddamn fool!"

He got his eyes open but everything was blurred. He tried to grin.

"Jesus," Parilli said.

"We ought to kill the son of a bitch."

"You shut your face," Parilli said.

"What? But, Jesus, boss—"

"Take him down and put him in a car and take him home."

"Home? Home? But for crissakes—"

"You wanta argue?"

"No, I don't wanna argue."

"I said take him home."

There was a silence. He could feel them carrying him. One of them said apologetically: "You gonna let him fight again boss?"

"He won't fight again."

"How you gonna stop him?"

"Lookit his hands. You can see the bones. He won't fight no more."

"But he's gettin' off light. Shouldn't we make a lesson on him?"

"Listen," Parilli said slowly. There was a pause. "I tell you what. We sit him down and let him come to. We give him a shot, just so's he can stand. Then you person'ly, all by yourself, you want to try to work him over?"

The other man did not say anything. Parilli laughed.

"Take him home," Parilli said.

He lay in the car with his head against the window and when they passed a streetlight he could see the rain falling in long silvery streaks. He watched the rain and the lights going by and was dumbly warmly happy. But he was not going home. One thing more. He grinned craftily to himself and gave the driver her address. He lay grinning against the window and hugging his stomach where it hurt and watching the rain. When they let him out he was able to walk and he made it up to her door.

He stopped here as he had at the other. He did not know why. Some of the joy of it went suddenly away. He thought that he must look pretty bad. He wiped his face, making his check bleed again, and tried to tuck his shirt in. His right hand hurt and he looked down at it and saw that it was broken. The knuckles were all hunched and bloody where the one had stepped on it. He began to feel the pain of it and the pain in his body. He thought that if you were going to do this at all you better do it quick. He pressed the bell.

She was a long while coming. When she came his eyes were blurred and he could not see her clearly. She put a hand to her throat and backed away.

"Sorry woke you up," he said. "Got somethin' to tell you." He saw the fear in her eyes. "Christ," he said, "I ain' gonna hurt you. I just want to tell you. I been over to see the Cyclone. We finished up at his place." He grinned widely and felt the dried blood cracking on his lips. "He ast me to his party. Vict'ry party. So I went on over there. You should've seen it. He couldn't run no more. I caught him there and I hung him. Oh, baby, I really, really, hung him . . ."

He raised his right hand and shook it and staggered with the effort.

"You," she said thickly, "you."

"So I just thought I'd drop by and tell you."

"You had to," she said. He saw her clearly. Her face above the white nightgown was all warped and strange.

"So I'll see you some time," he said.

"My God, will you ever," she said. "Will you ever, ever. Look what they've done, they've hurt you, you don't see what they've done." She pulled at his arm, her face twisted. "Can you see me? You look like you can't see me."

"I can see you."

"You need a doctor." She pulled at him and he went with her into the room. "Sit down. Sit there. You had to come here. You had to tell me. Oh, look at you." She turned and went away and he could hear her on the phone and then she came back with a wet, warm towel for his face. He looked down at her and he felt suddenly very thick and flowing inside. She was dabbing at his face and he was staring at her, and when she saw the expression on his face she stopped. He could feel it come welling up. But he couldn't say anything. He wanted to say it but he had no words. He sat gazing at her dumbly. Never any words, he thought, always the trouble—mad or happy, never any words, always choked up inside with big hot waves. Mad and you fight and happy you never said anything, never could, and she too—both of us like that—but think of it now.

"What's the matter?" she said.

"Honey?" he said.

"What's the matter?" she said again. He saw that she was crying.

"Ah," he said. He bent his head. He saw his hand, his bloody right hand. He raised it and held it before her eyes.

"See?" he said. "Honey?"

She stared at the hand. She reached out and touched it gently. She lay her head on his knee and he could feel the sobs racking her.

"Listen," he said. "Don't do that."

He reached out and put his good hand on her hair.

"Honey. Don't do that. Listen. You're getting the blood on you."

"Blood?" she said. She looked up at him. "Blood. All right. Let me get the blood on me. I need the blood on me. Think of all the people in the world never got blood on them."

She rose up and put her arms around his neck. His face was warm and dark against her bosom.

TIME PAYMENT

IT WAS REMARKABLY WARM FOR NOVEMBER. There was a gray haze over the lake and the sun behind it was rich and orange. I waited in the heat of the porch, fanning thick hot air into my face and gazing down absently into the coolness of the lake.

Ten minutes.

Twenty.

I looked at my watch. He would have to come soon.

And then I chuckled slightly, feeling a shiver of cool excitement. He could come back anytime, Pell could. Anytime at all.

I waited.

And then he came.

All of a sudden he was there on the porch, come out of nowhere. His eyes were bright and glistening, laughing. He held a fresh newspaper in his hand. He stood for a long moment looking at me and smiling, and I looked back at him smiling too, filled with awe and suspense and relief all at once.

"Where did you go?" I asked.

"Nineteen thirty-eight," he said.

Now that it was done, really and truly and irrevocably done, we sat wrapped in silence, unmindful of the heat. It was a great moment, of course, but now nothing made sense anymore and we were back at the Problem.

I had a bottle ready. I poured two stiff ones and we drank to ourselves. Then we drank to the future.

"How long was I gone?" he said.

"Thirty-four minutes."

He nodded, checking his watch.

"Exactly. I just had time to go into town and buy a

paper." He pushed it across the table toward me. It read *October 30, 1938*.

I grinned.

"Not a very impressive relic."

Pell shrugged.

"First attempt. Next time I'll bring back something with a little more color. Like Cleopatra's girdle, for instance." He laughed, flushed, and then his eyes widened. "God, Tom, it's unbelievable! I saw them all—all the children and the dead ones and the neighbors I used to know. I *talked* with them. And nobody recognized me. I could have stayed longer but I was weak, I was so excited . . . it's . . . it's . . . unbelievable."

He stared out over the lake, shaking his head slowly. We were both silent for a long while.

And then we faced the Problem.

Or rather Pell did. For me it was too hot and the day was too full of wonder. But we had worked and thought for many, many days, never really believing that a man could travel in time, and now of course Pell *had*, and therefore there was the Problem.

"Well," Pell said at last, "what about the future?"

I gestured weakly with my glass.

"To hell with it. Let it come."

"But it already has."

Pell lay back in his chair, smiling quietly, holding his glass to the light.

"The future exists," he said. "It exists *now*, Tom, just as the past exists now. That's proven. We've proved it ourselves."

"All right," I muttered, taking a long, deep cool one.

"But if *we* have time travel," Pell went on slowly, "then obviously men in the future have time travel. They will be able—*are* able to come back."

He paused, tinkling his glass absently.

"Tom," he said after a while, "where are they?"

I tried to let the question pass, to feel the warm sun and the pride of achievement. But I couldn't. There was something vaguely, weirdly wrong. For years Pell and I had worked with time travel, and all that discouraging time we had hunted for evidence—any evidence—that it could be done, that men had actually traveled in time. Because of course, if it *could* be done, then it would have been done already. But we never found a thing. Nowhere in history

—and we searched for years—was there a single believable case of a visitor from another time. There were certain unexplainable incidents—like the famous two ladies of the Tuilleries—but never anything at all that might have come from the future. And although it had been maddening then, it was worse now. Because now we actually had time travel, and if we had it, so did the future. But . . . where were they?

"Well, obviously," I said, breaking the long silence, "they must be visiting us all the time and we don't know about it."

Pell shook his head strongly.

"No," he said, "there is no evidence. And it's much too big a thing. There are too many years ahead, too many billions of them. Somewhere, sometime, they would have to betray themselves."

I shifted uncomfortably in my chair. The whole thing was too complex, much too incredibly involved for a man to understand. And in the midst of it, caught like a fly in the tangled threads, was a vague bulbous fear I could not define.

But God! I thought, coming suddenly to myself. How could we sit here brooding on the world's finest day? I jumped up from my chair.

"Oh, good Lord, man, let it pass!" I shouted, snatching at the lovely newspaper and waving it before Pell's eyes. "We've done it, we've done it, after all those years! Man, man, we've conquered Time!"

I began to pace back and forth excitedly as the living reality of what we had accomplished began to come home now for the first time. I wanted to go myself. With a great warm yearning, more than anything else in the world, I wanted to go myself. They were all there waiting—great God! how many were waiting! My brother, who died in the war. My mother, young and in peace before her sickness came . . .

It was while I was thinking all these things, phrasing the words I would say and planning the places and the times of my visits, that Pell discovered the answer.

"Listen," he said abruptly. At the sound of his voice I stopped pacing and looked at him. His face was white, stunned. He stared dazedly out toward the lake, toward where the Machine stood gleaming in the afternoon sun.

"We can't use it," he said.

I stared at him.

He rose and walked to the door, speaking slowly and numbly.

"We'll have to destroy the Machine."

I was too shocked to move. I think I began to stutter, but Pell cut me off.

"Tom. No one has ever come back from the future. Not even *us*, Tom. Not anybody at all. There's only one reason, do you see?"

He paused.

"Nobody has come back because there's nobody there. There is no future."

After a long moment, a long exploding moment, I sat down. My fingers crumpled the newspaper. I did not even begin to argue, because I realized at last that this was the tangle in the web, the thing I had seen but had tried to ignore. It was true—I believed it. I sat in a daze.

"Somewhere up ahead," Pell was saying, "man stops. It must be very soon. It must be—" He broke off and shook his head quickly, turned to me.

"All the while we were building this thing, all the while we were dreaming about it, did it ever once occur to you what a weapon it was? The Time Machine—a weapon! The Ultimate Weapon. You can't detect it, you can't anticipate it. You can't screen it out. The man who owns it controls space and time and the world. If we pass this thing on, it goes into the future. Into a future nobody comes back from."

He sat for a long while in silence.

Eventually I said, groping: "How do you know it's the Machine that's responsible? It might be a war that happens tomorrow. It might be"—I glanced involuntarily at the low red sun—"it might even be that the sun turns nova."

"Pell reached down and picked up his glass, from which the ice was long gone.

"We can't know. All we know is that if the future has time travel there are no men in it. If the future does not have time travel perhaps it is there right now, alive, secure. What can we do? Man has ten billion years to live. We can't pass on the Machine."

"But all the work, all the years . . ."

"All useless," Pell said. His voice was low and thick, but very steady.

"If we are wrong, there is only us to suffer. If we are right . . . other men will undoubtedly make the same discovery, will do—have already done—the same thing down

100

through the years. They have suppressed it—they will have suppressed it, every one of them down all the ages to come. Because the moment that a man fails to suppress it . . ." Pell shook himself. "This is too fine an evening for the end of the world."

He went quickly down the steps and over the hot grass toward the Machine.

Author's note:

The original ending said simply that one man looked at the other, knowing that time travel was impossible, unable to understand why no one seemed ever to come back. And then, staring at the sunset, they suddenly know. The sun is growing. It has begun to blow, to nova. Pell says, to this effect:

"Of course. No one comes back from the future . . ." —he lifts his glass in a toast to the blooming sun—"because there isn't any."

My editor didn't like that ending, so he printed this, with my grudging permission. Making it loving and human and blah. Too fine an evening for the end of the world—that was not my line.

CITIZEN JELL

NONE OF HIS NEIGHBORS KNEW MR. JELL'S great problem. None of his neighbors, in truth, knew Mr. Jell at all. He was only an odd old man who lived alone in a little house on the riverbank. He had the usual little mailbox, marked "E. Jell," set on a post in front of his house, but he never got any mail, and it was not long before people began wondering where he got the money he lived on.

Not that he lived well, certainly; all he ever seemed to do was just fish, or just sit on the riverbank watching the sky, telling tall stories to small children. And none of that took any money to do.

But still he *was* a little odd; people sensed that. The stories he told all his young friends, for instance—wild, weird tales about spacemen and other planets—people hardly expected tales like that from such an old man. Tales about cowboys and Indians they might have understood, but spaceships?

So he was definitely an odd old man, but just how odd, of course, no one ever really knew. The stories he told the children—stories about space travel, about weird creatures far off in the Galaxy—those stories were all true.

Mr. Jell was, in fact, a retired spaceman.

Now that was part of Mr. Jell's problem, but it was not all of it. He had very good reasons for not telling anybody the truth about himself—no one except the children—and he had even more excellent reasons for not letting his own people know where he was.

The race from which Mr. Jell had sprung did not allow this sort of thing—retirement to Earth. They were a fine, tolerant, extremely advanced people, and they had learned long ago to leave undeveloped races, like the one on Earth,

105

alone. Bitter experience had taught them that more harm than good came out of giving scientific advances to backward races, and often just the knowledge of their existence caused trouble among primitive peoples.

No, Mr. Jell's race had for a long while quietly avoided contact with planets like Earth, and if they had known Mr. Jell had violated the law, they would have come swiftly and taken him away—a thing Mr. Jell would have died rather than let happen.

Mr. Jell was unhuman, yes, but other than that he was a very gentle, usual old man. He had been born and raised on a planet so overpopulated that it was one vast city from pole to pole. It was the kind of place where a man could walk under the open sky only on rooftops, where vacant lots were a mark of incredible wealth. Mr. Jell had passed most of his long life under unbelievably cramped and crowded conditions—either in small spaceships or in the tiny rooms of unending apartment buildings.

When Mr. Jell had happened across Earth on a long voyage some years ago, he had recognized it instantly as the place of his dreams. He had had to plan very carefully, but when the time came for his retirement, he was able to slip away. The language of Earth was already on record; he had no trouble learning it, no trouble buying a small cottage on the river in a lovely warm place called Florida. He settled down quietly, a retired old man of one hundred and eighty-five, looking forward to the best days of his life.

And Earth turned out to be more wonderful than his dreams. He discovered almost immediately that he had a great natural aptitude for fishing, and though the hunting instinct had been nearly bred out of him and he could no longer summon up the will to kill, still he could walk in the open woods and marvel at the room, the incredible open, wide, and unoccupied room, live animals in a real forest, and the sky above, clouds seen through the trees—*real trees,* which Mr. Jell had seldom seen before. And, for a long while, Mr. Jell was certainly the happiest man on Earth.

He would arise, very early, to watch the sun rise. After that, he might fish, depending on the weather, or sit home just listening to the lovely rain on the roof, watching the mighty clouds, the lightning. Later in the afternoon, he might go for a walk along the riverbank, waiting for school to be out so he could pass some time with the children.

Whatever else he did, he would certainly go looking for the children.

A lifetime of too much company had pushed the need for companionship pretty well out of him, but then he had always loved children, and they made his life on the river complete. They *believed* him; he could tell them his memories in safety, and there was something very special in that —to have secrets with friends. One or two of them, the most trustworthy, he even allowed to see the Box.

Now the Box *was* something extraordinary, even to so advanced a man as Mr. Jell. It was a device which analyzed matter, made a record of it, and then duplicated it. The Box could duplicate anything.

What Mr. Jell would do, for example, would be to put a loaf of bread into the Box, and press a button, and presto, there would be *two* loaves of bread, each perfectly alike, atom for atom. It would be absolutely impossible for anyone to tell them apart. This was the way Mr. Jell made most of his food and all of his money. Once he had gotten one original dollar bill, the Box went on duplicating it— and bread, meat, potatoes, anything else Mr. Jell desired was instantly available at the touch of a button.

Once the Box duplicated a thing, anything, it was no longer necessary to have the original. The Box filed a record in its electronic memory, describing, say, bread, and Mr. Jell had only to dial a number anytime he wanted bread. And the Box needed no fuel except dirt, leaves, old pieces of wood, just anything made out of atoms—most of which it would arrange into bread or meat or whatever Mr. Jell wanted, and the rest of which it would use as a source of power.

So the Box made Mr. Jell entirely independent, but it did even more than that; it had one other remarkable feature. It could be used also as a transmitter and receiver. Of matter. It was, in effect, the Sears Roebuck catalogue of Mr. Jell's people, with its own built-in delivery service.

If there was an item Mr. Jell needed, any item at all, and that item was available on any of the planets ruled by Mr. Jell's people, Mr. Jell could dial for it, and it would appear in the Box in a matter of seconds.

The makers of the Box prided themselves on the speed of their delivery, the ease with which they could transmit matter instantaneously across light-years of space. Mr. Jell admired this property, too, but he could make no use of it.

For once he had dialed, he would also be billed. And of course his Box would be traced to Earth. That Mr. Jell could not allow.

No, he would make do with whatever was available on Earth. He had to get along without the catalogue.

And he really never needed the catalogue, not at least for the first year, which was perhaps the finest year of his life. He lived in perfect freedom, ever-continuing joy, on the riverbank, and made some special friends: one Charlie, aged five, one Linda, aged four, one Sam, aged six. He spent a great deal of his time with these friends, and their parents approved of him happily as a free baby-sitter, and he was well into his second year on Earth when the first temptation arose.

Bugs.

Try as he might, Mr. Jell could not learn to get along with bugs. His air-conditioned, antiseptic, neat, and odorless existence back home had been an irritation, yes, but he had never in his life learned to live with bugs of any kind, and he was too old to start now. But he had picked an unfortunate spot. The state of Florida was a heaven for Mr. Jell, but it was also a heaven for bugs.

There is probably nowhere on Earth with a greater variety of insects, large and small, winged and stinging, than Florida, and the natural portion of all kinds found their ways into Mr. Jell's peaceful existence. He was unable even to clear out his own house—never mind the endless swarms of mosquitoes that haunted the riverbank—and the bugs gave him some very nasty moments. And the temptation was that he alone, of all people on Earth, could have exterminated the bugs at will.

One of the best-selling export gadgets on Mr. Jell's home world was a small, flying, burrowing, electronic device which had been built specifically to destroy bugs on planets they traded with. Mr. Jell was something of a technician, and he might not even have had to order a Destroyer through the catalogue, but there were other problems.

Mr. Jell's people had not been merely capricious when they formed their policy of nonintervention. Mr. Jell's bug-destroyer would kill all the bugs, but it would undoubtedly ruin the biological balance upon which the country's animal life rested. The birds which fed on the bugs would die, and the animals which fed on the birds, and so on, down a

108

course which could only be disastrous. And even one of the little Destroyers would put an extraordinary dent in the bug population of the area; once sent out into the woods, it could not be recalled or turned off, and it would run for years.

No, Mr. Jell made the valiant decision to endure little itchy bumps on his arms for the rest of his days.

Yet that was only the first temptation. Soon there were others, much bigger and more serious. Mr. Jell had never considered this problem at all, but he began to realize at last that his people had been more right than he knew. He was in the uncomfortable position of a man who can do almost anything and does not dare do it. A miracle man who must hide his miracles.

The second temptation was rain. In the middle of Mr. Jell's second year, a drought began—a drought which covered all of Florida. He sat by helplessly, day after day, while the water level fell in his own beloved river, and fish died gasping breaths, trapped in little pockets upstream. Several months of that produced Mr. Jell's second great temptation. Lakes and wells were dry all over the country, farms and orange groves were dry, there were great fires in the woods, birds and animals died by the thousands.

All that while, of course, Mr. Jell could easily have made it rain. Another simple matter, although this time he would have had to send away for the materials, through the Box. But he couldn't do that. If he did, *they* would come for him, and he consoled himself by arguing that he had no right to make it rain. That was not strictly controllable either. It might rain and rain for several days, once started, filling up the lakes, yes, and robbing water from somewhere else, and then what would happen when the normal rainy season came?

Mr. Jell shuddered to think that he might be the cause, for all his good intentions, of vast floods, and he resisted the second temptation. But that was relatively easy. The third temptation turned out to be infinitely harder.

Little Charlie, aged five, owned a dog—a grave, sober, studious dog named Oscar. On a morning near the end of Mr. Jell's second year, Oscar was run over by a truck. And Charlie gathered the dog up, all crumpled and bleeding and already dead, and carried him tearfully but faithfully off to Mr. Jell, who could fix *anything*.

And Mr. Jell could certainly have fixed Oscar. Hoping to guard against just such an accident, he had already made a "recording" of Oscar several months before. The Box had scanned Oscar and discovered exactly how he was made—for the Box, as has been said, could duplicate anything—and Mr. Jell had only to dial Oscar's number to produce a new Oscar. A live Oscar, grave and sober, atom for atom identical with the Oscar that was dead.

But young Charlie's parents, who had been unable to comfort the boy, came to Mr. Jell's house with him. And Mr. Jell had to stand there, red-faced and very sad, and deny to Charlie that there was anything he could do, and watch the look in Charlie's eyes turn into black betrayal. And when the boy ran off crying, Mr. Jell had the worst temptation of all.

He thought so at the time, but he could not know that the dog had not been the worst. The worst was yet to come.

He resisted a great many temptations after that, but now for the first time doubt had begun to seep in to his otherwise magnificent existence. He swore to himself that he could never give this life up. Here on the riverbank, dry and buggy as it well was, was still the most wonderful life he had ever known—infinitely preferable to the drab crowds he would face at home. He was an old man, grimly aware of the passage of time. He would consider himself the luckiest of men to be allowed to die and be buried here.

But the temptations went on.

First there was the Red Tide, a fish-killing disease which often sweeps Florida's coast, murdering fish by the hundreds of millions. He could have cured that, but he would have had to send off for the chemicals.

Next there was an infestation of the Mediterranean fruit fly, a bug which threatened most of Florida's citrus crop and very nearly ruined little Linda's father, a farmer. There was a Destroyer available which could be set to kill just one type of bug, Mr. Jell knew, but he would have had to order it, again, from the catalogue. So he had to let Linda's father lose most of his life's savings.

Shortly after that, he found himself tempted by a young, gloomy couple, a Mr. and Mrs. Ridge, whom he visited one day looking for their young son, and found himself in the midst of a morbid quarrel. Mr. Ridge's incredible point of view was that this was too terrible a world to bring children into. Mr. Jell found himself on the verge of saying that he himself had personally visited forty-seven other worlds, and not one could hold a candle to this one.

110

He resisted that, at last, but it was surprising how close he had come to talking, even over such a relatively small thing as that, and he had concluded that he was beginning to wear under the strain, when there came the day of the last temptation.

Linda, the four-year-old, came down with a sickness. Mr. Jell learned with a shock that everyone on Earth believed her incurable.

He had no choice then. He knew that from the moment he heard of the illness, and he wondered why he had never until that moment anticipated this. There was, of course, nothing else he could do, much as he loved this Earth, and much as he knew little Linda would certainly have died in the natural order of things. All of that made no difference; it had finally come home to him that if a man is able to help his neighbors and does not, then he ends up something less than a man.

He went out on the riverbank and thought about it all that afternoon, but he was only delaying the decision. He knew he could not go on living here or anywhere with the knowledge of the one small grave for which he would be forever responsible. He knew Linda would not begrudge him those few moments, that one afternoon more. He waited, watching the sun go down, and then he went back into the house and looked through the catalogue. He found the number of the serum and dialed for it.

The serum appeared within less than a minute. He took it out of the Box and stared at it, the thought of the life it would bring to Linda driving all despair out of his mind. It was a universal serum; it would protect her from all disease for the rest of her life. *They* would be coming for him soon, but he knew it would take them a while to get here —perhaps even a full day. He did not bother to run. He was much to old to run and hide.

He sat for a while thinking of how to get the serum to her, but that was no problem. Her parents would give her anything she asked now, and he made up some candy, injecting the serum microscopically into the chunks of chocolate, and then suddenly had a wondrous idea. He put the chunks into the Box and went on duplicating candy until he had several boxes.

When he was finished with that, he went visiting all the houses of all the good people he knew, leaving candy for them and their children. He knew he should not do that,

111

but, he thought, it couldn't really do much harm, could it? Just those few lives altered, out of an entire world?

But the idea had started wheels turning in his mind, and toward the end of that night he began to chuckle with delight. Might as well be flashed for a rogg as a zilb.

He ordered out one special little bug Destroyer, from the Box, set to kill just one bug, the medfly, and sent it happily down the road toward Linda's farm. After that, he duplicated Oscar and sent the dog yelping homeward with a note on his collar. When he was done with that, he ordered a batch of chemicals, several tons of it, and ordered a conveyer to carry it down and dump it into the river, where it would be washed out to sea and so end the Red Tide.

By the time that was over, he was very tired; he had been up the whole night. He did not know what to do about young Mr. Ridge, the one who did not want children. He decided that if the man was that foolish, nothing could help him. But there was one other thing he could do. Praying silently that once he started this thing it would not get out of hand, he made rain.

In this way, he deprived himself of the last sunrise. There was nothing but gray sky, misty, blowing, when he went out onto the riverbank that morning. But he did not really mind. The fresh air and the rain on his face were all the good-bye he could have asked for. He was sitting on wet grass wondering the last thought—why in God's name don't more people here realize what a beautiful world this is?—when he heard a voice behind him.

The voice was deep and very firm.

"Citizen Jell," it said.

The old man sighed.

"Coming," he said, "coming."

THE DARK ANGEL

THE BOY WAS ALONE ON THE BACK PORCH when the sun went down. He was playing with the new set of soldiers and did not notice the darkness until it was suddenly there, all around him, as if someone had sneaked up on him and tried to scare him with it. He sat up in chilled light, his skin coming up in little pimples on his arms. The sun was gone. There was still light in the far sky, a gray pinkish glow beyond the black trees, but the night was coming—the endless darkness, the Angel. The boy sat very still and watched the light die. There was a nightmare coming. The Angel was waiting, with teeth like knives.

The boy began gathering up the soldiers and he could hear his grandmother in the kitchen, talking to his father. His grandmother's voice was crackly and sharp. She was saying that it was high time a boy his age went to Sunday school. A boy eight years old not going to church—what would people think? The boy stopped gathering the soldiers and listened, but his father said nothing. The boy peeked round the door and he could see his father sitting behind a newspaper. His grandmother was talking from the kitchen door. She talked for a long time about Sunday school, and the boy began to sense that she was making his father mad. After a while he saw his father put down the paper slowly, very slowly, and the boy cringed. His father was huge, incomprehensible, a giant with iron hands. The boy loved him with the absolute utter unquestioning devotion possible only to a small boy in a lonely and incomprehensible world. He did not want his father to be mad. But his father did not say anything. He just looked at the woman for a moment and the woman stopped talking as if she'd run out of breath, and then his father said slowly, in a cold iron whisper that froze the room, "Have you been talking to him about God?"

"No," the woman said, and the boy knew she was nervous.

She started to explain something, but his father went on in the freezing iron voice: "There'll be none of that. I've had enough of that. They had him last year and they filled him full of all that filth about hell. Burning in hell. A little boy. Burning in hell. I guarantee you, there'll be no more of *that*."

His father turned his head and saw the boy's thin face peering round the door. The boy didn't know what was going to happen, but the darkness went out of his father's face and he looked at the boy with that special look that was the finest thing in the boy's life.

"Hey," his father said. He was smiling. The boy came forward into the room, looking first cautiously toward his grandmother. She was backing into the kitchen. His father held out his arms and the boy went to be held in the great strength, the warm tobacco smell. Then his father whacked him on the fanny and told him to go wash up. The boy skipped off in delight, forgetting for just those moments the fear of the coming dark, but when he went into the bathroom the lone high window was black, he could already see the stars. The Angel was coming, the Angel was closer. The boy thought, I'll tell my father. But he looked at his own pale face in the mirror and knew he couldn't do that. His father didn't think much of things like that—churches and angels.

At supper his grandmother was still mad and nobody said anything. The boy ate carefully, watchfully, hoping nothing would happen. After a while his father said, grinning, "It isn't the Devil that'll get you if you're bad. No sir, laddie. You better worry about *me*."

His grandmother grunted and plunked more potatoes on his plate and complained about him not eating enough.

His father said, "Let him alone. It would help if you'd worry less about what's in his stomach and more about what's on his mind."

His grandmother said she *did* worry about that, and it went on from there into a strained silence. The boy was glad when his grandmother had to go home. She got his bed and bath all ready, and then started whispering to his father.

116

"You don't have to whisper," his father said. "He knows I'm going."

"Well. I thought you might at least . . . well, is everything all ready?"

"It won't be for another week," his father said.

"Yes, but I want to make sure he'll have everything he needs."

"He doesn't need much. Just make sure you take the right toys."

"Well, you might be away for some time—"

"Listen," his father said. "Couldn't you just stay here while I'm gone? It would be better for him to sleep in his own bed."

"No. I couldn't possibly. Why shouldn't he want to come to my house? And anyway, it's closer to the hospital and it'll be easier to come and visit you."

"I won't be wanting visitors for a while. I certainly don't want him to come up there unless I'm looking well. It might worry him too much. The last time he ever saw his mother was in that hospital."

The boy listened, but the voices faded away. He felt the fear wash over him in a numbing wave. But there was still time and he didn't have to go to bed right now. There would be time to sit for a little while at least and watch television with his father, and maybe to talk about the world and things. They often did that; it was the best part of the boy's day. But when he got out of the tub and went out on the porch, he could tell from the way his father was sitting, staring off into nothing, that his father wouldn't want to talk tonight.

So there was nothing to do but play awhile, and wait. He wished he could tell somebody. But when his father took him to bed, the man's face was distant—he was thinking about something sad and far away—and the boy couldn't say anything and didn't want to show he was afraid. He asked his father to please leave the light on in the hall and he did, and that helped some. His grandmother wouldn't have done that—she hated to leave lights on. She wouldn't leave the light on when he stayed with her, while his father went to the hospital. He . . . wanted to like his grandmother, but she didn't really look at him. He was a duty. She fussed all over him but she never truly looked at him. So he couldn't tell her. He wondered about his mother. He wondered, if the angels hadn't taken her all that time ago, so far back that she wasn't even real, only a name, a

117

look in his father's eye, a look that shut the boy out and made him very lonely, he wondered, could he have told *her?*

The Angel came down. It was the worst night of all. The Angel was a vast black floppy thing that grinned and hopped and fluttered, and there was the boy's father very far away, very small like a tiny boy, and the Angel swooped over him and caught him in the black wings, smothered him, swallowed, and grinned with the teeth like knives, the black wings rolling and flapping, and the boy screamed and woke up.

He sat up in bed, sobbing, his heart beating, and looked all around him frantically, trying to see familiar things. But the room was all shadowy and moving. He got out of bed still crying and hopped into the bathroom for the light, the blessed white light. The light gleamed and drove off the darkness and he stood for a long moment shaking, feeling the hard cold tile beneath his feet. Then he hopped up on the vanity and looked at himself in the mirror—the bright freckles, tears in the blue eyes. It was reassuring just to see himself, alive in a dull quiet bathroom. He sat there for a while and looked out the window and could see smooth shapes of clouds moving on the lawn. He had no idea what time it was. The night stretched out from his white island of light, black and endless in all directions.

He sat on the vanity for a long, long time. The fear went slowly away; he began to feel sleepy. But he could not go back to bed. He got down off the vanity and wandered out into the dark living room, wanting to feel the warm rug under his toes. As he came out of the hall he saw a soft warm glow far across the house—sweet yellow light coming from the back porch. He felt a surge of great joy, hopped across the rug and on toward the back, stopped in the door, and saw his father, his huge father. The man was sitting in a blue cloud of cigarette smoke, staring up at the moon.

"Hi," the boy said.

The man turned and saw him, surprised. Then the man slowly smiled and the boy felt wondrously fine. He skipped across the room and sat down on his father's footstool, tucking his hands between his knees and twisting them tightly together, grinning with relief and delight. His father reached down and brushed his hair, then let the big hand fall on the thin shoulder.

118

"How come you're awake?"

"Oh"—the boy shrugged, still clutching his hands tightly in his lap—"I had an ole nightmare."

The man smiled again.

"What about?"

"Oh, nothing much."

"Did it scare you?"

"It sure did."

"Well. It's all right now."

"I sure am happy you're up. Do I have to go back to bed?"

The man was watching him with kind, quiet eyes.

"No. In a little while, yes, but not right now."

"Please can I stay up?"

The man shook his head. "I'm going to bed myself in just a bit."

"Oh."

"Sure is a bright moon tonight."

"Yep," the boy said. "Sort of scary."

"Laddie," the man said, "what was it about?"

"The dream?"

"Uh-huh."

"Well. It was only an ole dream."

"Don't you want to tell me?"

"Well. You'll probably get mad." The boy's heart beat suddenly, thumped in fear.

"Mad?" His father stared down at him. He still had his hand on the boy's shoulder. "Why would I be mad?" The boy shrugged helplessly. He did not want to spoil anything. He was safe and happy now and he did not want to talk about it. But the man was waiting. The boy felt trapped.

"You don't like angels and bad things like that," the boy said, motioning with his hands.

"Were you dreaming about angels?" The man's face was soft and patient. The boy nodded, shivering.

"What about angels? Were they *bad* angels?" The boy nodded again. The man was deeply interested, not mad at all. The boy watched his eyes for a sign of anger, but there was nothing there but a quiet kindness.

"Go ahead and tell me. Please. I promise, I won't get mad."

So the boy took a deep breath and looked into his father's face and started to tell it, stumbling, anxious, searching his father's eyes alert and aware and then getting

119

lost in it, becoming more afraid as he told it. And then he began to pour it out, letting it all go like a vast thick weight—all about the Dark Angel and the other times—and his father sat listening gravely, silently, his face going all soft and strange. The boy finished and sat fearfully with his thin hands twisting in his lap.

"You're not mad?"

"No." The man smiled a strange soft smile. After a while he said, "The Dark Angel. Where did you hear about that?"

"I don't know." The boy shook his head.

"You must have heard it somewhere."

"I don't remember. But it wasn't grandma. She talks about angels, but she never said anything about the Dark Angel."

"Well." His father went on looking down on him with that odd, funny look. "Why were you so afraid to tell me?"

The boy fluttered his arms nervously. "Well . . . you don't like angels much, and all those people that talk about God and all . . ."

"God?" his father said. He put out his other arm and drew the boy closer. "Laddie, do you believe in God?"

"I do if *you* do," the boy said.

The man took a slow deep breath. He stopped smiling.

"Don't you think I believe in God?" he said.

"Well—" The boy was confused. He wanted desperately to please.

"Do you ever pray?"

The boy sat straight up. "No sir," he said.

The man went on looking into his face. The boy thought he must have said something wrong. "I wish," his father said—then he said nothing. The boy waited, hoping to understand. "I didn't mean," his father said—and then again he paused, and he did not look at the boy.

"The trouble was," the boy said, and suddenly he could feel tears coming and he did not want them and fought against them, "the Dark Angel was after *you*."

The man pulled him in close and put his arms around him. After a while his father held him back and looked into his face. His father seemed very uncertain—the boy didn't understand.

The man's face was still all soft and strange. His hand on the boy's shoulder loosened.

"What you want me to do," the man said slowly, "is tell you about God." The boy waited, confused. The man

120

did not look at him. After a moment the man said, stumbling, "I wish . . . I always thought it was better to wait. But . . ." He groped for the words and then he shrugged helplessly and shook his head. "I can't. I wish to heaven I could. But I can't tell you things I don't believe. I just can't."

The boy did not understand, did not know what to say. The man took hold of his shoulder again and looked down at him with that odd, sad, urgent look on his face, and the boy was jarred.

"I've hunted all my life," the man said slowly, "for a belief . . ." He stopped abruptly and shook his head. "No. It'll have to wait. Until you're older."

"Sure," the boy said. He knew that his father was disturbed and he knew also that the big warm man was ill and was going soon to the hospital for an operation, and he did not want to bother him anymore—he wanted only to sit here for a while and be warm and safe. He wondered if maybe he could sit here all the way till dawn. He rested in the circle of the arm.

But after a while he had to go. His father walked him hand in hand back to the bedroom, back to the dark, back toward the sleep and terror.

And what burst out then was something he could not control, something that rushed out with an urgency all its own and which he did not even know was coming until it came, but which was so terribly important he could not possibly have gone to bed without knowing.

"Daddy?" He held tightly to the hand.

"Yes."

"If you go to the hospital. And something happens to you. Something bad happens. Would I ever see you again? Ever?"

The man stopped. He straightened slightly. The boy could not see his face. He waited in an agony of suspense. He heard the man slowly sigh. Then the man knelt and circled him with his arms.

"Yes, you would, laddie," the man whispered with great tenderness. "Of course you would. You'll see me always."

And so it was all true, of course, because his father would never have said it, and therefore the fear fled away and the boy put his arms around his father's neck and hugged him, and the man held him close and patted his hair.

Then he took the boy back to bed under the window in

121

the moonlight, and tucked him in, and went away, back to his lonely place on the porch. And the boy lay there for a long time and could not sleep, for the Dark Angel still waited in the blackness beyond the window, waited in the shadows with gleaming teeth. And then after a while the boy got out of bed and got down on his knees and cupped his hands in front of him, the way he knew people sometimes did, and began to pray.

WAINER

THE MAN IN THE PURPLE ROBE WAS TOO OLD to walk or stand. He was wheeled upon a purple bench into the center of a marvelous room, where unhuman beings whom we shall call "They" had gathered and waited. Because he was such an old man, he commanded a great sum of respect, but he was nervous before Them and spoke with apology and sometimes with irritation, because he could not understand what They were thinking and it worried him.

Yet there was no one left like this old man. There was no one anywhere who was as old—but that does not matter. Old men are important not for what they have learned, but for whom they have known, and this old man had known Wainer.

Therefore he spoke and told Them what he knew, and more that he did not know he was telling. And They, who were not men, sat in silence and the deepest affection, and listened . . .

William Wainer died and was forgotten (said the old man) much more than a thousand years ago. I have heard it said that people are like waves, rising and riding and crumbling, and if a wave fell once on a shore long ago, then it left its mark on the beach and changed the shape of the world, but is not remembered. That is true, except for the bigger waves. There is nothing remarkable in Wainer's being forgotten then, because he was not a big wave. In his own time he was nothing at all—he even lived off the state—and the magnificent power that was in him and that he brought to the world was never fully recognized. But the story of his life is probably the greatest story I have ever heard. He was the beginning of You. I only wish I had known.

From his earliest days, as I remember, no one ever looked after Wainer. His father had been one of the last of the priests. Just before young Wainer was born in 2430, the government passed one of the great laws, the we-take-no-barriers-into-space edict, and religious missionaries were banned from the stars. Wainer's father never quite recovered from that. He went down to the end of his days believing that the Earth had gone over to what he called "Anti-Christ." He was a fretful man and he had no time for the boy.

Young Wainer grew up alone. Like everyone else, he was operated on at the age of five, and it turned out that he was a Reject. At the time, no one cared. His mother afterward said that she was glad, because Wainer's head even then was magnificently shaped and it would have been a shame to put a lump on it. Of course, Wainer knew that he could never be a doctor, or a pilot, or a technician of any kind, but he was only five years old and nothing was final to him. Some of the wonderful optimism he was to carry throughout his youth, and which he was to need so badly in later years, was already with him as a boy.

And yet You must understand that the world in which Wainer grew up was a good world, a fine world. Up to that time, it was the best world that ever was, and no one doubted that—

(Some of Them had smiled in Their minds. The old man was embarrassed.)

You must try to understand. We all believed in that world; Wainer and I and everyone believed. But I will explain as best I can and doubtless You will understand.

When it was learned, long before Wainer was born, that the electronic brains could be inserted within the human brain and connected with the main neural paths, there was no one who did not think it was the greatest discovery of all time. Do You know, can You have any idea, what the mind of Man must have been like before the brains? God help them, they lived all their lives without controlling themselves, trapped, showered by an unceasing barrage of words, dreams, totally unrelated, uncontrollable memories. It must have been horrible.

The brains changed all that. They gave Man freedom to think, freedom from confusion: they made him logical.

126

There was no longer any need to memorize, because the brains could absorb any amount of information that was inserted into them, either before or after the operation. And the brains never forgot, and seldom made mistakes, and computed all things with an inhuman precision.

A man with a brain—or "clerks," as they were called, after Le Clerq—knew everything, literally *everything*, that there was to know about his profession. And as new information was learned, it was made available to all men, and punched into the clerks of those who desired it. Man began to think more clearly than ever before, and thought with more knowledge behind him, and it seemed for a while that this was a godlike thing.

But in the beginning, of course, it was very hard on the Rejects.

Once in every thousand persons or so would come someone like Wainer whose brain would not accept the clerk, who would react as if the clerk were no more than a hat. After a hundred years, our scientists still did not know why. Many fine minds were ruined with their memory sections cut away, but then a preliminary test was devised to prove beforehand that the clerks would not work and that there was nothing that anyone could do to make them work. Year by year the Rejects, as they were called, kept coming, until they were a sizable number. The more fortunate men with clerks outnumbered the Rejects a thousand to one, and ruled the society, and were called "Rashes"—slang for Rationals.

Thus the era of the Rash and Reject.

Now, of course, in those days the Rejects could not hope to compete in a technical world. They could neither remember nor compute well enough, and the least of all doctors knew more than a Reject ever could, the worst of all chemists knew much more chemistry, and a Reject certainly could never be a space pilot.

As a result of all this, mnemonics was studied as never before, and Rejects were taught memory. When Wainer was fully grown, his mind was more ordered and controlled and his memory more exact than any man who had lived on Earth a hundred years before. But he was still a Reject and there was not much for him to do.

He began to feel it, I think, when he was about fifteen. He had always wanted to go into space, and when he realized at last that it was impossible, that even the meanest of jobs aboard ship was beyond him, he was very deeply

127

depressed. He told me about those days much later, when it was only a Reject's memory of his youth. I have lived a thousand years since then, and I have never stopped regretting that they did not let him go just once when he was young, before those last few days. It would have been such a little thing for them to do.

I first met Wainer when he was eighteen years old and had not yet begun to work. We met in one of those music clubs that used to be in New York City, one of the weird, smoky, crowded little halls where Rejects could gather and breathe their own air away from the—as we called them—"lumpheads." I remember young Wainer very clearly. He was a tremendous man, larger even than You, with huge arms and eyes, and that famous mass of brownish hair. His size set him off from the rest of us, but it never bothered him, and although he was almost painfully awkward, he was never laughed at.

I don't quite know how to describe it, but he was very big—ominous, almost—and he gave off an aura of tremendous strength. He said very little, as I remember; he sat with us silently and drank quite a bit, and listened to the music and to us, grinning from time to time with a wonderfully pleasant smile. He was very likable.

He was drawn to me, I think, because I was a *successful* Reject—I was just then becoming known as a surgeon. I sincerely believed that he envied me.

At any rate, he was always ready to talk to me. In the early days I did what I could to get him working, but he never really tried. He had only the Arts, You see, and they never really appealed to him.

(There was a rustle of surprise among Them. The old man nodded.)

It is true. He never wanted to be an artist. He had too much need for action in him, and he did not want to be a lonely man. But because of the Rashes, he had no choice.

The Rashes, as You know, had very little talent. I don't know why. Perhaps it was the precision, the methodicity with which they lived, or perhaps—as we proudly claimed —the Rejects were Rejects because they had talent. But the result was wonderfully just: the Rejects took over the Arts and all other fields requiring talent. I myself had good hands; I became a surgeon. Although I never once operated without a Rash by my side, I was a notably successful surgeon.

It was a truly splendid thing. That is why I say it was a good world. The Rash and Reject combined in society and made it whole. And one thing more was in favor of the Reject: he was less precise, less logical, and therefore more glamorous than the Rash. Hence Rejects always had plenty of women, and Reject women did well with men.

But the Rash, in the end, had everything that really counted.

Well, there was only such work that a Reject could do. But none of it fitted Wainer. He tried all the arts at one time or another before he finally settled on music. In music there was something vast and elemental; he saw that he could build. He began, and learned, but did little actual work. In those beginning years he could be found almost always out by the Sound, or wandering among the cliffs across the River, his huge hands fisted and groping for something to do, wondering, wondering, why he was a Reject.

The first thing he wrote was the *Pavanne*, which came after his first real love affair. I cannot remember the girl, but in a thousand years I have not forgotten the music. It may surprise You to learn that the *Pavanne* was a commercial success. It surprised Wainer, too. The Rashes were actually the public, and their taste was logical. Most of all they liked Bach and Mozart, some Beethoven and Greene, but nothing emotional and obscure. The *Pavanne* was a success because it was a love piece, wonderfully warm and gay and open. Wainer never repeated that success.

That was one of the few times I ever saw him with money. He received the regular government fee and a nice sum in royalties, but not quite enough for a trip into space, so he drank it all up. He was happy for a while. He went back to the music clubs and stayed away from the beaches, but when I asked him if he was working on anything else, he said no, he had nothing else to write.

Right after that, he fell in love again, this time with his mother.

The longevity treatment was still fairly new; few had stopped to consider that, as men grew older, their mothers remained young, as tender and fresh as girls in school, and there is no woman as close to a man as his mother. Inevitably, a great many men fell in love that way. Wainer was one. His mother, poor girl, never suspected, and it was pure anguish for him. It was some time before he had recovered enough to talk about it, and by then he was thirty. One of the ways he recovered was by writing more music.

There were a lot of lesser works, and then came the First Symphony.

Looking back over the centuries, I cannot understand how the thing was so controversial. The Rashes wrote of it harshly in all their papers. The Rejects almost unanimously agreed that it was a masterpiece. I myself, when I heard it, became aware that Wainer was a great man.

Because of the controversy which raged for a while, Wainer made some money, but the effect of the criticism was to keep him from writing for years. There is something in that First Symphony of the Wainer of later years, some of the hungry, unfinished, incomprehensible strength. Wainer knew that if he wrote anything else, it would be much like the First, and he recoiled from going through it all again. He went back to the beaches.

He had something rare in those days—a great love for the sea. I suppose it was to him what space is to others. I know that the next thing he wrote was a wild, churning, immortal thing which he called Water Music; and I know that he himself loved it best of anything he wrote, except, of course, the Tenth Symphony. But this time was worse than the last. The only ones who paid any attention to Water Music were the Rejects, and they didn't count.

If Wainer had been a true composer, he would have gone on composing whether anyone cared or not, but as I have said, he was not really an artist. Despite the fact that he was the greatest composer we have ever known, music was only a small thing to him. He had a hint, even then, that although he had been born on Earth there was something in him that was alien, and that there was so much left to do, so much to be seen, and because he could not understand what it was that fired him, he ground himself raw, slowly, from within, while walking alone by the rocks on the beaches.

When I saw him again, after I took ship as a surgeon to Altair, he was forty, and he looked—I borrow the phrase —like a man from a land where nobody lived. Having written no music at all, he was living again on government charity. He had a room, of sorts, and food, but whatever money he got he drank right up, and he was such a huge

130

and haggard man that even Rejects left him carefully alone. I did what I could for him, which wasn't much except keep him drunk. It was then that he told me about his feeling for space, and a great many other things, and I remember his words: "I will have to go out into space someday. It is almost as if I used to live there."

Shortly after that, the coughing began. But it came very seldom and seemed no more than a common thing. Because there was no longer any such thing as disease, neither Wainer nor I thought much about it, except that Wainer went and got some pills from the government. For a long while—we may be thankful for that, at least—the cough did not bother him.

And so the years passed.

When Wainer was forty-two, he met the girl. Her name was Lila. She was a Rash, a teacher of mnemonics, and all I can remember of her are the dark-brown lovely eyes and the warm, adoring face. She was the only woman that Wainer ever really loved, except perhaps his mother, and he chose to have his child by her.

Because of the population problem, a man could have one child then every hundred years. Wainer had his child by Lila, and although he was very happy that the boy turned out to be a Rash, he never paid him much attention.

He was about fifty then and beginning to break down. So that he could see Lila often and with pride, he wrote a great deal during those years, and his lungs were collapsing all that while. It was out of that period that he wrote all his symphonies from the Second to the Ninth.

It is unbelievable; they were all purely commercial. He tossed them out with a part of his mind. I cannot help but wonder what the rest of that mind was doing.

I can see him now, that gaunt and useless man, his great muscled arms chained to a pen, his stony, stretching legs cramped down beneath a desk . . .

I did not see him again for almost ten years, because he went away. He left New York for perhaps the only time in his life, and began to wander across the inland of the American continent. I heard from him rarely. I think it was in one of those letters that he first mentioned the pain that was beginning in his lungs.

I never knew what he did, or how he lived during those ten years. Perhaps he went into the forests and worked and lived like a primitive, and perhaps he just walked. He had no transportation. I know that he was not wholly sane then, and never was again until the end of his life. He was like a magnificent machine which has run out of tune for too many years—the delicate gears were strained and cracking.

(The old man paused in the utter silence, while several tears dropped down his cheek. None of Them moved, and at last he went on.)

Near the end of the ten years, I received a package from him in the mail. In it was a letter and the manuscript to the Storm in Space Overture. He wanted me to register the work and get the government fee, and he asked me the only favor he had ever asked of anyone— that I get him the money, because he was going into space.

He came back some weeks later, on foot. I had gotten the money from Rejects—they had heard the Overture—it was enough. He brought Lila with him and was going to make reservations. He was heading, I think, only as far as Alpha Centauri.

It was too late.

They examined him, as someone should have a long time ago, as someone would have if he had only ever asked, but in the end it would have made no difference either way, and it was now that they found out about his lungs.

There was nothing anyone could do. At first I could not believe it. People did not get sick and die. *People just did not die!* Because I was only a Reject and a surgeon, no Rash doctor had ever told me that this had happened before, many times, to other men. I heard it not from the Rashes, but from Wainer.

His lungs were beginning to atrophy. They were actually dying within his body, and no one as yet knew why or could stop it. He could be kept alive without lungs, yes, for a long while. I asked if we could graft a lung into him and this is what I was told: Because no one had yet synthesized human tissue, the graft would have to be a human lung, and in this age of longevity there were only a few available. Those few, of course, went only to important men, and Wainer was nothing.

I volunteered a lung of my own, as did Lila, as did many Rejects. There was hope for a while, but when I looked into Wainer's chest I saw for myself that there was no way to connect. So much was wrong, so much inside him was twisted and strange that I could not understand how he had lived at all. When I learned of the other men who had been like this, I asked what had been done. The answer was that nothing had been done at all.

So Wainer did not go out into space. He returned instead to his single room to sit alone and wait, while the cool world around him progressed and revolved, while the city and its people went on without notice, while a voucher was being prepared somewhere, allowing the birth of another child because citizen Wainer would soon be dead.

What could the man have thought, that huge, useless man? When he sat by his window and watched the world moving by, and looked up at night to the stars, and when he drank cool water, or breathed morning air, or walked or sat or lay down, what was there for him to think?

He had one life, the same as any man, one time to be upon the Earth, and it was ending now as a record of nothing, as a piece of loneliness carved with great pain, as a celestial abortion, withered, wasted. There was nothing in his life, nothing, nothing, which he had ever wanted to be, and now he was dying without reason in a world without reason, unused, empty, collapsing, alone.

He went down to the beach again.

In the days that came he was a shocking sight. What was happening became known, and when he walked the streets people stared at the wonder, the sickness, the man who was dying. Therefore he went out to the beaches and slept and took no treatments and no one will ever know what was in his mind, his million-faceted mind, as he waited to die.

Well, it was told to me at last because I knew Wainer, and they needed him. It was told hesitantly, but when I heard it I broke away and ran, and in the clean air of the beach I found Wainer and told him.

At first he did not listen. I repeated it several times. I told him what the Rashes had been able to learn. He stood breathing heavily, face to the Sun, staring out over the incoming sea. Then I knew what he was thinking.

The Rashes had told me this:

The atrophy of the lungs was not all that happened, but it was the major thing, and it came only to Rejects. After years of study, it could be stated, cautiously, that the disease seemed to be in the nature of an *evolutionary* change.

For many years they had probed for the cause of the Rejects, and the final conclusion—to be kept from the people—was that there was some variation in the brain of the Reject, something subtly, unfathomably different from the brain of a Rash. And so it was also with the lungs, and with other parts of the body. And the scientists thought it was Evolution.

I told this to Wainer, and more, while peace spread slowly across his rugged face. I said that the nature of life was to grow and adapt, and that no one knew why. The first cells grew up in the sea and then learned to live on land, and eventually lifted themselves to the air, and now certainly there was one last step to be taken.

The next phase of change would be into space, and it was clear now what Wainer was, what all the Rejects were.

Wainer was a link, incomplete, groping, unfinished. A link.

It meant more to him, I think, than any man can ever really understand. He had a purpose, after all, but it was more than that. He was a creature with a home. He was part of the Universe more deeply than any of us had ever been. In the vast eternal plan which only You and Your kind can see, Wainer was a beginning, vital part. All the long years were not wasted. The pain of the lungs was dust and air.

Wainer looked at me and I shall never forget his face. He was a man at peace who has lived long enough.

(Because They knew much more than the old man could ever know, They were utterly, nakedly absorbed, and the silence of the room was absolute. The old man tired and closed to the end, while They—unbreathing, undying, telepathic and more, the inconceivable next phase in the Evolution of Man—listened and learned.)

He lived for another six months—long enough to take part in the experiments the Rashes had planned and to write the Tenth Symphony. Even the Rashes could not ignore the Tenth.

It was Wainer's valedictory, a sublime, triumphant summation, born of his hope for the future of Man. It was more than music: it was a cathedral in sound. It was Wainer's soul.

Wainer never lived to hear it played, to hear himself become famous, and in the end, I know, he did not care. Although we could have saved him for a little while, al-

134

though I pleaded with him to remain for the sake of his woman and his music, Wainer knew that the pattern of his life was finished, that the ending time was now.

For Wainer went out into space at last, into the sweet dark home between the stars, moving toward the only great moment he would ever have.

The Rashes wanted to see how his lungs would react in alien atmospheres. Not in a laboratory—Wainer refused—but out in the open sun, out in the strange alien air of the worlds themselves, Wainer was set down. On each of a dozen poisonous worlds he walked. He opened his helmet while we tiny men watched. He breathed.

And he lived.

He lived through methane, through carbon dioxide, through nitrogen and propane. He existed without air at all for an incredible time, living all the while as he never had before, with a wonderful, glowing excitement. And then, at last, there was that final world which was corrosive. It was too much, and Wainer smiled regretfully, holding himself upright with dignity by the base of an alien rock, and still smiling, never once moving to close his helmet, he died.

There was a long pause. The old man was done.

They looked at him with the deep compassion that his own race had denied to those who were different or lesser than themselves.

One of Them arose and gently spoke.

"And now you are the last of your kind, as alone as Wainer was. We are sorry."

There was no bitterness in the old man's voice. "Don't be. Wainer was content to die, knowing that he was the link between us and You. Yet neither he nor You could have been if humanity had never existed. We had our place in the endless flow of history. We were, so to speak, Wainer's parents and Your grandparents. I, too, am content, proud of the children of Man."

Great were the Antha, so reads the One Book of History, greater perhaps than any of the Galactic Peoples, and they were brilliant and fair, and their reign was long, and in all things they were great and proud, even in the manner of their dying—

Preface to Loab: History of the Master Race

135

ALL THE WAY BACK

THE HUGE RED BALL OF A SUN HUNG GLOWING upon the screen.

Jansen adjusted the traversing knob, his face tensed and weary. The sun swung off the screen to the right, was replaced by the live black of space and the million speckled lights of the farther stars. A moment later the sun glided silently back across the screen and went off at the left. Again there was nothing but space and the stars.

"Try it again?" Cohn asked.

Jansen mumbled, "No. No use," and he swore heavily. "Nothing. Always nothing. Never a blessed thing."

Cohn repressed a sigh, began to adjust the controls.

In both of their minds was the single, bitter thought that there would be only one more time, and then they would go home. And it was a long way to come to go home with nothing.

When the controls were set there was nothing left to do. The two men walked slowly aft to the freeze room. Climbing up painfully onto the flat steel of the beds, they lay back and waited for the mechanism to function, for the freeze to begin.

Turned in her course, the spaceship bore off into the open emptiness. Her ports were thrown open, she was gathering speed as she moved away from the huge red star.

The object was sighted upon the last leg of the patrol, as the huge ship of the Galactic Scouts came across the edge of the Great Desert of the Rim, swinging wide in a long slow curve. It was there on the massometer as a faint *blip,* and, of course, the word went directly to Roymer.

"Report," he said briefly, and Lieutenant Goladan—a

young and somewhat pompous Higiandrian—gave the Higiandrian equivalent of a cough and then reported.

"Observe," said Lieutenant Goladan, "that it is not a meteor, for the speed of it is much too great."

Roymer nodded patiently.

"And again, the speed is decreasing"—Goladan consulted his figures—"at the rate of twenty-four dines per segment. Since the orbit appears to bear directly upon the star Mina, and the decrease in speed is of a certain arbitrary origin, we must conclude that the object is a spaceship."

Roymer smiled.

"Very good, lieutenant." Like a tiny nova, Goladan began to glow and expand.

A good man, thought Roymer tolerantly. His is a race of good men. They have been two million years in achieving space flight; a certain adolescence is to be expected.

"Would you call Mind-Search, please?" Roymer asked.

Goladan sped away, to return almost immediately with the heavy-headed nonhuman Trian, chief of the Mind-Search Section.

Trian cocked an eyelike thing at Roymer with grave inquiry.

"Yes, commander?"

The thought message popped clearly into Roymer's mind. Those of Trian's race had no vocal apparatus. In the aeon-long history of their race it had never been needed.

"Would you stand by, please?" said Roymer, and he pressed a button and spoke to the engaging crew. "Prepare for alien contact."

The abrupt change in course was noticeable only on the viewplate, as the stars slid silently by. The patrol vessel veered off, swinging around and into the desert, settled into a parallel course with the strange new craft, keeping a discreet distance of—approximately—a light-year.

The scanners brought the object into immediate focus, and Goladan grinned with pleasure. A spaceship, yes. Alien, too. Undoubtedly a primitive race. He voiced these thoughts to Roymer.

"Yes," the commander said, staring at the strange, small, projectilelike craft. "Primitive type. It is to be wondered what they are doing in the desert."

Goladan assumed an expression of intense curiosity.

"Trian," said Roymer pleasantly, "would you contact?"

The huge head bobbed up and down once and then stared into the screen. There was a moment of profound silence. Then Trian turned back to stare at Roymer, and there was a distinctly human expression of surprise in his eyelike things.

"Nothing," came the thought. "I can detect no presence at all."

Roymer raised an eyebrow.

"Is there a barrier?"

"No"—Trian had turned to gaze back into the screen— "a barrier I could detect. But there is nothing at all. There is no sentient activity on board that vessel."

Trian's word had to be taken, of course, and Roymer was disappointed. A spaceship empty of life—Roymer shrugged. A derelict, then. But why the decreasing speed? Preset controls would account for that, of course, but why? Certainly, if one abandoned a ship, one would not arrange for it to—

He was interrupted by Trian's thought.

"Excuse me, but there is nothing. May I return to my quarters?"

Roymer nodded and thanked him, and Trian went ponderously away. Goladan said, "Shall we prepare to board it, sir?"

"Yes."

And then Goladan was gone to give his proud orders.

Roymer continued to stare at the primitive vessel which hung on the plate. Curious. It was very interesting, always, to come upon derelict ships. The stories that were told, the silent tombs that had been drifting, perhaps, for millions of years in the deep sea of space. In the beginning Roymer had hoped that the ship would be manned, and alien, but— nowadays, contact with an isolated race was rare, extremely rare. It was not to be hoped for, and he would be content with this, this undoubtedly empty, ancient ship.

And then, to Roymer's complete surprise, the ship at which he was staring shifted abruptly, turned on its axis, and flashed off like a live thing upon a new course.

When the defrosters activated and woke him up, Jansen lay for a while upon the steel table, blinking. As always with the freeze, it was difficult to tell at first whether anything had actually happened. It was like a quick blink and no more, and then you were lying, feeling exactly the same, thinking the same thoughts even, and if there was anything at all different it was maybe that you were a little numb. And yet in the blink time took a great leap, and the months went by like—Jansen smiled—like fenceposts.

He raised a languid eye to the red bulb in the ceiling. Out. He sighed. The freeze had come and gone. He felt vaguely cheated, reflected that this time, before the freeze, he would take a little nap.

He climbed down from the table, noted that Cohn had already gone to the control room. He adjusted himself to the thought that they were approaching a new sun, and it came back to him suddenly that this would be the last one —now they would go home.

Well, then, let this one have planets. To have come all this way, to have been gone from home for eleven years, and yet to find nothing—

He was jerked out of the old feeling of despair by a lurch of the ship. That would be Cohn taking her off the auto. And now, he thought, we will go in and run out the telescope and have a look, and there won't be a thing.

Wearily, he clumped off over the iron deck, going up to the control room. He had no hope left now, and he had been so hopeful at the beginning. As they are all hopeful, he thought, as they have been hoping now for three hundred years. And they will go on hoping, for a little while, and then men will become hard to get, even with the freeze, and then the starships won't go out anymore. And Man will be doomed to the System for the rest of his days.

Therefore, he asked humbly, silently, let this one have planets.

Up in the dome of the control cabin Cohn was bent over the panel, pouring power into the board. He looked up, nodded briefly as Jansen came in. It seemed to both of them that they had been apart for five minutes.

"Are they all hot yet?" asked Jansen.

"No, not yet."

The ship had been in deep space with her ports thrown open. Absolute cold had come in and gone to the core of her, and it was always a while before the ship was reclaimed and her instruments warmed. Even now there was a sharp chill in the air of the cabin.

Jansen sat down idly, rubbing his arms.

"Last time around, I guess."

"Yes," said Cohn, and added laconically, "I wish Weizsäcker was here."

Jansen grinned. Weizsäcker, poor old Weizsäcker. He was

142

long dead and it was a good thing, for he was the most maligned human being in the System.

For a hundred years his theory on the birth of planets, that every sun necessarily gave birth to a satellite family, had been an accepted part of the knowledge of Man. And then, of course, there had come space flight.

Jansen chuckled wryly. Lucky man, Weizsäcker. Now, two hundred years and a thousand stars later, there had been discovered just four planets. Alpha Centauri had one: a barren, ice-crusted mote no larger than the Moon; and Pollux had three, all dead lumps of cold rock and iron. None of the other stars had any at all. Yes, it would have been a great blow to Weizsäcker.

A hum of current broke into Jansen's thought as the telescope was run out. There was a sudden beginning of light upon the screen.

In spite of himself and the wry, hopeless feeling that had been in him, Jansen arose quickly, with a thin trickle of nervousness in his arms. There is always a chance, he thought, after all, there is always a chance. We have only been to a thousand suns, and in the Galaxy a thousand suns are not anything all. So there is always a chance.

Cohn, calm and methodical, was manning the radar.

Gradually, condensing upon the center of the screen, the image of the star took shape. It hung at last, huge and yellow and flaming with an awful brilliance, and the prominences of the rim made the vast circle uneven. Because the ship was close and the filter was in, the stars of the background were invisible, and there was nothing but the one great sun.

Jansen began to adjust for observation.

The observation was brief.

They paused for a moment before beginning the tests, gazing upon the face of the alien sun. The first of their race to be here and to see, they were caught up for a time in the ancient, deep thrill of space and the unknown Universe.

They watched, and into the field of their vision, breaking in slowly upon the glaring edge of the sun's disk, there came a small black ball. It moved steadily away from the edge, in toward the center of the sun. It was unquestionably a planet in transit.

When the alien ship moved, Roymer was considerably rattled.

143

One does not question Mind-Search, he knew, and so there could not be any living thing aboard that ship. Therefore, the ship's movement could be regarded only as a peculiar aberration in the still-functioning drive. Certainly, he thought, and peace returned to his mind.

But it did pose an uncomfortable problem. Boarding that ship would be no easy matter—not if the thing was inclined to go hopping away like that, with no warning. There were two hundred years of conditioning in Roymer —it would be impossible for him to put either his ship or his crew into an unnecessarily dangerous position. And wavery, erratic spaceships could undoubtedly be classified as dangerous.

Therefore, the ship would have to be disabled.

Regretfully, he connected with Fire Control, put the operation into the hands of the Firecon officer, and settled back to observe the results of the action against the strange craft.

And the alien moved again.

Not suddenly, as before, but deliberately now, the thing turned once more from its course, and its speed decreased even more rapidly. It was still moving in upon Mina, but now its orbit was tangential and no longer direct. As Roymer watched the ship come about, he turned up the magnification for a larger view, checked the automatic readings on the board below the screen. And his eyes were suddenly directed to a small, conical projection which had begun to rise up out of the ship, which rose for a short distance and stopped, pointed in on the orbit toward Mina at the center.

Roymer was bewildered, but he acted immediately. Firecon was halted, all protective screens were reestablished, and the patrol ship backtracked quickly into the protection of deep space.

There was no question in Roymer's mind that the movements of the alien had been directed by a living intelligence and not by any mechanical means. There was also no doubt in Roymer's mind that there was no living being on board that ship. The problem was acute.

Roymer felt the scalp of his hairless head beginning to crawl. In the history of the galaxy, there had been discovered but five nonhuman races, yet never a race which did not betray its existence by the telepathic nature of its thinking. Roymer could not conceive of a people so alien that even the fundamental structure of their thought process was entirely different from the Galactics.

Extra-Galactics? He observed the ship closely and shook his head. No. Not an extra-Galactic ship certainly—much too primitive a type.

Extraspatial? His scalp crawled again.

Completely at a loss as to what to do, Roymer again contacted Mind-Search and requested that Trian be sent to him immediately.

Trian was preceded by a puzzled Goladan. The orders to alien contact, then to Firecon, and finally for a quick retreat, had affected the lieutenant deeply. He was a man accustomed to a strictly logical and somewhat ponderous course of events. He waited expectantly for some explanation to come from his usually serene commander.

Roymer, however, was busily occupied in tracking the alien's new course. An orbit about Mina, Roymer observed, with that conical projection laid on the star; a device of war; or some type of measuring instrument?

The stolid Trian appeared—walking would not quite describe how—and was requested to make another attempt at contact with the alien. He replied with his usual eerie silence and in a moment, when he turned back to Roymer, there was surprise in the transmitted thought.

"I cannot understand. There is life there now."

Roymer was relieved, but Goladan was blinking.

Trian went on, turning again to gaze at the screen.

"It is very remarkable. There are two life-beings. Human-type race. Their presence is very clear, they are"—he paused briefly—"explorers, it appears. But they were not there before. It is extremely unnerving."

So it is, Roymer agreed. He asked quickly: "Are they aware of us?"

"No. They are directing their attention on the star. Shall I contact?"

"No. Not yet. We will observe them first."

The alien ship floated upon the screen before them, moving in slow orbit about the star Mina.

Seven. There were seven of them. Seven planets, and three at least had atmospheres, and two might even be inhabitable. Jansen was so excited he was hopping around the control room. Cohn did nothing but grin widely with a wondrous joy, and the two of them repeatedly shook hands and gloated.

"Seven!" roared Jansen. "Old lucky seven!"

Quickly then, and with extreme nervousness, they ran

145

spectrograph analyses of each of those seven fascinating worlds. They began with the central planets, in the favorable temperature belt where life conditions would be most likely to exist, and they worked outward.

For reasons which were as much sentimental as they were practical, they started with the third planet of this fruitful sun. There was a thin atmosphere, fainter even than that of Mars, and no oxygen. Silently they went on to the fourth. It was cold and heavy, perhaps twice as large as Earth, had a thick envelope of noxious gases. They saw with growing fear that there was no hope there, and they turned quickly inward toward the warmer area nearer the sun.

On the second planet—as Jansen put it—they hit the jackpot.

A warm, green world it was, of an Earthlike size and atmosphere; oxygen and water vapor lines showed strong and clear in the analysis.

"This looks like it," said Jansen, grinning again.

Cohn nodded, left the screen, and went over to man the navigating instruments.

"Let's go down and take a look."

"Radio check first." It was the proper procedure. Jansen had gone over it in his mind a thousand times. He clicked on the receiver, waited for the tubes to function, and then scanned for contact. As they moved in toward the new planet he listened intently, trying all lengths, waiting for any sound at all. There was nothing but the rasping static of open space.

"Well," he said finally, as the green planet grew large upon the screen, "if there's any race there, it doesn't have radio."

Cohn showed his relief.

"Could be a young civilization."

"Or one so ancient and advanced that it doesn't *need* radio."

Jansen refused to let his deep joy be dampened. It was impossible to know what would be there. Now it was just as it had been three hundred years ago, when the first Earth ship was approaching Mars. And it will be like this, Jansen thought, in every other system to which we go. How can you picture what there will be? There is nothing at all in your past to give you a clue. You can only hope.

The planet was a beautiful green ball on the screen.

*   *   *

The thought which came out of Trian's mind was tinged with relief.

"I see how it was done. They have achieved a complete statis, a perfect state of suspended animation which they produce by an ingenious usage of the absolute zero of outer space. Thus, when they are—frozen, is the way they regard it—their minds do not function, and their lives are not detectable. They have just recently revived and are directing their ship."

Roymer digested the new information slowly. What kind of a race was this? A race which flew in primitive star ships, yet it had already conquered one of the greatest problems in Galactic history, a problem which had baffled the Galactics for millions of years. Roymer was uneasy.

"A very ingenious device," Trian was thinking. "They use it to alter the amount of subjective time consumed in their explorations. Their star ship has a very low maximum speed. Hence, without this—freeze—their voyage would take up a good portion of their lives."

"Can you classify the mind-type?" Roymer asked with growing concern.

Trian reflected silently for a moment.

"Yes," he said, "although the type is extremely unusual. I have never observed it before. General classification would be Human-Four. More specifically, I would place them at the Ninth level."

Roymer started. "The *Ninth* level?"

"Yes. As I say, they are extremely unusual."

Roymer was now clearly worried. He turned away and paced the deck for several moments. Abruptly, he left the room and went to the files of alien classification. He was gone for a long time, while Goladan fidgeted and Trian continued to gather information plucked across space from the alien minds. Roymer came back at last.

"What are they doing?"

"They are moving in on the second planet. They are about to determine whether the conditions are suitable there for an establishment of a colony of their kind."

Gravely, Roymer gave his orders to navigation. The patrol ship swung into motion, sped off swiftly in the direction of the second planet.

There was a single, huge blue ocean which covered an entire hemisphere of the new world. And the rest of the surface was a young jungle—wet and green and empty of

147

any kind of people, choked with queer growths of green and orange. They circled the globe at a height of several thousand feet, and to their amazement and joy, they never saw a living thing—not a bird or a rabbit or the alien equivalent, in fact nothing alive at all. And so they stared in happy fascination.

"This is it," Jansen said again, his voice uneven.

"What do you think we ought to call it?" Cohn was speaking absently. "New Earth? Utopia?"

Together they watched the broken terrain slide by beneath them.

"No people at all. It's ours." And after a while Jansen said, "New Earth. That's a good name."

Cohn was observing the features of the ground intently. "Do you notice the kind of . . . circular appearance of most of those mountain ranges? Like on the Moon, almost, but grown over and eroded. They're all almost perfect circles."

Pulling his mind away from the tremendous visions he had of the colony which would be here, Jansen tried to look at the mountains with an objective eye. Yes, he realized with faint surprise, they were round, like Moon craters.

"Peculiar," Cohn muttered. "Not natural, I don't think. Couldn't be. Meteors not likely in this atmosphere. What in—?"

Jansen jumped. "Look there," he cried suddenly, "a round lake!"

Off toward the northern pole of the planet a lake which was a perfect circle came slowly into view. There was no break in the rim other than that of a small stream which flowed in from the north.

"That's not natural," Cohn said briefly. "Someone built that."

They were moving on to the dark side now, and Cohn turned the ship around. The sense of exhilaration was too new for them to be let down, but the strange sight of a huge number of perfect circles, existing haphazardly like the remains of great splashes on the surface of the planet, was unnerving.

It was the sight of one particular crater, a great barren hole in the midst of a wide red desert, which rang a bell in Jansen's memory, and he blurted: "A war! There was a war here. That one there looks just like a fusion bomb crater."

Cohn stared, then raised his eyebrows.

148

"I'll bet you're right."

"A bomb crater, do you see? Pushes up hills on all sides in a circle, and kills—" A sudden, terrible thought hit Jansen. Radioactivity. Would there be radioactivity here?

While Cohn brought the ship in low over the desert, he tried to calm Jansen's fears.

"There couldn't be much. Too much plant life. Jungles all over the place. Take it easy, man."

"But there's not a living thing on the planet. I'll bet that's why—there was a war. It got out of hand—the radioactivity got everything. We might have done this to Earth!"

They glided in over the flat emptiness of the desert, and the counters began to click madly.

"That's it," Jansen said conclusively. "Still radioactive. It might not have been too long ago."

"Could have been a million years, for all we know."

"Well, most places are safe, apparently. We'll check before we go down."

As he pulled the ship up and away, Cohn whistled.

"Do you suppose there's really not a living thing? I mean, not a bug or a germ or even a virus? Why, it's like a clean new world, a nursery!" He could not take his eyes from the screen.

They were going down now. In a very little while they would be out and walking in the sun. The lust of the feeling was indescribable. They were Earthmen freed forever from the choked home of the System, Earthmen gone out to the stars, landing now upon the next world of their empire.

Cohn could not control himself.

"Do we need a flag?" he said, grinning. "How do we claim this place?"

"Just set her down, man," Jansen roared.

Cohn began to chuckle.

"Oh, brave new world," he laughed, "that has *no* people in it."

"But why do we have to contact them?" Goladan asked impatiently. "Could we not just—"

Roymer interrupted without looking at him.

"The law requires that contact be made and the situation explained before action is taken. Otherwise it would be a barbarous act."

Goladan brooded.

The patrol ship hung in the shadow of the dark side, tracing the alien by its radioactive trail. The alien was going down for a landing on the daylight side.

Trian came forward with the other members of the Alien Contact Crew, reported to Roymer. "The aliens have landed."

"Yes," said Roymer, "we will let them have a little time. Trian, do you think you will have any difficulty in the transmission?"

"No. Conversation will not be difficult. Although the confused and complex nature of their thought patterns does make their inner reactions somewhat obscure. But I do not think there will be any problem."

"Very well. You will remain here and relay the messages."

"Yes."

The patrol ship flashed quickly up over the north pole, then swung inward toward the equator, circling the spot where the alien had gone down. Roymer brought his ship in low and with the silence characteristic of a Galactic, landed her in a wooded spot a mile east of the alien. The Galactics remained in their ship for a short while as Trian continued his probe for information. When at last the Alien Contact Crew stepped out, Roymer and Goladan were in the lead. The rest of the crew faded quietly into the jungle.

As he walked through the young orange brush, Roymer regarded the world around him. Almost ready for repopulation, he thought. In another hundred years the radiation will all be gone and we will come back. One by one the worlds of that war will be reclaimed.

He felt Trian's directions pop into his mind.

"You are approaching them. Proceed with caution. They are just beyond the next small rise. I think you had better wait, since they are remaining close to their ship."

Roymer sent back a silent yes. Motioning Goladan to be as quiet as possible, Roymer led the way up the last rise. In the jungle around him the Galactic crew moved silently.

The air was perfect; there was no radiation. Except for the wild orange color of the vegetation, the spot was a Garden of Eden. Jansen felt instinctively that there was no danger here, no terrible blight or virus or any harmful thing. He felt a violent urge to get out of his spacesuit and run and breathe, but it was forbidden. Not on the first

150

trip. That would come later, after all the tests and experiments had been made and the world pronounced safe.

One of the first things Jansen did was get out the recorder and solemnly claim this world for the Solar Federation, recording the historic words for the archives of Earth. And he and Cohn remained for a while by the air lock of their ship, gazing around at the strange yet familiar world into which they had come.

"Later on we'll search for ruins," Cohn said. "Keep an eye out for anything that moves. It's possible that there are some of them left and who knows what they'll look like. Mutants, probably, with five heads. So keep an eye open."

"Right."

Jansen began collecting samples of the ground, of the air, of the nearer foliage. The dirt was Earth-dirt—there was no difference. He reached down and crumbled the soft moist sod with his fingers. The flowers may be a little peculiar—probably mutated, he thought—but the dirt is honest to goodness dirt, and I'll bet the air is Earth-air.

He rose and stared into the clear, open blue of the sky, feeling again an almost overpowering urge to throw open his helmet and breathe, and as he stared at the sky and at the green and orange hills, suddenly, a short distance from where he stood, a little old man came walking over a hill.

They stood facing each other across the silent space of a foreign glade. Roymer's face was old and smiling; Jansen looked back at him with absolute astonishment.

After a short pause, Roymer began to walk out onto the open soil, with Goladan following, and Jansen went for his heat gun.

"Cohn!" he yelled in a raw, brittle voice, "Cohn!"

And as Cohn turned and saw and froze, Jansen heard words being spoken in his brain. They were words coming from the little old man.

"Please do not shoot," the old man said, his lips unmoving.

"No, don't shoot," Cohn said quickly. "Wait. Let him alone." The hand of Cohn, too, was at his heat gun.

Roymer smiled. To the two Earthmen his face was incredibly old and wise and gentle. He was thinking: Had I been a nonhuman they would have killed me.

He sent a thought back to Trian. The Mind-Searcher

151

picked it up and relayed it into the brains of the Earthmen, sending it through their cortical centers and then up into their conscious minds, so that the words were heard in the language of Earth.

"Thank you," Roymer said gently.

Jansen's hand held the heat gun leveled on Roymer's chest. He stared, not knowing what to say.

"Please remain where you are." Cohn's voice was hard and steady.

Roymer halted obligingly. Goladan stopped at his elbow, peering at the Earthmen with mingled fear and curiosity. The sight of fear helped Jansen very much.

"Who are you?" Cohn said clearly, separating the words.

Roymer folded his hands comfortably—across his chest—he was still smiling.

"With your leave, I will explain our presence."

Cohn just stared.

"There will be a great deal to explain. May we sit down and talk?"

Trian helped with the suggestion. They sat down.

The sun of the new world was setting, and the conference went on. Roymer was doing most of the talking. The Earthmen sat transfixed.

It was like growing up suddenly, in the space of a second.

The history of Earth and of all Mankind just faded and dropped away. They heard of great races and worlds beyond number, the illimitable government which was the Galactic Federation. The fiction, the legends, the dreams of a thousand years had come true in a moment, in the figure of a square little old man who was not from Earth. There was a great deal for them to learn and accept in the time of a single afternoon, on an alien planet.

But it was just as new and real to them that they had discovered an uninhabited, fertile planet, the first to be found by Man. And they could not help but revolt from the sudden realization that the planet might well be someone else's property—that the Galactics owned everything worth owning.

It was an intolerable thought.

"How far," asked Cohn, as his heart pushed up in his throat, "does the Galactic League extend?"

Roymer's voice was calm and direct in their minds.

"Only throughout the central regions of the galaxy.

152

There are millions of stars along the rim which have not as yet been explored."

Cohn relaxed, bowed down with relief. There was room then for Earthmen.

"This planet. Is it part of the Federation?"

"Yes," said Roymer, and Cohn tried to mask his thought. Cohn was angry, and he hoped that the alien could not read his mind as well as he could talk to it. To have come this far—

"There was a race here once," Roymer was saying, "a humanoid race which was almost totally destroyed by war. This planet has been uninhabitable for a very long time. A few of its people who were in space at the time of the last attack were spared. The Federation established them elsewhere. When the planet is ready, the descendants of those survivors will be brought back. It is their home."

Neither of the Earthmen spoke.

"It is surprising," Roymer went on, "that your home world is in the desert. We had thought that there were no habitable worlds—"

"The desert?"

"Yes. The region of the galaxy from which you have come is that which we call the desert. It is an area almost entirely devoid of planets. Would you mind telling me which star is your home?"

Cohn stiffened.

"I'm afraid our government would not permit us to disclose any information concerning our race."

"As you wish. I am sorry you are disturbed. I was curious to know—" He waved a negligent hand to show that the information was unimportant. We will get it later, he thought, when we decipher their charts. He was coming to the end of the conference. He was about to say what he had come to say.

"No doubt you have been exploring the stars about your world?"

The Earthmen both nodded. But for the question concerning Sol, they long ago would have lost all fear of this placid old man and his wide-eyed, silent companion.

"Perhaps you would like to know," said Roymer, "why your area is a desert."

Instantly, both Jansen and Cohn were completely absorbed. This was it, the end of three hundred years of searching. They would go home with the answer.

153

Roymer never relaxed.

"Not too long ago," he said, "approximately thirty thousand years by your reckoning, a great race ruled the desert, a race which was known as the Antha, and it was not a desert then. The Antha ruled hundreds of worlds. They were perhaps the greatest of all the Galactic peoples; certainly they were as brilliant a race as the galaxy has ever known.

"But they were not a good race. For hundreds of years, while they were still young, we tried to bring them into the Federation. They refused, and of course we did not force them. But as the years went by the scope of their knowledge increased amazingly; shortly they were the technological equals of any other race in the galaxy. And then the Antha embarked upon an era of imperialistic expansion.

"They were superior—they knew it and were proud. And so they pushed out and enveloped the races and worlds of the area now known as the desert. Their rule was a tyranny unequaled in Galactic history."

The Earthmen never moved, and Roymer went on.

"But the Antha were not members of the Federation, and, therefore, they were not answerable for their acts. We could only stand by and watch as they spread their vicious rule from world to world. They were absolutely ruthless.

"As an example of their kind of rule, I will tell you of their crime against the Apectans.

"The planet of Apectus not only resisted the Antha, but somehow managed to hold out against their approach for several years. The Antha finally conquered and then, in retaliation for the Apectans' valor, they conducted the most brutal of their mass experiments.

"They were a brilliant people. They had been experimenting with the genes of heredity. Somehow they found a way to alter the genes of the Apectans, who were humanoids like themselves, and they did it on a mass scale. They did not choose to exterminate the race—their revenge was much greater. Every Apectan born since the Antha invasion has been born without one arm."

Jansen sucked in his breath. It was a very horrible thing to hear, and a sudden memory came into his brain. Caesar did that, he thought. He cut off the right hands of the Gauls. Peculiar coincidence. Jansen felt uneasy.

Roymer paused for a moment.

"The news of what happened to the Apectans set the

154

Galactic peoples up in arms, but it was not until the Antha attacked a Federation world that we finally moved against them. It was the greatest war in the history of Life.

"You will perhaps understand how great a people the Antha were when I tell you that they alone, unaided, dependent entirely upon their own resources, fought the rest of the Galactics, and fought them to a standstill. As the terrible years went by we lost whole races and planets—like this one, which was one the Antha destroyed—and yet we could not defeat them.

"It was only after many years, when a Galactic invented the most dangerous weapon of all, that we won. The invention—of which only the Galactic Council has knowledge—enabled us to turn the suns of the Antha into novae, at long-range. One by one we destroyed the Antha worlds. We hunted them through all the planets of the desert; for the first time in history the edict of the Federation was death—death for an entire race. At last there were no longer any habitable worlds where the Antha had been. We burned their worlds and ran them down in space. Thirty thousand years ago, the civilization of the Antha perished."

Roymer had finished. He looked at the Earthmen out of grave, tired old eyes.

Cohn was staring in openmouthed fascination, but Jansen—unaccountably—felt a chill. The story of Caesar remained uncomfortably in his mind. And he had a quick, awful suspicion.

"Are you sure you got all of them?"

"No. Some surely must have escaped. There were too many in space, and space is without limits."

Jansen wanted to know: "Have any of them been heard of since?"

Roymer's smile left him as the truth came out. "No. Not until now."

There were only a few more seconds. He gave them time to understand. He could not help telling them that he was sorry—he even apologized. And then he sent the order with his mind.

The Antha died quickly and silently, without pain.

Only thirty thousand years, Roymer was thinking, but thirty thousand years and they came back out to the stars. They have no memory now of what they were or what they have done. They started all over again, the old history

155

of the race has been lost, and in thirty thousand years they came all the way back.

Roymer shook his head with sad wonder and awe. The most brilliant people of all.

Goladan came in quietly with the final reports.

"There are no charts," he grumbled, "no maps at all. We will not be able to trace them to their home star."

Roymer did not know, really, what was right—to be disappointed or relieved. We cannot destroy them now, he thought, not right away. He could not help being relieved. Maybe this time there will be a way, and they will not have to be destroyed. They could be—

He remembered the edict—the edict of death. The Antha had forged it for themselves and it was just. He realized that there wasn't much hope.

The reports were on his desk and he regarded them with a wry smile. There was indeed no way to trace them back. They had no charts, only a regular series of course-check coordinates which were preset on their home planet and which were not decipherable. Even at this stage of their civilization they had already anticipated the consequences of having their ship fall into alien hands. And this although they lived in the desert.

Goladan startled him with an anxious question. "What can we do?"

Roymer was silent.

We can wait, he thought. Gradually, one by one, they will come out of the desert, and when they come we will be waiting. Perhaps one day we will follow one back and destroy their world, and perhaps before then we will find a way to save them.

Suddenly, as his eyes wandered over the report before him and he recalled the ingenious mechanism of the freeze, a chilling, unbidden thought came into his brain.

And perhaps, he thought calmly, for he was a philosophical man, they will come out already equipped to rule the Galaxy.

2066: ELECTION DAY

EARLY THAT AFTERNOON PROFESSOR LARKIN crossed the river into Washington, a thing he always did on Election Day, and sat for a long while in the Polls. It was still called the Polls, in this year 2066 A.D., although what went on inside bore no relation at all to the elections of primitive American history. The Polls was now a single enormous building which rose out of the green fields where the ancient Pentagon had once stood. There was only one of its kind in Washington, only one Polling Place in each of the fifty states, but since few visited the Polls nowadays, no more were needed.

In the lobby of the building a great hall was reserved for visitors. Here you could sit and watch the many-colored lights dancing and flickering on the huge panels above, listen to the weird but strangely soothing hum and click of the vast central machine. Professor Larkin chose a deep soft chair near the long line of booths and sat down. He sat for a long while smoking his pipe, watching the people go in and out of the booths with strained, anxious looks on their faces.

Professor Larkin was a lean, boyish-faced man in his late forties. With the pipe in his hand he looked much more serious and sedate than he normally felt, and it often bothered him that people were able to guess his profession almost instantly. He had a vague idea that it was not becoming to look like a college professor, and he often tried to change his appearance—a loud tie here, a sport coat there—but it never seemed to make any difference. He remained what he was, easily identifiable, Professor Harry L. (Lloyd) Larkin, Ph.D., Dean of the Political Science Department at a small but competent college just outside of Washington.

It was his interest in Political Science which drew him regularly to the Polls at every election. Here he could sit and feel the flow of American history in the making and recognize, as he did now, perennial candidates for the presidency. Smiling, he watched a little old lady dressed in pink, very tiny and very fussy, flit doggedly from booth to booth. Evidently her test marks had not been very good. She was clutching her papers tightly in a black-gloved hand, and there was a look of prim irritation on her face. But *she* knew how to run this country, by George, and one of these days *she* would be President. Harry Larkin chuckled.

But it did prove one thing. The great American dream was still intact. The tests were open to all. And anyone could still grow up to be President of the United States.

Sitting back in his chair, Harry Larkin remembered his own childhood, how the great battle had started. There were examinations for everything in those days—you could not get a job streetcleaning without taking a civil-service examination—but public office needed no qualifications at all. And first the psychologists, then the newspapers, had begun calling it a national disgrace. And, considering the caliber of some of the men who went into public office, it *was* a national disgrace. But then psychological testing came of age, really became an exact science, so that it was possible to test a man thoroughly—his knowledge, his potential, his personality. And from there it was a short but bitterly fought step to—SAM.

SAM. UNCLE SAM, as he had been called originally, the last and greatest of all electronic brains. Harry Larkin peered up in unabashed awe at the vast battery of lights which flickered above him. He knew that there was more to SAM than just this building, more than all the other fifty buildings put together, that SAM was actually an incredibly enormous network of electronic cells which had its heart in no one place, but its arms in all. It was an unbelievably complex analytical computer which judged a candidate far more harshly and thoroughly than the American public could ever have judged him. And crammed in its miles of memory banks lay almost every bit of knowledge mankind had yet discovered. It was frightening—many thought of it as a monster—but Harry Larkin was unworried.

The thirty years since the introduction of SAM had been

thirty of America's happiest years. In a world torn by continual war and unrest, by dictators, puppet governments, the entire world had come to know and respect the American President for what he was: the best possible man for the job. And there was no doubt that he was the best. He had competed for the job in fair examination against the cream of the country. He had to be a truly remarkable man to come out on top.

The day was long since past when just any man could handle the presidency. A full century before men had begun dying in office, cut down in their prime by the enormous pressures of the job. And that was a hundred years ago. Now the job had become infinitely more complex, and even now President Creighton lay on his bed in the White House, recovering from a stroke, an old, old man after one term of office.

Harry Larkin shuddered to think what might have happened had America not adopted the system of "the best qualified man." All over the world this afternoon men waited for word from America, the calm and trustworthy words of the new President, for there had been no leader in America since President Creighton's stroke. His words would mean more to the people, embroiled as they were in another great crisis, than the words of their own leaders. The leaders of other countries fought for power, bought it, stole it, only rarely earned it. But the American President was known the world over for his honesty, his intelligence, his desire for peace. Had he not those qualities, "old UNCLE SAM" would never have elected him.

Eventually, the afternoon nearly over, Harry Larkin rose to leave. By this time the President was probably already elected. Tomorrow the world would return to peace. Harry Larkin paused in the door once before he left, listened to the reassuring hum from the great machine. Then he went quietly home, walking quickly and briskly toward the most enormous fate on Earth.

"My name is Reddington. You know me?"

Harry Larkin smiled uncertainly into the phone.

"Why . . . yes, I believe so. You are, if I'm not mistaken, general director of the Bureau of Elections."

"Correct," the voice went on quickly, crackling in the receiver, "and you are supposed to be an authority on Political Science, right?"

161

"Supposed to be?" Larkin bridled. "Well, it's distinctly possible that I—"

"All right, all right," Reddington blurted. "No time for politeness. Listen, Larkin, this is a matter of urgent national security. There will be a car at your door—probably be there when you put this phone down. I want you to get into it and hop on over here. I can't explain further. I know your devotion to the country—if it wasn't for that I would not have called you. But don't ask questions. Just come. No time. Good-bye."

There was a click. Harry Larkin stood holding the phone for a long shocked moment, then he heard a pounding at the door. The housekeeper was out, but he waited automatically before going to answer it. He didn't like to be rushed, and he was confused. Urgent national security? Now what in blazes—

The man at the door was an Army major. He was accompanied by two young but very large sergeants. They identified Larkin, then escorted him politely but firmly down the steps into a staff car. Larkin could not help feeling abducted, and a completely characteristic rage began to rise in him. But he remembered what Reddington had said about national security and so sat back quietly with nothing more than an occasional grumble.

He was driven back into Washington. They took him downtown to a small but expensive apartment house he could neither identify nor remember, and escorted him briskly into an elevator. When they reached the suite upstairs they opened the door and let him in, but did not follow him. They turned and went quickly away.

Somewhat ruffled, Larkin stood for a long moment in the hall by the hat table, regarding a large rubber plant. There was a long sliding door before him, closed, but he could hear an argument going on behind it. He heard the word "SAM" mentioned many times, and once he heard a clear sentence: ". . . Government by machine. I will not tolerate it!" Before he had time to hear any more, the doors slid back. A small, square man with graying hair came out to meet him. He recognized the man instantly as Reddington.

"Larkin," the small man said. "Glad you're here." The tension on his face showed also in his voice. "That makes all of us. Come in and sit down." He turned back into the large living room. Larkin followed.

"Sorry to be so abrupt," Reddington said, "but it was

162

necessary. You will see. Here, let me introduce you around."

Larkin stopped in involuntary awe. He was used to the sight of important men, but not so many at one time, and never so close. There was Secretary Kell, of Agriculture, Wachsmuth, of Commerce, General Vines, Chief of Staff, and a battery of others so imposing that Larkin found his mouth hanging embarrassingly open. He closed it immediately.

Reddington introduced him. The men nodded one by one, but they were all deathly serious, their faces drawn, and there was now no conversation. Reddington waved him to a chair. Most of the others were standing, but Larkin sat.

Reddington sat directly facing him. There was a long moment of silence during which Larkin realized that he was being searchingly examined. He flushed, but sat calmly with his hands folded in his lap. After a while Reddington took a deep breath.

"Dr. Larkin," he said slowly, "what I am about to say to you will die with you. There must be no question of that. We cannot afford to have any word of this meeting, any word at all, reach anyone not in this room. This includes your immediate relatives, your friends, anyone— anyone at all. Before we continue, let me impress you with that fact. This is a matter of the gravest national security. Will you keep what is said here in confidence?"

"If the national interests—" Larkin began, then he said abruptly, "of course."

Reddington smiled slightly.

"Good. I believe you. I might add that just the fact of your being here, Doctor, means that you have already passed the point of no return . . . well, no matter. There is no time. I'll get to the point."

He stopped, looking around the room. Some of the other men were standing and now began to move in closer. Larkin felt increasingly nervous, but the magnitude of the event was too great for him to feel any worry. He gazed intently at Reddington.

"The Polls close tonight at eight o'clock." Reddington glanced at his watch. "It is now six eighteen. I must be brief. Doctor, do you remember the prime directive that we gave to SAM when he was first built?"

"I think so," said Larkin slowly.

"Good. You remember then that there was one main

163

order. SAM was directed to elect, quote, *the best qualified man.* Unquote. Regardless of any and all circumstances, religion, race, so on. The orders were clear—the best qualified man. The phrase has become world famous. But unfortunately"—he glanced up briefly at the men surrounding him—"the order was a mistake. Just whose mistake does not matter. I think perhaps the fault lies with all of us, but —it doesn't matter. What matters is this: SAM will not elect a President."

Larkin struggled to understand. Reddington leaned forward in his chair.

"Now follow me closely. We learned this only late this afternoon. We are always aware, as you no doubt know, of the relatively few people in this country who have a chance for the presidency. We know not only because they are studying for it, but because such men as these are marked from their childhood to be outstanding. We keep close watch on them, even to assigning the Secret Service to protect them from possible harm. There are only a very few. During this last election we could not find more than fifty. All of those people took the tests this morning. None of them passed."

He paused, waiting for Larkin's reaction. Larkin made no move.

"You begin to see what I'm getting at? *There is no qualified man.*"

Larkin's eyes widened. He sat bolt upright.

"Now it hits you. If none of those people this morning passed, there is no chance at all for any of the others tonight. What is left now is simply crackpots and malcontents. They are privileged to take the tests, but it means nothing. SAM is not going to select anybody. Because sometime during the last four years the presidency passed the final limit, the ultimate end of man's capabilities, and with scientific certainty we know that there is probably no man alive who is, according to SAM's directive, qualified."

"But," Larkin interrupted, "I'm not quite sure I follow. Doesn't the phrase 'elect the best qualified man' mean that we can at least take the best we've got?"

Reddington smiled wanly and shook his head.

"No. And that was our mistake. It was quite probably a psychological block, but none of us ever considered the possibility of the job surpassing human ability. Not then, thirty years ago. And we also never seemed to remember that SAM is, after all, only a machine. He takes the words

164

to mean exactly what they say: Elect the best, comma, *qualified,* comma, man. But do you see, if there is *no* qualified man, SAM cannot possibly elect the best. So SAM will elect no one at all. Tomorrow this country will be without a President. And the result of that, more than likely, will mean a general war."

Larkin understood. He sat frozen in his chair.

"So you see our position," Reddington went on wearily. "There's nothing we can do. Reelecting President Creighton is out of the question. His stroke was permanent—he may not last the week. And there is no possibility of tampering with SAM, to change the directive. Because, as you know, SAM is foolproof—had to be. The circuits extend through all fifty states. To alter the machine at all requires clearing through all fifty entrances. We can't do that. For one thing, we haven't time. For another, we can't risk letting the world know there is no qualified man.

"For a while this afternoon, you can understand, we were stumped. What could we do? There was only one answer—we may come back to it yet. Give the presidency itself to SAM—"

A man from across the room, whom Larkin did not recognize, broke in angrily.

"Now Reddington, I told you, that is government by machine! And I will not stand—"

"What else can you *do!*" Reddington whirled, his eyes flashing, his tension exploding now into rage. "Who else knows all the answers? Who else can compute in two seconds the tax rate for Mississippi, the parity levels for wheat, the probable odds on a military engagement? Who else but SAM! And why didn't we do it long ago—just feed the problems to *him,* SAM—and not go on killing man after man, great men, *decent* men like poor Jim Creighton, who's on his back now and dying because people like you—" He broke off suddenly and bowed his head. The room was still. No one looked at Reddington. After a moment he shook his head. His voice, when he spoke, was husky. "Gentlemen, I'm sorry. This leads nowhere." He turned back to Larkin.

Larkin had begun to feel the pressure. But the presence of these men, of Reddington's obvious profound sincerity, reassured him. Creighton had been a great President. He had surrounded himself with some of the finest men in the country. Larkin felt a surge of hope that such men as these were available for one of the most critical hours in American history. For critical it was, and Larkin knew as clearly as anyone there what the absence of a President in the morning—no deep reassurance, no words of hope—would mean. He sat waiting for Reddington to continue.

"Well, we have a plan. It may work, it may not. We may all be shot. But this is where you come in. I hope for all our sakes you're up to it."

Larkin waited.

"The plan," Reddington went on, slowly, carefully, "is this. SAM has one defect. We can't tamper with it. But we *can* fool it. Because when the brain tests a man, it does not at the same time identify him. We do the identifying ourselves. So if a man named Joe Smith takes the personality tests and another man also named Joe Smith takes the Political Science tests, the machine has no way of telling them apart. Unless our guards supply the difference SAM will mark up the results of both tests to one Joe Smith. We can clear the guards—no problem there. The first problem was to find the eight men to take the eight tests."

Larkin understood. He nodded.

"Exactly. Eight specialists," Reddington said. "General Vines will take the Military; Burden, Psychology; Wachsmuth, Economics; and so on. You, of course, will take the Political Science. We can only hope that each man will come out with a high enough score in his own field so that the combined scores of our mythical 'candidate' will be enough to qualify him. Do you follow me?"

Larkin nodded dazedly. "I think so. But—"

"It should work. It has to work."

"Yes," Larkin murmured, "I can see that. But who, who will actually wind up—"

"As President?" Reddington smiled very slightly and stood up.

"That was the most difficult question of all. At first we thought there was no solution. Because a President must be so many things—consider. A President blossoms instantaneously, from nonentity, into the most important job on earth. Every magazine, every newspaper in the country immediately goes to work on his background, digs out his life story, anecdotes, sayings, and so on. Even a very strong fraud would never survive it. So the first problem was believability. The new President must be absolutely believable. He must be a man of obvious character, of obvious intelligence, but more than that, his former life must fit the

166

facts: he must have had both the time and the personality to prepare himself for the office.

"And you see immediately what all that means. Most businessmen are out. Their lives have been too social—they wouldn't have had the time. For the same reason all government and military personnel are also out, and we need hardly say that anyone from the Bureau of Elections would be immediately suspect. No. You see the problem. For a while we thought that the time was too short, the risk too great. But then the only solution, the only possible chance, finally occurred to us.

"The only believable person would be—a professor. Someone whose life has been serious but unhurried, devoted to learning but at the same time isolated. The only really believable person. And not a scientist, you understand, for a man like that would be much too overbalanced in one direction for our purpose. No, simply a professor, preferably in a field like political science, a man whose sole job for many years has been teaching, who can claim to have studied in his spare time, his summers—never really expected to pass the tests and all that—a humble man, you see—"

"Political Science," Larkin said.

Reddington watched him. The other men began to close in on him.

"Yes," Reddington said gently. "Now do you see? It is our only hope. Your name was suggested by several sources, you are young enough, your reputation is well known. We think that you would be believable. And now that I've seen you"—he looked around slowly—"I for one am willing to risk it. Gentlemen, what do you say?"

Larkin, speechless, sat listening in mounting shock while the men agreed solemnly, one by one. In the enormity of the moment he could not think at all. Dimly, he heard Reddington.

"I know. But, Doctor, there is no time. The Polls close at eight. It is now almost seven."

Larkin closed his eyes and rested his head on his hands. Above him Reddington went on inevitably.

"All right. You are thinking of what happens after. Even if we pull this off and you are accepted without question, what then? Well, it will simply be the old system all over again. You will be at least no worse off than Presidents before SAM. Better even, because if worst comes to worst there is always SAM. You can feed all the bad ones to him.

167

You will have the advice of the cabinet, of the military staff. We will help you in every way we can—some of us will sit with you on all conferences. And you know more about this than most of us—you have studied government all your life.

"But all this, what comes later is not important. Not now. If we can get through tomorrow, the next few days, all the rest will work itself out. Eventually we can get around to altering SAM. But we must have a President in the morning. You are our only hope. You can do it. We all know you can do it. At any rate there is no other way, no time. Doctor"—he reached out and laid his hand on Larkin's shoulder—"shall we go to the Polls?"

It passed, as most great moments in a man's life do, with Larkin not fully understanding what was happening to him. Later he would look back to this night and realize the enormity of the decision he had made, the doubts, the sleeplessness, the responsibility and agony toward which he moved. But in that moment he thought nothing at all. Except that it was Larkin's country, Larkin's America. And Reddington was right. There was nothing else to do. He stood up.

They went to the Polls.

At 9:30 that evening, sitting alone with Reddington back at the apartment, Larkin looked at the face of the announcer on the television screen and heard himself pronounced President-elect of the United States.

Reddington wilted in front of the screen. For a while neither man moved. They had come home alone, just as they had gone into the Polls one by one in the hope of arousing no comment. Now they sat in silence until Reddington turned off the set. He stood up and straightened his shoulders before turning to Larkin. He stretched out his hand.

"Well, may God help us," he breathed, "we did it."

Larkin took his hand. He felt suddenly weak. He sat down again, but already he could hear the phone ringing in the outer hall. Reddington smiled.

"Only a few of my closest friends are supposed to know about that phone. But every time anything big comes up—" He shrugged. "Well," he said, still smiling, "let's see how it works."

He picked up the phone and with it an entirely different manner. He became amazingly light and cheerful, as if he

168

was feeling nothing more than the normal political good-will.

"Know him? Of course I know him. Had my eye on the guy for months. Really nice guy—wait'll you meet him . . . yup, college professor, Political Science, written a couple of books . . . must know a hell of a lot more than Polly Sci, though. Probably been knocking himself out in his spare time. But those teachers—you know how it is—they don't get any pay, but all the spare time in the world . . . Married? No, not that I know of—"

Larkin noticed with wry admiration how carefully Reddington had slipped in that bit about spare time, without seeming to be making an explanation. He thought wearily to himself, I hope that I don't have to do any talking myself. I'll have to do a lot of listening before I can chance any talking.

In a few moments Reddington put down the phone and came back. He had on his hat and coat.

"Had to answer a few," he said briefly, "make it seem natural. But you better get dressed."

"Dressed? Why?"

"Have you forgotten?" Reddington smiled patiently. "You're due at the White House. The Secret Service is already tearing the town apart looking for you. We were supposed to alert them. Oh, by the saints, I hope that wasn't too bad a slip."

He pursed his mouth worriedly while Larkin, still dazed, got into his coat. It was beginning now. It had already begun. He was tired but it did not matter. That he was tired would probably never matter again. He took a deep breath. Like Reddington, he straightened his shoulders.

The Secret Service picked them up halfway across town. That they knew where he was, who he was, amazed him and worried Reddington. They went through the gates of the White House and drove up before the door. It was opened for him as he put out his hand. He stepped back in a reflex action from the sudden blinding flares of the photographer's flashbulbs. Reddington behind him took him firmly by the arm. Larkin went with him gratefully, unable to see, unable to hear anything but the roar of the crowd from behind the gates and the shouted questions of the reporters.

Inside the great front doors it was suddenly peaceful again, very quiet and pleasantly dark. He took off his hat instinctively. Luckily he had been here before. He recognized the lovely hall and felt not awed but at home. He was introduced quickly to several people whose names made no impression on him. A woman smiled. He made an effort to smile back. Reddington took him by the arm again and led him away. There were people all around him, but they were quiet and hung back. He saw the respect on their faces. It sobered him, quickened his mind.

"The President's in the Lincoln Room," Reddington whispered. "He wants to see you. How do you feel?"

"All right."

"Listen."

"Yes."

"You'll be fine. You're doing beautifully. Keep just that look on your face."

"I'm not trying to keep it there."

"You aren't?" Reddington looked at him. "Good. Very good." He paused and looked again at Larkin. Then he smiled.

"It's done it. I thought it would but I wasn't sure. But it does it every time. A man comes in here—no matter what he was before, no matter what he is when he goes out, but he feels it. Don't you feel it?"

"Yes. It's like—"

"What?"

"It's like . . . when you're in here . . . you're *responsible.*"

Reddington said nothing. But Larkin felt a warm pressure on his arm.

They paused at the door of the Lincoln Room. Two Secret Service men, standing by the door, opened it respectfully. They went on in, leaving the others outside.

Larkin looked across the room to the great, immortal bed. He felt suddenly very small, very tender. He crossed the soft carpet and looked down at the old man.

"Hi," the old man said. Larkin was startled, but he looked down at the broad weakly smiling face, saw the famous white hair and the still-twinkling eyes, and found himself smiling in return.

"Mr. President," Larkin said.

"I hear your name is Larkin." The old man's voice was surprisingly strong, but as he spoke now Larkin could see that the left side of his face was paralyzed. "Good name for a President. Indicates a certain sense of humor. Need a sense of humor. Reddington, how'd it go?"

"Good as can be expected, sir." He glanced briefly at

Larkin. "The President knows. Wouldn't have done it without his O.K. Now that I think of it, it was probably he who put the Secret Service on us."

"You're doggone right," the old man said. "They may bother the by-jingo out of you, but those boys are necessary. And also, if I hadn't let them know we knew Larkin was material—" He stopped abruptly and closed his eyes, took a deep breath. After a moment he said: "Mr. Larkin?"

"Yes, sir."

"I have one or two comments. You mind?"

"Of course not, sir."

"I couldn't solve it. I just . . . didn't have time. There were so many other things to do." He stopped and again closed his eyes. "But it will be up to you, son. The presidency . . . must be preserved. What they'll start telling you now is that there's only one way out, let SAM handle it. Reddington, too." The old man opened his eyes and gazed sadly at Reddington. "He'll tell you the same thing, but don't you believe it.

"Sure, SAM knows all the answers. Ask him a question on anything—on levels of parity tax rates, on anything. And right quick SAM will compute you out an answer. So that's what they'll try to do—they'll tell you to take it easy and let SAM do it.

"Well, all right, up to a certain point. But Mr. Larkin, understand this. SAM is like a book. Like a book, he knows the answers. *But only those answers we've already found out.* We gave SAM those answers. A machine is not creative, neither is a book. Both are only the product of creative minds. Sure, SAM could hold the country together. But growth, man, there'd be no more growth! No new ideas, new solutions, change, progress, development! And America *must* grow, must progress—"

He stopped, exhausted. Reddington bowed his head. Larkin remained idly calm. He felt a remarkable clarity in his head.

"But, Mr. President," he said slowly, "if the office is too much for one man, then all we can do is cut down on his powers—"

"Ah," the old man said faintly, "there's the rub. Cut down on what? If I sign a tax bill, I must know enough about taxes to be certain that the bill is the right one. If I endorse a police action, I must be certain that the strategy involved is militarily sound. If I consider farm prices . . . you see, you see, what will you cut? The office is respon-

171

sible for its acts. It must remain responsible. You cannot take just someone else's word for things like that—you must make your own decisions. Already we sign things we know nothing about—bills for this, bills for that—on somebody's word."

"What do you suggest?"

The old man cocked an eye toward Larkin, smiled once more with half his mouth, anciently worn, only hours from death, an old, old man with his work not done, never to be done.

"Son, come here. Take my hand. Can't lift it myself."

Larkin came forward, knelt by the side of the bed. He took the cold hand, now gaunt and almost translucent, and held it gently.

"Mr. Larkin," the President said. "God be with you, boy. Do what you can. Delegate authority. Maybe cut the term in half. But keep us human, please—keep us growing, keep us alive." His voice faltered, his eyes closed. "I'm very tired. God be with you."

Larkin laid the hand gently on the bedcover. He stood for a long moment looking down. Then he turned with Reddington and left the room.

Outside he waited until they were past the Secret Service men and then turned to Reddington.

"Your plans for SAM. What do you think now?"

Reddington winced.

"I couldn't see any way out."

"But what about now? I have to know."

"I don't know. I really don't know. But . . . let me tell you something."

"Yes."

"Whatever I say to you from now on is only advice. You don't have to take it. Because understand this: however you came in here tonight you're going out the President. You were elected. Not by the people maybe, not even by SAM. But you're President by the grace of God and that's enough for me. From this moment on you'll be President to everybody in the world. We've all agreed. Never think that you're only a fraud, because you aren't. You heard what the President said. You take it from here."

Larkin looked at him for a long while. Then he nodded once briefly.

"All right," he said.

"One more thing."

"Yes?"

172

"I've got to say this. Tonight, this afternoon, I didn't really know what I was doing to you. I thought ... well ... the crisis came. But you had no time to think. That wasn't right. A man shouldn't be pushed into a thing like this without time to think. The old man just taught me something about making your own decisions. I should have let you make yours."

"It's all right."

"No, it isn't. You remember him in there. Well. That's you four years from tonight. If you live that long."

Now it was Larkin who reached out and patted Reddington on the shoulder.

"That's all right, too," he said.

Reddington said nothing. When he spoke again Larkin realized he was moved.

"We have the greatest luck, this country," he said tightly. "At all the worst times we always seem to find all the best people."

"Well," Larkin said hurriedly, "we'd better get to work. There's a speech due in the morning. And the problem of SAM. And ... oh, I've got to be sworn in."

He turned and went off down the hall. Reddington paused a moment before following him. He was thinking that he could be watching the last human President the United States would ever have. But—once more he straightened his shoulders.

"Yes, sir," he said softly, "Mr. President."

BORDER INCIDENT

WHEN HE REACHED THE BORDER IT WAS LATE afternoon: the sun was a soft yellow ball over dusty blue hills. He drove down past a long row of gray tanks, a mass of trucks, through a gap in a barbed wire fence. He stopped before a long white building and got out of the car into the silence, the heat. There were no other cars. In a field near the buildings troops were marching soundlessly, boots stirring dust but not very high, only up to their knees, so that they seemed to be marching on a flat cloud. On the other side of the building was more barbed wire, and the border. The border was a black iron gate set in the barbed wire. He looked down past the gate and saw the road running out in to No Mans Land: a narrow gray path fading out into dust.

He gave a guard his papers. He was an American in a rented car, traveling alone. The guard took him into a building and he filled out a form. After a while an officer came into the room and stood looking at him. The officer had a quiet, pale face, with a black mustache. He had that mechanized air, that gun-oil smell of efficiency which was not so much ruthless as simply inhuman, like the gate, the tanks, the rolling wire.

"And where are you going?" the officer said.

"Jerusalem," the American said.

"You have passed through here before," the officer said, stating it as a mechanical fact.

"Yes."

"Why do you go again?"

The American thought: because it's there. He smiled.

"I would like to see it again."

"Why?"

The American shrugged, still smiling. But he was uncomfortable. He became aware suddenly that the officer was one of those who hated Americans. It was nothing the man did—the man did not even move. There was no flick of expression or even a shading in the eye, but it was there in the air, like a smell; it had been there all along, drifting out toward the American, blown by the dark silent wind in the officer's head, and now the American knew it and pulled back from it. The officer watched him with calibrated eyes.

"What is your occupation?"

"I am retired," the American said. He found himself suddenly unable to cooperate. It was always this way with soldiers. He sat mute, unopened, indomitable as a stubborn child facing the implacable parent. But that was foolish, because he wanted to get out of here.

"You are not very old," the officer said.

"I tire easily," the American said.

The officer turned abruptly and went out of the room. The American stood staring at the empty door. He knew what would happen. The officer would take the papers into the next room and let them sit there. He would let them sit for an hour or two, and in the meantime he would have a cup of coffee and smoke a cigarette or return to a card game, and then, when the papers had rested there the proper length of time and he had exercised the necessary restraint, the professional caution, he would come back in and sit and stare and brood, and then slowly, carefully, with one small tinge of fear that he might be making a mistake, but with a sense of satisfaction that he had not made all this easy or simple, had made it seem a cautious and wary and perhaps even dangerous business, he would sign the papers.

The American took a deep breath and went outside and stood looking at the gate and the road beyond. He looked at his watch. The border closed at six o'clock. After six they let no one through. He had little more than an hour. He wanted to be on his way. It was not that he really had to be anywhere—no, he had all the time in the world. But he wanted to be out of here, past the gate, out on the narrow road. No one was waiting in Jerusalem. No one was waiting anywhere. But the American was a tired man. He was tired of many things: guns and troops and borders. He knew that if he stayed much longer he would lose his temper. He had not yet lost his temper but this time it was possible. He only wanted to go to Jerusalem.

178

After the proper time the guard came out. By then it was very nearly six o'clock and the sun was a fragment of fire behind a round hill. The guard gave him the passport reluctantly and he got into the car and drove up to the gate. At the gate he waited. He sat under the barbed wire; black loops of shadow rolled over his car. Then the gate came open, scream of a metal hinge. He drove through and out into the open land.

It was more than a mile to the other border. The American drove slowly into the darkness, the silence. The road ran straight between a cleft in gray rocks, down into a valley. He was out of sight of the barbed wire. He slowed. The land was empty. He came out onto the plain between two countries. Bare flat ground on both sides of the road, ending far off in the haze of evening. There was nothing alive anywhere, it was desert country. On each side of the road there were black signs warning tourists to stay on the roads—the fields were mined.

He drove slowly toward the center of the plain. He began to feel an extraordinary peace. He had come this way before and there had been people in the car; he remembered them all complaining about what terrible bleak land it was. But it was not that way at all—it was a land of vast soft silence. He stopped the car.

He waited in the center of the road, turned the engine off so he could hear the silence. The air was gentler now, the sun was down, there was a fine light breeze moving over his face. Suddenly the evening was enormously beautiful. The American thought: I wasn't going to Jerusalem at all. I came back for this.

He relaxed in the car, mindless and free, at rest in the silence. After a while he got out of the car and walked along the road, looked down at the black signs. Too bad they had to mine it. Why did they have to mine it? But the mines did not show. The land beyond the signs was flat and clean. He saw an oleander, one lone bush rising out of a cleft in the rocks. Something lived, then. And there would be small animals: bugs, lizards. But no people. No people anywhere.

He could not see ahead to the other border. There was a rise of hill behind him and another rise ahead; he was in a corridor of emptiness between two worlds. He looked down the corridor and had a peculiar vision: this band of emptiness led all round the earth—if you could walk between the mines you could walk round the world.

179

He knelt down in the dirt by the side of the road. Six o'clock came, passed. He was aware of it. He was unable to leave. The silence was blessed, the moment was blessed. He was utterly unable to leave.

Later, in the darkness, he went back to the car. The night air was clear, some of the stars were colored. He saw one that was red, and one that was orange, and many that were blue. He sat on the hood of the car, watching for stars to fall, a thing he had not done for more than thirty years, and he began to remember days from that time with an incredible clarity; he could see it all again and smell it, taste it—all the mornings with frost on the window, the steaming hot breakfast, the smell of his mother's hands, soap and love, his father's huge shoes, the cat by the fireplace.

Just after midnight a meteor flared. He had heard about that but he had never seen it. All night long the stars were falling—pale lean sparks against the vaulted black—and then one came in directly above him and blossomed like a match, brilliant, soundless, and died. He stood breathlessly waiting for another. He passed the night in memory, watching the stars.

Just before dawn he began to be aware that he was in trouble. At the border ahead they would see the time on his passport, they would know he had been out here all night. They would want to know why. What had he done? Had he disarmed the mines? Who had he seen? He had visions of metal faces, alarmed, efficient, bending over him. He felt a stunning weariness. He could not go back. He took one long deep breath and let it all go out of his mind, like a small sand hill washed by a wave. He could see the first light in the east, exactly as it was: a fire behind the hills. He walked out onto the road.

He looked off down the corridor of empty land. Of course you couldn't live there. No water, no food. No way to plant anything. It was all desert and nothing would grow. People could bring you food. They could hand it over the wire. But they wouldn't. The soldiers wouldn't let them.

I've gone out of my mind, he thought. If my friends could see me. They'll wonder, when they hear.

But he was not out of his mind. He considered that carefully, standing in the road staring upward toward the glow in the east. His mind was wholly at rest. His mind was perfectly clear. But he was very tired. He was too tired to move ahead to the wire.

I wonder what will happen if I stay?

But that would be no good. A car will come. Other cars. They'll talk about me. Troops will be waiting, at both ends. Finally someone will come.

He thought of himself being dragged. Because he would have to be dragged. Because he was unable to leave.

The glow in the east was higher, beginning to wash out the stars. In a little while he'd feel a wind. He carefully lighted a cigarette, cupped the fire in his hands, breathed deeply. He was free, but the sun was coming. Still smoking the cigarette, he closed the door of the car. When he felt the first wind he walked down off the road and past the black sign and began to walk patiently westward, one hand in his pocket, away from the sun.

STARFACE

MONDAY, MARCH 8: SHE CAME BACK HOME today. She was—no other word—stunning. I stood there. Stunned. She's taller now, about three inches, maybe more. She—blossoms. The figure is superb, yes, but slimmer than she was. The breasts are smaller, but even so, somehow, oh, indescribable. That *face*. My girl. And dark hair now, very dark, no more that golden blonde—and dark eyes that *glow* and a sharp-pointed nose—seen in profile—but that didn't take long, we had no time for profile, we were in bed and there I lay with this slim lovely dark-haired pointy-nosed *doll*—absolutely beautiful, and all that was still Myra, *my* Myra, all that was still the old Myra was that same soft squeaky voice, the only thing unchanged, and so we lay side by side talking and, old friend, it's been a rare day. A different woman. But only on the outside. The same voice—in the dark it was the same soft gentle Myra's voice, but even in the dark they were not *her* breasts, and that rattled me, must admit. I was making love to my woman, but—in the dark—to new and lovely breasts. Oh, it has been a magnificent job they did. She looks at herself in the mirror now and admires herself; she's wanted to be narrower now for a long time, and she seems much happier now, dazzled, and so the surgery is complete and the job is acceptable. She's not really *very* different—not really. It's still my Myra there—well, at least partly internally mine—and what it was was only delicate surgery on the face, and more extensive work on the legs and breasts, and so on, but none of that changes Myra. Not really. It's only the mechanical parts, really—Myra's tools, as they say— and it's rather pleasant to think that anybody can have that done now any way he wants it—trade in your hand for a new one, lungs this year, kidneys the next—now even the

185

face and hair—but I'm a bit behind the times. I've never changed much myself—well, yes, new hand once, long ago, forgot all about that, but only a hand, never anything like—my face.

Gives a man pause.

Women do it all the time now, but they usually look, well, similar. But my Myra now is different. When I woke just a while ago, next to that tall dark radiant girl—well, must be me. Old-fashioned. The Quiet Man. But—she was *gorgeous*. And we went right back to it again. But there was something—in the bright light—I have to get used to. She was not—that body. So. Well. Nothing has really changed. But I lay in bed watching her. And she moved from the bed in a different way. I was watching—something strange. Well. Remember: it's—exciting. In a few weeks we'll be in tune again. I just have to get over the shock. You're an oldie, Mac. Maybe it's the dark hair? Well. Minor change. We'll see.

Saturday, March 13: She's gone off with a new one. For the nite. Okay, write it down. We've always been open with this stuff, but—she says it's a new world. I thought it was only a new face. But she says, for Chrissake, she feels that she's been "born again." Wonder if the new world includes me. Hell. A flingo. All the girls—their lives depend so much on what they look like. But Myra—changed? No. Not possible. After all those years. Fling, and come back. I wait. And we'll share it all, the future, the present.

Monday, March 15: Didn't come back. No phone call. Well. Fling for a few days. Man tells her over and over again how beautiful she is. As they always do. Nowadays, Mac, all the girls are lovely. Nothing special. If they don't like the face, why not change it? But that doesn't change the girl.—Can't.

Friday, March 19: Myra left today. Will live with the other chap. I don't know his name.

She came by. She was so—clean. Hair black and glistening and shiney. She called me "dear" as she does talking to little boys. Will always look back on these days of our youth. But now the new man calls to her. Name is John Something. Love at first sight. She says that's true—there really is love at first sight. And she's stepped through the Looking Glass—into the other world. She said: "Mac,

I'm not the same. Things are just . . . different. People treat me, well, they *look* at me. And I thought that was only because of the new face, not much like the old, but no—you see, people I've known, not even old friends, suddenly want to know me better. This man—he says he looked at me, and I was suddenly—the most valuable thing in the world."

Self swore. Naturally. Words. But—can't argue. It means nothing. If it was only—temporary. Maybe it will be temporary? These passion-type things just—don't last. A quick flame. I know that. But I also know—she won't be back.

Nope.

And so—amen.

I'm the Quiet Man.

Ah.

Thursday, April 8: Okay, so why not? What the hell. See one of those blokes. Tear up no more pages. Sweat no more. Quiet Man.

Snarl.

Friday, April 9: A tall fella. Impressive. Doesn't look like a medic, certainly not like a surgeon. I asked if much work had been done on him, on his face, and he said cheerily: "Oh, yes, but not as you can see, by any real artist. And in this job what you need is an artist."

Artist?

But he talks well and gives the impression of—competence. I trust. Already. But he spent much time just sitting there gazing, from side to side, then he closed his eyes and said not a word, and then went on, woke up, looked again. Made one of those holo photos of my head in the three-dim look. Sizing me up, sizing me down. But the Quiet Man (me) was practical. Cost?

"Can't say yet. You want only the face?"

"Well, you've seen it all. What you think? Ole buddy?"

He didn't say much. I really don't know what to expect —except—I'm tired of *me*. S'truth. I'm a blah. Always have been a blah. And I know surgery won't make much difference—hell, I don't want to be no unicorn—but somehow, maybe something will happen. God knows. I may even—wake up. So. He didn't find out what I wanted to look like, didn't seem to care, and didn't name a price, and didn't try to sell anything, or promise anything, said he needed some time—*he* needs time—and so here I sit. Waiting. For what?

Tuesday, April 13: Saw Dr. Amstell again today. He said he needed to *study* me. He seems interested in a—peculiar way. Gay? Don't think so. Don't underestimate this bloke. Went to him mainly because he's *new,* still relatively cheap, but also familiar with the new stuff, new technique, all the latest, and what little I've heard of him has been very good. He does, so they say, marvelous things. They call him, already, the New Headmaster. Hee. Well, he does seem to know what the hell he's doing to me, and I get the message just by being with the bloke for a few minutes. Good feeling. *His* face? Wonder if he did anything to his own face? It sure is—cheery. They do those things to themselves?

I've seen pix of what people used to look like, in general, back in the days when faces were left what they had to call "normal."

Yuck.

Wednesday, April 14: Amstell: we start Friday. I said: okay. Of the price he said this: "You pay when I'm done, but only if you like what I've done. If you do not like what I've done, there is no fee, and I will return you exactly to the face you wear now."

This rattles me a bit. Fees are usually stiff, and of course, people can always get the retread. But he won't show me what he plans. So I wonder. Experiment? He said, "Yes." I said, "What the hell's that mean?" And he said, in this patient peculiar manner, "Sir, there is something unique in the structure of your face. Something that links with the tone of voice behind it, something—yes—*inspiring.* I cannot —explain this except by showing it to you. And that is what I will do. If you do not permit this—but if you will, and it is done, and then you do not approve of the face I have created, then you may, of course, have it instantly changed, to anything you desire, at no expense. But I have had, I must say"—and the fella had gleaming eyes—"I've had an absorbing week! Let me go to work, sir, and we shall see!"

Chilled me a bit.

But I have faith in the chap. Don't know why. So. What the hell. Anybody can change back. And becom- old man Blah again. Me. Do I have friends?

188

No.

The Quiet Man.

Who will miss him?

When I look in the mirror, which I just did again, I know I won't even miss myself. Goodbye, old chap. I'll not be seeing you.

Tuesday, April 27: I can *see!*

So: can write a bit. But even now—only one eye is free. They insist the other is all right, whoopee, but Amstell apparently has even widened the position of the eyes—which is rather rare. But he says the eye he replaced—the right eye—was going bad to begin with, and there's no problem, that's even an improvement, saving the cost of eye operation, maybe, but who the hell knows? So here I sit—one-eyed Mac—and it is strange. I do *feel* different. All mental, right? Even with a new eye. Inside here, back in the dark, when I've closed the eye—nothing has changed.

Mmmmm.

Sunday, May 2: Today things come off. But I do not see. No mirror yet. Urp. Here comes A. He says I need "a bit of training."

So. Trained. And quite groggy. Now. Will sleep. And here come some of those remarkable dreams.

Monday: Trained again. Amstell, I tell you, is weird. He says, they all say: Masterpiece. I feel . . . drugged.

Wednesday: Amstell said, "When do you want to see yourself?"

I said, "Why the hell ask?"

He said, "Each day that passes, you get better. So. The later you see, the better t'will be. But if you *must* see your face, you can do that now."

I said, "You mean there's no problem?"

He said, "No."

"But *you* want me to wait?"

"Yes."

"All right. How long?"

"Not long. Three days."

"I have strange dreams."

"My friend, worry not. You are . . . a masterpiece."

189

"Don't kid me," I said.

He said, "But I'm not."

Nurses keep popping by to look at me. One called me: Starface.

Boy, I'm tired.

Friday: And so today, being of sound mind and body, I saw myself.

And it's not me.

Hello out there.

Big fella.

The *eyes.*

I look back at myself and it's not me out there in the mirror—it's a man with a broad forehead and great dark eyes and a bigger mouth and bigger teeth and something rather—*pleasant* somewhere—something in the eyes, in the shape of it, of all of it. Well. So there I am. Likeable guy. Out *there.* In front. Cheery? I seem to be—serious. But not harmful. But not—the Quiet Man.

Not anymore.

Who am I?

I'll think on that.

Wednesday, Someday: I left today. They all came out to say good-bye. It was a good time, with good people. I'll miss them too. Marian, that lovely nurse, met me tonight for dinner and stayed over, and she was, ah, magnificent. She sleeps now, as I write here, having come home with my new face. She called me, again, Starface. But the way she speaks to me, they all speak to me—she opened so quickly —Amstell said one thing: "You were always a quiet man, Mac, yes, you were always soft of speech. Now do this: continue the quiet, do not speak now, not too much, because your face is now an enigmatic face, and many people will be curious now—do you see?" And he was right—and he said, "I want to see you learn to react to what is out there, as it reacts to you. The thing out there that sees you, that thing is also different now. Because it sees something else. Ah, wait, my friend, watch, and wait, and listen. And learn."

And so I'm again, in my own way, the Quiet Man. But it was always because no one seemed interested much. Or was it? Now people seem drawn to me. They come. They look at me with—lights in their eyes. Starface. Amstell says, repeatedly, that I am his first masterpiece, and that he will be known now, from this day onward, as a great artist. Well. Today, at the hospital, as I left, they broke into applause. And somehow, dammit, it was not laughable. I am—gifted.

Monday: No more time. Dream, perhaps comes true. My presence is now charismatic. Were I to stay here I would be known always as Amstell's first great work and I am grateful. But I go now, as Myra did, into that brave new world. I never knew how much my life depended on the shape of the face, the color of the eyes, but because I've changed, the world around me has changed—people smile, and this charming magnetism is feelable within. I am something of value now, however small—I see that in their eyes—and I shall now leave this job forever, and go —to office? Where? Starface?

I have written into this book all my life, talking to— myself. A very small diary. But it ends now, is done today, for there is now a world out there. So goodbye, old book, but not farewell. I'll be back again, someday.

THE PEEPING TOM PATROL

Mundy cut the lights and the patrol car glided down silently through the trees onto the beach. The moon was high and full; they saw the car parked back under the trees just about the same time the people in the car saw them. Mundy swore and jumped out, grabbing for his flashlight. Redmond came out the other side, feeling ridiculous.

Mundy lunged heavily through the sand up to the parked car, blazed the powerful flashlight beam through the window. The boy and girl were both up, both clothed, blinking in the light. The boy had taken his arms away from the girl, but the girl was startled and was hanging on to him tightly.

"All right, son," Mundy grunted. "You have to get out of here." Redmond could hear his disappointment and grinned cheerfully into the dark.

"This ain't no public beach," Mundy said, "you kids go do that stuff somewhere else. You never know what can happen out here."

"Yes sir," the boy said instantly. He was about eighteen.

"Never can tell. Lots of queer characters hang out around places like this. One of them jump out on you one of these nights, be hell to pay."

"Yes sir," the boy said. He started the car.

"So get on home."

The boy nodded, the girl still hanging on to him, and drove off. Mundy watched them go, kicking fretfully at the sand.

"Crap," he said. "They must of seen us coming."

Redmond said nothing. Mundy was senior man. Mundy made all the decisions. But Redmond felt very good. They went back to the cruiser.

"Well," Mundy said after a while, his optimism coming back, "I know lots more spots. We'll see who else is diddling who."

He ran down the beach, then up a dirt road through the woods. He followed the road for a long while, occasionally slowing to a crawl and cutting his lights. He found absolutely nothing. After a while Redmond said, "Shouldn't we better get back downtown? What happens if we get a call?"

Mundy shrugged. "Don't worry about it. This is Wednesday. Nothing happens Wednesday. And if we get a call and we're too far away, they call somebody else."

They turned down another short road leading to the sea. They flushed another couple but did not catch them in the act. When they came out and headed for still another spot Mundy knew, Redmond was irritated.

"Listen," he said, "we going to do this all night?"

Mundy chuckled. "You got a better idea?"

"Well, what the hell, this is no way—"

"Relax."

"But it's none of our business. These people aren't hurting anybody."

Mundy swung the car down another lonely road.

"You never can tell," he said cheerfully. "Couple times I found suicides this way, sneakin' up on parked cars. One guy in there been dead a week. Hell of a note, a guy lays out here dead all that while and somebody else finds him. Makes the cops look bad. We got to investigate. How do *you* know what's goin' on in them cars? People could be murderin' people."

"Sure," Redmond said.

Mundy went on whistling absently. After a while he said without concern, "You'll learn, after you been around awhile. How long you been on the force?"

"Three months."

"Where they put you?"

"North Traffic Cruiser. Accident car. Last month they had me walking Ninth and Central."

Mundy chuckled. "Man, that Ninth and Central. That's the beat, hah? More quiff down there than a man could use in a hundred years. Bet you went for that stuff, hah?"

Mundy waited for him to say something, but he didn't.

"Best damn beat in town," Mundy reaffirmed fondly, remembering. "All the girls in them stores, the bank. Man, when I walked that beat I was busy all day. I had coffee with five hundred different women on the city's time. And then on *my* time—" He laughed fatly, then went on to tell some highly unlikely sexual adventures.

Bored, Redmond let his mind wander. But it was true what Mundy said about the downtown beat. There were women all over the place, and most of them happy to talk to you. He wondered why. The uniform, yes, but it was more. The gun. Authority. He stared thoughtfully up at the moon. He remembered vague tales some of the men told about the way women acted around the gun. How one of them had even wanted the man to wear it to bed. The gun, yes. And all the power it represented. Authority. The Law.

He glanced at Mundy. The Law, he thought. This is the Law.

Mundy was sighing reflectively. "But that was a good beat. Yes *sir*. Few good months of that could kill a man." He chortled, then broke it off. "Crap," he said with feeling. "I could sure use a little of that. They ain't had me on that beat in three years."

"Wonder why," Redmond said wryly.

"Ah, they don't know what they're doin'." Mundy brooded. He said some very brutal things about the brass upstairs. He told Redmond to stick with him, that he would learn something.

"Too bad you only ride with me one night a week," he said. "You'd learn fast, boy. But ridin' relief is all right. Who else you ride with?"

"I only ride two nights a week. Other nights I walk, four to midnight."

"Walk? Ninth and Central?"

"Yep. I walk that tomorrow."

"Jesus," Mundy breathed heavily, and wagged his head. "You must know somebody."

They rode on for a while in silence, Mundy brooding about the injustice of it. Redmond hoping there weren't many more cops like this. Mundy took it out on the next couple they flushed.

The girl was badly flustered. She had buttoned her blouse before they got there but she had done it too quickly and when Mundy's light shone in, her open middle buttons had come back open. Mundy gave the two kids a vicious lecture. Redmond turned away from it and went back to the cruiser.

"Listen," he said, when Mundy was done, "you keep at

197

this long enough, and one of these days you're gonna run across somebody you know."

"Nah," Mundy said, grinning. "Only the kids come out here. Only the amateurs. The smart money finds a motel or stays home. The old pros got their own places. All you get out here is the ones that don't know their way around. Sometimes you get *old* couples. Jesus. And I got a doctor once, *him* I knew. He and his nurse, goin' at it hot and heavy. And him married with four kids. You should've heard the way I give it to *him*."

Mundy glowed with satisfaction. Redmond looked away from him.

"There's one more good spot up ahead," Mundy said. "I've been savin' it till it got late. We check that out and then we go home. Best place I've got. Always get somebody there."

He turned off down another dirt road. He cut the lights again, and when he could see the ocean gleaming beyond the trees he stopped the car. He grinned excitedly at Redmond.

"From here we walk. Take no chances this time. Keep damned quiet."

"I'll stay here," Redmond said.

"The hell you will." Mundy's voice was quietly ugly. "Suppose that son of a bitch decides to get rough? You're my partner, boy. Where I go, you go."

"All right," Redmond said. He got out of the car.

"Keep good and goddamn quiet," Mundy whispered.

They walked off down the road. Redmond breathed deeply in the cool night air. "Watch your senior man," he thought. He remembered the captain saying it: "Watch your senior man, boys, *learn* from him! Watch him in action!" Redmond grunted in disgust. Mundy in action!

He looked up ahead and watched Mundy in action. The older man was stepping lightly down the ruts in the road, lightly and ridiculously, walking on eggs. Redmond could not bring himself to be careful. He couldn't help it. He told himself that Mundy up there was the Law, old John Law, and he giggled aloud. A twig snapped. He saw Mundy's angry turn. He grinned back, knowing his face couldn't be seen. Then he saw the car.

It was parked out in the open, on the beach. Real amateurs, Redmond thought. It was facing the ocean and Mundy was going in on it from behind. The moonlight was very strong and Redmond could see straight through the

198

car and see the ocean through the windshield, but he could see nobody in it.

Mundy went in very close, beginning to crouch. Redmond walked more silently without realizing it. He watched Mundy go up to the car. He knew this one was it, that Mundy had them this time, cleanly and without hope, and a shiver went through him. He thought of shouting. He didn't. He walked in close and waited.

He saw Mundy waving him down. Obediently, he knelt. He waited for Mundy to shine the light, but the older man didn't; he rose slowly and looked in the rear window. Redmond could not see his face. But he was in close enough now and he could hear the car moving, hear the people moving inside it. Jesus, he thought, chilled. He did not go up to look. He waited by the rear of the shaking car.

After a very long while Mundy exploded the light. It blasted into the car and the couple inside jumped frantically. Redmond felt his face grow hot; he had to look down at the ground with shame. He heard Mundy begin to speak.

"All right now," Mundy was saying happily, "come on out of there. *Now.*" He pulled the door open wide. "I said *now.* Or do you want me to run you in?"

The commotion inside the car stopped. A man got out the front door. He had his pants on but nothing else. Redmond felt himself irresistibly drawn around to the other side of the car.

He watched the girl get out in the glare of Mundy's light. She was clutching her clothes desperately to the front of her, her face an agony of shock. She was completely nude.

"All right, sister," Mundy said, "you can put your dress on now."

The girl turned to face the car. They all watched, all three men. She dropped all her clothes, her fingers horribly nervous, and bent to separate her dress from the rest. She raised her arms and put the dress on over her head and for an instant her whole body was gleaming and bare in the light of Mundy's flash. Nobody said anything while she put the dress on. When she was done she turned and the light fell again on her face, and Redmond realized dumbly that he knew her.

Mundy let the man put his shirt on, beginning to question him. When the man told who he was and who the girl was and showed his driver's license, Mundy asked him for one good reason why he shouldn't run him in. The man asked for a break. Redmond watched the girl.

She worked in the insurance office on the corner of Ninth and Central. She was about twenty years old and so pretty she made him shy. He had seen her every day when he was walking the downtown beat, seen her coming to work and going home and stepping out now and then for coffee, but he had never spoken to her. He knew all the girls in her office, he had had coffee dates with most of them and dated some of them, but never her. She was too pretty. He remembered that the other girls had not liked her for it, but they had never said anything against her. She was too remote. Cold and remote, and beautiful. He continued to stare at her, unable to move.

Once she had her dress on, Mundy took the light away from her. She had her head down, she did not see him. The dress was still open at the neck; she began to button it slowly, fumbling with the buttons. Her hair was wild and hung down in black streaks across her face. Without shoes she looked smaller than he remembered her. He wanted suddenly very much to help her. But he did not move.

He went on watching her, looked down once at the soft white pile of underclothes around her bare feet. He could feel his heart beat violently under his badge. She knelt in the sand and began to gather her clothes, lifting one hand to brush the black hair from her eyes, and then looked up and saw him.

She recognized him. She froze with her hand in her hair, on her knees, staring at him. It was the first time in his life Redmond had ever seen anyone look at him with terror.

He turned his eyes away. He heard the man trying painfully to be friendly with Mundy, asking him please to be a regular guy. Redmond began to want badly to kill Mundy. After a while Mundy turned toward him.

"Well," he said slowly, drawing it out, sucking it, feeding on it, "well, Red, what do you think? Should we give 'em a break? Hah?"

You son of a bitch, Redmond thought, oh, you lousy son of a dirty bitch. Because Mundy knew already he would let them go—he always let them go. Because then afterward, when he thought back on it and saw the girl naked and in agony and felt the thrill of it, he could still be virtuous, still be clean, because he had been a good joe, he had let them go. And I ought to take you, Redmond thought, I ought to open you up right here and now, you son of a bitch. But there was a kind of sick paralysis in his belly, and he could not move. He had to stand looking at the girl and he said finally, huskily, "Yes, let them go."

He listened while Mundy turned back to the man and told him how rough it would be if he got pulled in on a charge like this. He might lose his job. And how about the girl's reputation? He ought to think before he did a thing like this again. The man waited, smiled sickly, sweating. Redmond looked again at the girl's face.

She was standing now, her underclothes held crumpled in her hands, against her breast. He could not see her face clearly, but her eyes were wide and dark in the moonlight, and he understood. She thought he would talk about it. She thought he would tell it all over Ninth and Central. The paralysis was going away, he began to feel ugly. He thought this business better end quickly. She waited in front of him, unbearably tense, the white silk shining in her hands, like an offering. Something broke in him and he turned to Mundy.

"All right," he said. "That's enough." He spun and walked away, his feet thick and heavy in the sand.

Mundy was left alone. He did not like it but he had to break off. He told them both to get the hell out of there and came stalking back down the road. Redmond watched him come and behind him watched the soft light flowing down the girl's body.

"Now just what the hell—"

"You," Redmond said. "You. Listen. Nothing, you son of a bitch, nothing. Don't say anything. I'm telling you. I'm telling you this one time, don't say anything. Not a word. Not a goddamn other word."

There was this thing in his voice, this cold and enormous thing, that Mundy had heard before. He was an old cop and patient and not a fool. He said nothing. They checked off duty and Redmond went home and thought about the girl standing with her underwear in her hands.

The next day was his day at Ninth and Central. He checked on at four and went over to the corner by the bank and waited. He had thought about it all day and the more he thought the worse it got. Because no matter which way you looked at it, it had been sexy. It was a damn dirty thing to do but he had felt the thrill and it

201

shook him to admit it. Now it was necessary for him to make it right. He had to talk to her, to apologize, to make her see that he would never tell anybody.

She came out of the bank. She looked up to the corner and saw him and stopped, staring at him.

She was neat and small and shockingly pretty. She wore a light pink dress which swirled around her legs as she moved. She looked toward him for a long moment and he could see no expression on her face, no expression at all. She came and walked straight to him and stopped.

"Got time for a cup of coffee?" he said.

She gazed at him blankly, her eyes cold and clear. After a moment she nodded. They went silently across the street into Sam's and sat down in a booth. He had trouble beginning it. She was older than he had thought, more woman than girl, and it startled him to see that she was more composed than he was.

"I just wanted to tell you," he began, "about last night . . ."

She watched him calmly, still without expression, lighting a cigarette as he talked. A cool customer, he thought admiringly, a cool, cool customer. He saw her eyes go down to his badge and then back up to his face and an odd, thoughtful look came into her eyes. He became suddenly and joltingly aware of her body. He could not help thinking of how she had looked last night.

But he went on with it. When he was done he told her he would feel a damn sight better if she would say something. A slight smile came over her face, along with the odd look still in her wide, dark eyes. She said simply that she believed him.

He relaxed and was able to grin. The coffee came and they sat making conversation and it was gradually and surprisingly very pleasant. She chatted briefly about nothing, but her voice was low and warm and her smile delightful and he began to wonder just what in hell was behind that puzzling look in her eyes. The vision of her in the night kept coming back. He passed through one of those moments when it was absolutely necessary to reach out and touch her. But he didn't move. And you can't ask her out, he thought. How the hell could he ask her? She'd think it was blackmail.

"It must be very interesting," she was saying, "being a cop."

202

"Yep," Redmond said. He started to rise. "Well, I better get back to the beat."

She made no move to go. She sat looking up at him, smiling, something rare and delightful dancing in her eyes.

"I feel very peculiar about you," she said. "You know all about me."

"Not all," Redmond said.

"You know what I mean. I . . . don't have to hide anything from you. We're not trying to . . . well, *kid* each other. You see? It's odd."

He didn't quite understand. His eyes went automatically down the front of her dress and she leaned back suddenly and moved her arms away from in front of her and smiled at him softly, lazily.

"I know what you're thinking," she said.

"I'll bet you do."

"Why don't you ask?"

"You know damn well why."

"Why?"

"You'd think it was only—"

"And it wouldn't be?"

Redmond took a deep breath.

"So you won't even ask?" the girl said. She was still smiling but her eyes had closed slightly and there was no mistaking the look in her face, and it came to him in that moment with an enormous shock how little he knew about women.

"All right," she said softly, "if *you* won't ask. When you get off duty tonight, Mr. Policeman, why don't you come on by and pick me up?"

THE ORPHANS OF THE VOID

IN THE REGION OF THE COAL SACK NEBULA, on the dead fourth planet of a star called Tyban, Captain Steffens of the Mapping Command stood counting buildings. Eleven. No, twelve. He wondered if there was any significance in the number. He had no idea.

"What do you make of it?" he asked.

Lieutenant Ball, the executive officer of the ship, almost tried to scratch his head before he remembered that he was wearing a spacesuit.

"Looks like a temporary camp," Ball said. "Very few buildings, and all built out of native materials, the only stuff available. Castaways, maybe?"

Steffens was silent as he walked up onto the rise. The flat weathered stone jutted out of the sand before him.

"No inscriptions," he pointed out.

"They would have been worn away. See the wind grooves? Anyway, there's not another building on the whole damn planet. You wouldn't call it much of a civilization."

"You don't think these are native?"

Ball said he didn't. Steffens nodded.

Standing there and gazing at the stone, Steffens felt the awe of great age. He had a hunch, deep and intuitive, that this was old—*too* old. He reached out a gloved hand, ran it gently over the smooth stone ridges of the wall. Although the atmosphere was very thin, he noticed that the buildings had no airlocks.

Ball's voice sounded in his helmet. "Want to set up shop, Skipper?"

Steffens paused. "All right, if you think it will do any good."

"You never can tell. Excavation probably won't be

207

much use. These things are on a raised rock foundation, swept clean by the wind. And you can see that the rock itself is native"—he indicated the ledge beneath their feet —"and was cut out a long while back."

"How long?"

Ball toed the sand uncomfortably. "I wouldn't like to say offhand."

"Make a rough estimate."

Ball looked at the captain, knowing what was in his mind. He smiled wryly and said: "Five thousand years? Ten thousand? I don't know."

Steffens whistled.

Ball pointed again at the wall. "Look at the striations. You can tell from that alone. It would take even a brisk Earth wind *at least* several thousand years to cut that deep, and the wind here has only a fraction of that force."

The two men stood for a long moment in silence. Man had been in interstellar space for three hundred years and this was the first uncovered evidence of an advanced, space-crossing, alien race. It was an historic moment, but neither of them was thinking about history.

Man had been in space for only three hundred years. Whatever had built these had been in space for thousands of years.

Which ought to give *them,* thought Steffens uncomfortably, one hell of a good head start.

While the excav crew worked steadily, turning up nothing, Steffens remained alone among the buildings. Ball came out to him, looked dryly at the walls.

"Well," he said, "whoever they were, we haven't heard from them since."

"No? How can you be sure?" Steffens grunted. "A space-borne race was roaming this part of the Galaxy while men were still pitching spears at each other, *that* long ago. And this planet is only a parsec from Varius II, a civilization as old as Earth's. Did whoever built these get to Varius? Or did they get to Earth? How can you know?"

He kicked at the sand distractedly. "And most important, where are they now? A race with several thousand years . . ."

"Fifteen thousand," Ball said. When Steffens looked up, he added: "That's what the geology boys say. Fifteen thousand, at the least."

Steffens turned to stare unhappily at the buildings. When he realized now how really old they were, a sudden thought struck him.

"But why buildings? Why did they have to build in stone, to last? There's something wrong with that. They shouldn't have had a need to build unless they were castaways. And castaways would have left *something* behind. The only reason they would need a camp would be—"

"If the ship left and some of them stayed."

Steffens nodded. "But then the ship must have come back. Where did it go?" He ceased kicking at the sand and looked up into the blue-black midday sky. "We'll never know."

"How about the other planets?" Ball asked.

"The report was negative. Inner too hot, outer too heavy and cold. The third planet is the only one with a decent temperature range, but *it* has a CO_2 atmosphere."

"How about moons?"

Steffens shrugged. "We could try them and find out."

The third planet was a blank, gleaming ball until they were in close, and then the blankness resolved into folds and piling clouds and dimly, in places, the surface showed through. The ship went down through the clouds, falling the last few miles on her brakers. They came into the misty gas below, leveled off, and moved along the edge of the twilight zone.

The moons of this solar system had yielded nothing. The third planet, a hot, heavy world which had no free oxygen and from which the monitors had detected nothing, was all that was left. Steffens expected nothing, but he had to try.

At a height of several miles, the ship moved up the zone, scanning, moving in the familiar slow spiral of the Mapping Command. Faint dark outlines of bare rocks and hills moved by below.

Steffens turned the screen to full magnification and watched silently.

After a while he saw a city.

The main screen being on, the whole crew saw it. Someone shouted and they stopped to stare, and Steffens was about to call for altitude when he saw that the city was dead.

He looked down on splintered walls that were like cloudy glass pieces rising above a plain, rising in a shattered circle.

209

Near the center of the city, there was a huge, charred hole at least three miles in diameter and very deep. In all the piled rubble nothing moved.

Steffens went down low to make sure, then brought the ship around and headed out across the main continent into the bright area of the sun. The rocks rolled by below, there was no vegetation at all, and then there were more cities—all with the black depression, the circular stamp that blotted away and fused the buildings into nothing.

No one on the ship had anything to say. None had ever seen a war, for there had not been war on Earth or near it for more than three hundred years.

The ship circled around to the dark side of the planet. When they were down below a mile, the radiation counters began to react. It became apparent, from the dials, that there could be nothing alive.

After a while Ball said: "Well, which do you figure? Did our friends from the fourth planet do this, or were they the same people as these?"

Steffens did not take his eyes from the screen. They were coming around to the daylight side.

"We'll go down and look for the answer," he said. "Break out the radiation suits."

He paused, thinking. If the ones on the fourth planet were alien to this world, they were from outer space, could not have come from one of the other planets here. They had starships and were warlike. Then, thousands of years ago. He began to realize how important it really was that Ball's question be answered.

When the ship had gone very low, looking for a landing site, Steffens was still by the screen. It was Steffens, then, who saw the thing move.

Down far below, it had been a still black shadow, and then it moved. Steffens froze. And he knew, even at that distance, that it was a robot.

Tiny and black, a mass of hanging arms and legs, the thing went gliding down the slope of a hill. Steffens saw it clearly for a full second, saw the dull ball of its head tilt upward as the ship came over, and then the hill was past.

Quickly Steffens called for height. The ship bucked beneath him and blasted straight up; some of the crew went crashing to the deck. Steffens remained by the screen, increasing the magnification as the ship drew away. And he saw another, then two, then a black gliding group, all matched with bunches of hanging arms.

Nothing alive but robots, he thought, *robots*. He adjusted to full close-up as quickly as he could and the picture focused on the screen. Behind him he heard a crewman grunt in amazement.

A band of clear, plasticlike stuff ran round the head— it would be the eye, a band of eye that saw all ways. On the top of the head was a single round spot of the plastic, and the rest was black metal, joined, he realized, with fantastic perfection. The angle of sight was now almost perpendicular. He could see very little of the branching arms of the trunk, but what had been on the screen was enough. They were the most perfect robots he had ever seen.

The ship leveled off. Steffens had no idea what to do; the sudden sight of the moving things had unnerved him. He had already sounded the alert, flicked out the defense screens. Now he had nothing to do. He tried to concentrate on what the League Law would have him do.

The Law was no help. Contact with planet-bound races was forbidden under any circumstances. But could a bunch of robots be called a race? The Law said nothing about robots because Earthmen had none. The building of imaginative robots was expressly forbidden. But at any rate, Steffens thought, he had made contact already.

While Steffens stood by the screen, completely bewildered for the first time in his space career, Lieutenant Ball came up, hobbling slightly. From the bright new bruise on his cheek, Steffens guessed that the sudden climb had caught him unaware. The exec was pale with surprise.

"What were they?" he said blankly. "Lord, they looked like robots!"

"They were."

Ball stared confoundedly at the screen. The things were now a confusion of dots in the mist.

"Almost humanoid," Steffens said, "but not quite."

Ball was slowly absorbing the situation. He turned to gaze inquiringly at Steffens.

"Well, what do we do now?"

Steffens shrugged. "They saw us. We could leave now and let them quite possibly make a . . . a legend out of our visit, or we could go down and see if they tie in with the buildings on Tyban IV."

"Can we go down?"

"Legally? I don't know. If they are robots, yes, since

211

robots cannot constitute a race. But there's another possibility." He tapped his fingers on the screen confusedly. "They don't have to be robots at all. They could be the natives."

Ball gulped. "I don't follow you."

"They could be the original inhabitants of this planet—the brains of them, at least, protected in radiation-proof metal. Anyway," he added, "they're the most perfect mechanicals I've ever seen."

Ball shook his head, sat down abruptly. Steffens turned from the screen, strode nervously across the Main Deck, thinking.

The Mapping Command, they called it. Theoretically, all he was supposed to do was make a close-up examination of unexplored systems, checking for the presence of life-forms as well as for the possibilities of human colonization. Make a check and nothing else. But he knew very clearly that if he returned to Sirius base without investigating this robot situation, he could very well be court-martialed one way or the other, either for breaking the Law of Contact or for dereliction of duty.

And there was also the possibility, which abruptly occurred to him, that the robots might well be prepared to blow his ship to hell and gone.

He stopped in the center of the deck. A whole new line of thought opened up. If the robots were armed and ready . . . could this be an outpost?

An outpost!

He turned and raced for the bridge. If he went in and landed and was lost, then the League might never know in time. If he went in and stirred up trouble . . .

The thought in his mind was scattered suddenly, like a mist blown away. A voice was speaking in his mind, a deep calm voice that seemed to say:

"Greetings. Do not be alarmed. We do not wish you to be alarmed. Our desire is only to serve . . ."

"Greetings, it said! Greetings!" Ball was mumbling incredulously through shocked lips.

Everyone on the ship had heard the voice. When it spoke again, Steffens was not sure whether it was just one voice or many voices.

"We await your coming," it said gravely, and repeated: "Our desire is only to serve."

And then the robots sent a *picture*.

212

As perfect and as clear as a tridim movie, a rectangular plate took shape in Steffen's mind. On the face of the plate, standing alone against a background of red-brown bare rocks, was one of the robots. With slow, perfect movement, the robot carefully lifted one of the hanging arms of its side, of its *right* side, and extended it toward Steffens, a graciously offered hand.

Steffens felt a peculiar, compelling urge to take the hand, realized right away that the urge to take the hand was not entirely his. The robot mind had helped.

When the picture vanished, he knew that the others had seen it. He waited for a while; there was no further contact, but the feeling of the robot's urging was still strong within him. He had an idea that, if they wanted to, the robots could control his mind. So when nothing more happened, he began to lose his fear.

While the crew watched in fascination, Steffens tried to talk back. He concentrated hard on what he was saying, said it aloud for good measure, then held his own hand extended in the robot manner of shaking hands.

"Greetings," he said, because it was what *they* had said, and explained: "We have come from the stars."

It was overly dramatic, but so was the whole situation. He wondered baffledly if he should have let the Alien Contact crew handle it. Order someone to stand there, feeling like a fool, and *think* a message?

No, it was his responsibility; he had to go on.

"We request—we respectfully request permission to land upon your planet."

Steffens had not realized that there were so many.

They had been gathering since his ship was first seen, and now there were hundreds of them clustered upon the hill. Others were arriving even as the skiff landed; they glided in over the rocky hills with fantastic ease and power, so that Steffens felt a momentary anxiety. Most of the robots were standing with the silent immobility of metal. Others threaded their way to the fore and came near the skiff, but none touched it, and a circle was cleared for Steffens when he came out.

One of the near robots came forward alone, moving, as Steffens now saw, on a number of short, incredibly strong and agile legs. The black thing paused before him, extended a hand as it had done in the picture. Steffens took

213

it, he hoped, warmly—felt the power of the metal through the glove of his suit.

"Welcome," the robot said, speaking again to his mind, and now Steffens detected a peculiar alteration in the robot's tone. It was less friendly now, less—Steffens could not understand—somehow less *interested*, as if the robot had been—expecting someone else.

"Thank you," Steffens said. "We are deeply grateful for your permission to land."

"Our desire," the robot repeated mechanically, "is only to serve."

Suddenly, Steffens began to feel alone, surrounded by machines. He tried to push the thought out of his mind, because he knew that they *should* seem inhuman. But . . .

"Will the others come down?" asked the robot, still mechanically.

Steffens felt his embarrassment. The ship lay high in the mist above, jets throbbing gently.

"They must remain with the ship," Steffens said aloud, trusting to the robot's formality not to ask him why. Although, if they could read his mind, there was no need to ask.

For a long while, neither spoke, long enough for Steffens to grow tense and uncomfortable. He could not think of a thing to say, the robot was obviously waiting, and so, in desperation, he signaled the Aliencon men to come on out of the skiff.

They came, wonderingly, and the ring of robots widened. Steffens heard the one robot speak again. The voice was now much more friendly.

"We hope you will forgive us for intruding upon your thought. It is our—custom—not to communicate unless we are called upon. But when we observed that you were in ignorance of our real—nature—and were about to leave our planet, we decided to put aside our custom, so that you might base your decision upon sufficient data."

Steffens replied haltingly that he appreciated their action.

"We perceive," the robot went on, "that you are unaware of our complete access to your mind, and would perhaps be—dismayed—to learn that we have been gathering information from you. We must—apologize. Our only purpose was so that we could communicate with you. Only that information was taken which is necessary for communication and—understanding. We will enter your minds henceforth only at your request."

Steffens did not react to the news that his mind was being probed as violently as he might have. Nevertheless it was a shock, and he retreated into observant silence as the Aliencon men went to work.

The robot which seemed to have been doing the speaking was in no way different from any of the others in the group. Since each of the robots was immediately aware of all that was being said or thought, Steffens guessed that they had sent one forward just for appearance's sake, because they perceived that the Earthmen would feel more at home. The picture of the extended hand, the characteristic handshake of Earthmen, had probably been borrowed, too, for the same purpose of making him and the others feel at ease. The one jarring note was the robot's momentary lapse, those unexplainable few seconds when the things had seemed almost disappointed. Steffens gave up wondering about that and began to examine the first robot in detail.

It was not very tall, being at least a foot shorter than the Earthmen. The most peculiar thing about it, except for the circling eye-band of the head, was a mass of symbols which were apparently engraved upon the metal chest. Symbols in row upon row—numbers, perhaps—were upon the chest, and repeated again below the level of the arms, and continued in orderly rows across the front of the robot, all the way down to the base of the trunk. If they were numbers, Steffens thought, then it was a remarkably complicated system. But he noticed the same pattern on the nearer robots, all apparently identical. He was forced to conclude that the symbols were merely decoration and let it go tentatively at that, although the answer seemed illogical.

It wasn't until he was on his way home that Steffens remembered the symbols again. And only then did he realize what they were.

After a while, convinced that there was no danger, Steffens had the ship brought down. When the crew came out of the airlock, they were met by the robots, and each man found himself with a robot at his side, humbly requesting to be of service. There were literally thousands of the robots now, come from all over the barren horizon. The mass of them stood apart, immobile on a plain near the ship, glinting in the sun like a vast, metallic field of black wheat.

The robots had obviously been built to serve. Steffens began to *feel* their pleasure, to sense it in spite of the blank, expressionless faces. They were almost like children in their eagerness, yet they were still reserved. Whoever had built them, Steffens thought in wonder, had built them well.

Ball came to join Steffens, staring at the robots through the clear plastic of his helmet with baffledly widened eyes. A robot moved out from the mass in the field, allied itself to him. The first to speak had remained with Steffens.

Realizing that the robot could hear every word he was saying, Ball was for a while apprehensive. But the sheer unreality of standing and talking with a multilimbed, intelligent hunk of dead metal upon the bare rock of a dead, ancient world, the unreality of it slowly died. It was impossible not to like the things. There was something in their very lines which was pleasant and relaxing.

Their builders, Steffens thought, had probably thought of that, too.

"There's no harm in them," said Ball at last, openly, not minding if the robots heard. "They seem actually glad we're here. My God, whoever heard of a robot being glad?"

Steffens, embarrassed, spoke quickly to the nearest mechanical. "I hope you will forgive us our curiosity, but—yours is a remarkable race. We have never before made contact with a race like yours." It was said haltingly, but it was the best he could do.

The robot made a singularly human nodding motion of its head.

"I perceive that the nature of our construction is unfamiliar to you. Your question is whether or not we are entirely 'mechanical.' I am not exactly certain as to what the word 'mechanical' is intended to convey—I would have to examine your thought more fully—but I believe that there is fundamental similarity between our structures."

The robot paused. Steffens had a distinct impression that it was disconcerted.

"I must tell you," the thing went on, "that we ourselves are—curious." It stopped suddenly, struggling with a word it could not comprehend. Steffens waited, listening with absolute interest. It said at length: "We know of only two types of living structure. Ours, which is largely metallic,

216

and that of the *Makers,* which would appear to be some-what more like yours. I am not a—doctor—and therefore cannot acquaint you with the specific details of the Makers' composition, but if you are interested I will have a doctor brought forward. It will be glad to be of assistance."

It was Steffens's turn to struggle, and the robot waited patiently while Ball and the second robot looked on in silence. The Makers, obviously, were whoever or whatever had built the robots, and the "doctors," Steffens decided, were probably just that—doctor-robots, designed specifically to care for the apparently flesh-bodies of the Makers.

The efficiency of the things continued to amaze him, but the question he had been waiting to ask came out now with a rush.

"Can you tell us where the Makers are?"

Both robots stood motionless. It occurred to Steffens that he couldn't really be sure which was speaking. The voice that came to him spoke with difficulty.

"The Makers—are not here."

Steffens stared in puzzlement. The robot detected his confusion and went on.

"The Makers have gone away. They have been gone for a very long time."

Could that be *pain* in its voice, Steffens wondered, and then the specter of the ruined cities rose harsh in his mind.

War. The Makers had all been killed in that war. And these had not been killed.

He tried to grasp it, but he couldn't. There were robots here in the midst of a radiation so lethal that *nothing, nothing* could live; robots on a dead planet, living in an atmosphere of carbon dioxide.

The carbon dioxide brought him up sharp.

If there had been life here once, there would have been plant life as well, and therefore oxygen. If the war had been so long ago that the free oxygen had since gone out of the atmosphere—good God, how old were the robots? Steffens looked at Ball, then at the silent robots, then out across the field to where the rest of them stood. The black wheat. Steffens felt a deep chill.

Were they immortal?

"Would you like to see a doctor?"

Steffens jumped at the familiar words, then realized to what the robot was referring.

217

"No, not yet," he said, "thank you." He swallowed hard as the robots continued waiting patiently.

"Could you tell me," he said at last, "how old you are? Individually?"

"By your reckoning," said his robot, and paused to make the calculation, "I am forty-four years, seven months, and eighteen days of age, with ten years and approximately nine months yet to be alive."

Steffens tried to understand that.

"It would perhaps simplify our conversations," said the robot, "if you were to refer to me by a name, as is your custom. Using the first—letters—of my designation, my name would translate as Elb."

"Glad to meet you," Steffens mumbled.

"You are called 'Stef,'" said the robot obligingly. Then it added, pointing an arm at the robot near Ball: "The age of—Peb—is seventeen years, one month, and four days. Peb has therefore remaining some thirty-eight years."

Steffens was trying to keep up. Then the life span was obviously about fifty-five years. But the cities, and the carbon dioxide? The robot, Elb, had said that the Makers were similar to him, and therefore oxygen and plant life would have been needed. Unless—

He remembered the buildings on Tyban IV.

Unless the Makers had not come from this planet at all.

His mind helplessly began to revolve. It was Ball who restored order.

"Do you build yourselves?" the exec asked.

Peb answered quickly, that faint note of happiness again apparent, as if the robot was glad for the opportunity of answering.

"No, we do not build ourselves. We are made by the"—another pause for a word—"by the *Factory*."

"The Factory?"

"Yes. It was built by the Makers. Would you care to see it?"

Both of the Earthmen nodded dumbly.

"Would you prefer to use your—skiff? It is quite a long way from here."

It was indeed a long way, even by skiff. Some of the Aliencon crew went along with them. And near the edge of the twilight zone, on the other side of the world, they saw the Factory outlined in the dim light of dusk. A huge, fantastic block, wrought of gray and cloudy metal, lay in a valley between two worn mountains. Steffens went down low, circling in the skiff, stared in awe at the size of the building. Robots moved outside the thing, little black bugs in the distance—moving around their birthplace.

The Earthmen remained for several weeks. During that time, Steffens was usually with Elb, talking now as often as he listened, and the Aliencon team roamed the planet freely, investigating what was certainly the strangest culture in history. There was still the mystery of those buildings on Tyban IV; that, as well as the robots' origin, would have to be cleared up before they could leave.

Surprisingly, Steffens did not think about the future. Whenever he came near a robot, he sensed such a general, comfortable air of good feeling that it warmed him, and he was so preoccupied with watching the robots that he did little thinking.

Something he had not realized at the beginning was that he was as unusual to the robots as they were to him. It came to him with a great shock that not one of the robots had ever seen a living thing. Not a bug, a worm, a leaf. They did not know what flesh was. Only the doctors knew that, and none of them could readily understand what was meant by the words "organic matter." It had taken them some time to recognize that the Earthmen wore suits which were not parts of their bodies, and it was even more difficult for them to understand why the suits were needed.

But when they did understand, the robots did a surprising thing.

At first, because of the excessive radiation, none of the Earthmen could remain outside the ship for long, even in radiation suits. And one morning, when Steffens came out of the ship, it was to discover that hundreds of the robots, working through the night, had effectively decontaminated the entire area.

It was at this point that Steffens asked how many robots there were. He learned to his amazement that there were more than nine million. The great mass of them had politely remained a great distance from the ship, spread out over the planet, since they were highly radioactive.

Steffens, meanwhile, courteously allowed Elb to probe into his mind. The robot extracted all the knowledge of matter that Steffens held, pondered over the knowledge and tried to digest it, and passed it on to the other robots. Steffens, in turn, had a difficult time picturing the mind of a thing that had never known life.

219

He had a vague idea of the robots' history—more, perhaps, than they knew themselves—but he refrained from forming an opinion until Aliencon made its report. What fascinated him was Elb's amazing philosophy, the only outlook, really, that the robot could have had.

"What do you *do?*" Steffens asked.

Elb replied quickly, with characteristic simplicity: "We can do very little. A certain amount of physical knowledge was imparted to us at birth by the Makers. We spend the main part of our time expanding that knowledge wherever possible. We have made some progress in the natural sciences, and some in mathematics. Our purpose in being, you see, is to serve the Makers. Any ability we can acquire will make us that much more fit to serve when the Makers return."

"When they return?" It had not occurred to Steffens until now that the robots expected the Makers to do so.

Elb regarded him out of the band of the circling eye. "I see you had surmised that the Makers were not coming back."

If the robot could have laughed, Steffens thought it would have, then. But it just stood there, motionless, its tone politely emphatic.

"It has always been our belief that the Makers would return. Why else would we have been built?"

Steffens thought the robot would .go on, but it didn't. The question, to Elb, was no question at all.

Although Steffens knew already what the robot could not possibly have known—that the Makers were gone and would never come back—he was a long time understanding. What he did was push this speculation into the back of his mind, to keep it from Elb. He had no desire to destroy a faith.

But it created a problem in him. He had begun to picture for Elb the structure of human society, and the robot —a machine which did not eat or sleep—listened gravely and tried to understand. One day Steffens mentioned God.

"God?" the robot repeated without comprehension. "What is God?"

Steffens explained briefly, and the robot answered: "It is a matter which has troubled us. We thought at first that you were the Makers returning"—Steffens remembered the brief lapse, the seeming disappointment he had sensed— "but then we probed your minds and found that you were not, that you were another kind of being, unlike either the Makers or ourselves. You were not even"—Elb caught himself—"you did not happen to be telepaths. Therefore we troubled over who made you. We did detect the word 'Maker' in your theology, but it seemed to have a peculiar"—Elb paused for a long while—"an untouchable, intangible meaning which varies among you."

Steffens understood. He nodded.

The Makers were the robots' God, were all the God they needed. The Makers had built them, the planet, the universe. If he were to ask them who made the Makers, it would be like their asking him who made God.

It was an ironic parallel, and he smiled to himself.

But on that planet, it was the last time he smiled.

The report from Aliencon was finished at the end of the fifth week. Lieutenant Ball brought it in to Steffens in his cabin, laid it on the desk before him.

"Get set," Ball advised stiffly, indicating the paper. There was a strained, brittle expression on his face. "I sort of figured it, but I didn't know it was this bad."

When Steffens looked up in surprise, Ball said, "You don't know. Read it. Go ahead." The exec turned tautly and left the room.

Steffens stared after him, then looked down at the paper. The hint he had of the robots' history came back into his mind. Nervously, he picked up the report and started to read.

The story unfolded objectively. It was clear and cold, the way formal reports must always be. Yet there was a great deal of emotion in it. Even Aliencon couldn't help that.

What it told was this:

The Makers had been almost humanoid. Almost, but with certain notable exceptions. They were telepaths—no doubt an important factor in their remarkable technological progress—and were equipped with a secondary pair of arms. The robot-doctors were able to give flawless accounts of their body chemistry, which was similar to Earth-type, and the rubble of the cities had given a certain amount of information concerning their society and habits. An attached paper described the sociology, but Steffens put it aside until sometime later.

There had been other Factories. The remains of them had been found in several places, on each of the other continents. They had been built sometime prior to the war, and all but one of the Factories had subsequently been destroyed.

Yet the Makers were not, as Steffens had supposed, a warlike people. Telepathy had given them the power to know each others' minds and to interchange ideas, and their record of peace was favorable, especially when compared with Earth's. Nevertheless, a war had begun, for some reason Aliencon could not find, and it had obviously gotten out of hand.

Radiation and bacteria eventually destroyed the Makers; the last abortive efforts created enough radiation to destroy life entirely. There were the germs and the bombs and the burning rays, and in the end everything was blasted and died—everything, that is, but the one lone Factory. By a pure, blind freak, it survived.

And, naturally, it kept turning out robots.

It was powered by an atomic pile, stocked with materials which, when combined with the returning, worn-out robots, enabled it to keep producing indefinitely. The process, even of repair, was entirely automatic.

Year after year, the robots came out in a slow, steady stream. Ungoverned, uninstructed, they gathered around the Factory and waited, communicated only rarely among themselves. Gradually the memory of war, of life—of everything but that which was imprisoned in their minds at birth—was lost.

The robots kept coming, and they stood outside the Factory.

The robot brain, by far the finest thing the Makers had ever built, was variable. There was never a genius brain and never a moron brain, yet the intelligence of the robots varied considerably in between. Slowly, over the long years, the more intelligent among them began to communicate with each other, to inquire, and then to move away from the Factory, searching.

They looked for someone to serve and, of course, there was no one. The Makers were gone, but the crime was not in that alone. For when the robots were built, the Makers had done this:

Along with the first successful robot brain, the Makers had realized the necessity of creating a machine which could never turn against them. The present robot brain was the result. As Steffens had already sensed, *the robots could feel pain.* Not the pain of physical injury, for there were

222

no nerves in the metal bodies, but the pain of frustration, the pressure of thwarted emotion, *mental* pain.

And so, into the robot brain the Makers had placed this prime Directive: the robots could only feel content, free from the pain, as long as they were serving the Makers. The robots must act for the Makers, must be continually engaged in carrying out the wishes of the Makers, or else there was a slowly growing irritation, a restlessness and discontent which mounted as the unserving days went by.

And there were no more Makers to serve.

The pain was not unbearable. The Makers themselves were not fully aware of the potentialities of the robot brain, and therefore did not risk deranging it. So the pressure reached a peak and leveled off, and for all of the days of the robots' lives, they felt it never-ending, awake and aware, each of them, for fifty-five years.

And the robots never stopped coming.

A millenium passed, during which the robots began to move and to think for themselves. Yet it was much longer before they found a way in which to serve.

The atomic pile which powered the Factory, having gone on for almost five thousand years, eventually wore out. The power ceased. The Factory stopped.

It was the first *event* in the robots' history. Never before had there been a time when they had known anything at all to alter the course of their lives, except the varying weather and the unvarying pain. There was one among them now that began to reason.

It saw that no more robots were being produced, and although it could not be sure whether or not this was as the Makers had ordained, it formed an idea. If the purpose of the robots was to serve, then they would fail in that purpose if they were to die out. The robot thought this and communicated it to the others, and then, together, they began to rebuild the pile.

It was not difficult. The necessary knowledge was already in their minds, implanted at birth. The significance lay in the fact that, for the first time in their existence, the robots had acted upon their own initiative, had begun to serve again. Thus the pain ceased.

When the pile was finished, the robots felt the return of the pain and, having once begun, they continued to attempt to serve. A great many examined the Factory, found that they were able to improve upon the structure of their

223

bodies, so that they might be better able to serve the Makers when they returned. Accordingly, they worked in the Factory, perfecting themselves—although they could not improve the brains—and many others left the Factory and began to examine mathematics and the physical universe.

It was not hard for them to build a primitive spaceship, for the Makers had been on the verge of interstellar flight, and they flew it hopefully throughout the solar system, looking to see if the Makers were there. Finding no one, they left the buildings on Tyban IV as a wistful monument, with a hope that the Makers would someday pass this way and be able to use them.

Millennia passed. The pile broke down again, was rebuilt, and so the cycle was repeated. By infinitesimal steps, the robots learned and recorded their learning in the minds of new robots. Eventually they reached the limits of their capability.

The pain returned and never left.

Steffens left his desk, went over and leaned against the screen. For a long while he stood gazing through the mists of carbon air at the pitiful, loyal mechanicals who thronged outside the ship. He felt an almost overwhelming desire to break something, anything, but all he could do was swear to himself.

Ball came back, looked at Steffens' eyes and into them. His own were sick.

"Twenty-five thousand years," he said thickly, "that's how long it was. *Twenty-five thousand years . . .*"

Steffens was pale and wordless. The mass of the robots outside stood immobile, ageless among rock which was the same, hurting, hurting. A fragment of an old poem came across Steffens's mind. "They also serve who only stand and wait . . ."

Not since he was very young had he been so deeply moved. He stood up rigidly and began to talk to himself, saying in his mind:

It is all over now. To hell with what is past. We will take them away from this place and let them serve and, by God . . .

He faltered. But the knowledge of what could be done strengthened him. Earthmen would have to come in ships to take the robots away. It would be a little while, but after all those years a little while was nothing, less than

224

nothing. He stood there thinking of the things the robots could do, of how, in the Mapping Command alone, they would be invaluable. Temperature and atmosphere meant nothing to them. They could land on almost any world, could mine and build and develop . . .

And so it would be ended. The robots would serve Man.

Steffens took one long, painful breath. Then he strode from the room without speaking to Ball, went forward to the lockers and pulled out a suit, and a moment later he was in the airlock.

He had one more thing to do, and it would be at once the gladdest and most difficult job that he had ever attempted. He had to tell the robots.

He had to go out into the sand and face them, tell them that all of the centuries of pain had been for nothing, that the Makers were dead and would never return, that every robot built for twenty-five thousand years had been just surplus, purposeless. And yet—and this was how he was able to do it—he was also coming to tell them that the wasted years were over, that the years of doing had begun.

As he stepped from the airlock he saw Elb standing, immobile, waiting by the ship. In the last few seconds Steffens realized that it was not necessary to put this into words.

When he reached the robot, he put forth a hand and touched Elb's arm, and said very softly, "Elb, my friend, you must look into my mind—"

And the robot, as always, obeyed.

DEATH OF A HUNTER

NIELSON SAT WITHIN A BUSH, OUT OF SIGHT, his head bent low and his eyes closed. A few feet behind his back the forest opened onto a wide stream, and on the other side of the stream was a steep, bare rise which flattened out at the top into a small plateau. There were several men on the plateau. If Nielson had looked he would have seen them, sitting among the rocks at the top. He did not look but he knew they were there. On the other side of the forest there were more men coming toward him. They were firing into the bush as they came and occasionally he could hear the quick snaps and hisses of their guns. It was late afternoon. Nielson raised half-closed eyes to stare at the sky. No sign of rain. All day long he had hoped for rain. Still, it was already late afternoon and if the men coming toward him were cautious enough they might not get to him before the sun went down. He rested his head again on his chest, breathing slowly and heavily.

For three days he had not eaten, because he had not had time to stop and get something. He was also very thirsty. He thought of the stream a few feet away, the dust in his throat, the streaked stiff dirt on his face. Briefly he thought of what it would be like to go swimming. But the thought did not last. He was very tired. He wondered if he went to sleep in the bush here they might just possibly pass him by. And then he would awake in the middle of the night, the dark lovely night and stars shining through the trees, and all alone he would be, and then he would go swimming in the stream . . .

The psychologist sat on a rock at the top of the plateau, staring down into the forest. He was a young man, dressed in street clothes, bushy haired and nervous, unarmed. If the hunters captured the man down there alive, or if he lived for a while after they caught him, it would be the psychologist's job to find out why the hunted man was what he was. But the odds against them getting him alive were very small, and besides, the spectacle of many men hunting another is never uplifting, and the psychologist was gloomy now as well as nervous.

Near him on the ground was the leader of the hunt, a much older man in rough clothes, heavily armed. This man's name was Walter George. His hat was off and his silvery hair shone in the sun. He had a small portable radio by his side, into which he spoke from time to time, but mostly he spent his time looking from the sun to his watch to the forest. He also was nervous.

"How much light is there?" the psychologist asked.

"About an hour and a half."

"How does it look?"

"It'll be close."

"And if you don't get him before night?"

"Then we light up the woods as well as we can and sit it out until morning. He'll try to break out during the night. We'll have to keep very quiet."

The psychologist fidgeted.

"No chance at all of him giving up, I suppose?"

The older man shrugged.

"You're sure everyone knows that he's to be taken alive if at all possible?"

"Take it easy," George said. "Everybody knows, but don't expect anything. If you get him you get him, if you don't you don't. I been hunting him myself already for three years."

"And now, at last, it's become politically important," the psychologist said wryly. "Three years to get one man."

"It's a big continent," the older man said, apparently calm, "and he's an odd man."

"You said it," the psychologist muttered.

"The longer you look at it the odder it gets. The whole thing. You know how many men we have out there?" He waved an arm crookedly at the woods. "More than ten thousand. Ten thousand men spread out along a fifteen-mile front. Almost a thousand to the mile. Sometimes in the last three years we had even more. And helicopters and dogs and professional hunters. And altogether he killed twenty-seven of us and I don't recall as anybody ever saw him. Man, after a while you get superstitious."

230

"He's only a man."

"True. But a man can be a remarkable thing."

The psychologist looked up for a moment, frowning. Then he looked down into cool shadow of the stream.

"The unfortunate thing is that why he did it will die with him. How can we stamp that sort of thing out if we don't know the reason?"

"I wonder if he knew himself," the older man said.

"Listen," the psychologist said. "They told me back at the base that you might be able to tell me something."

George looked at him without expression.

"At least you spoke to him once or twice. That's more than anybody else around here."

"Yes," George said. He breathed once deeply and squinted into the sun. "I guess I could tell you something."

The psychologist took out a small black notebook.

"What was your impression of him? Were there any particular habits . . . ?"

The older man spoke as if he hadn't heard.

"I guess I really might just possibly be able to tell you something. Sure, now, I might just as well. Anyway, if we sit here all afternoon we can't help thinking of him down there in the dust, can we? So I might just as well tell you a little about it. It ought to help pass the time of day."

He leaned back comfortably and folded his arms across his rifle, ignoring the psychologist, who was staring at him with surprise. He was not sure yet just how much of it he would tell, but, as he said, it may have been after all that now was the time.

"Well, now," George said, "if the facts are of help, I have a great many. But what kind of man Nielson was? He did not know himself. Son of a government clerk, he was of a thin gloomy Swede father who collected stamps and buried his family for twenty years in a dim dark home on one of the lower levels of New York and of whom it is said that he never once saw a leaf in its natural state or peered upwards once into the sky, or wished to, from his tenth year on, but passed his life reading books on philosophy and the care of ancient paper. And so he unwittingly imparted to his young Swede son a serious emptiness which the chance sight of a real jungle later on was certainly not enough to fill, but more than enough to magnetize, so that the young man possibly went into the woods as a flower turns to the sun because of that, because

231

of too much closeness and dimness and pressure as a boy, but perhaps not for that reason at all. Perhaps for some reason lost with the now-lost books of his father, which he read and made a serious attempt to understand while too young, and from which he no doubt derived too much misunderstood philosophy too young. At any rate, a woodsman, a professional hunter. And yet more, for it is a long, long complicated path he led to the woods in which he sits now below, and there is about it a strange brutal darkness.

"So who was he?

"A hunter. A man who chose for his lifelong profession the killing of animals. A man who chose mostly to live alone.

"How came he to Morgan? Why?

"Well, these are the facts.

"He came to Morgan in the first year, when it was still young, just after it was discovered and before the colonists landed. When he came there were only a few thousand men on the planet: a motley bearded construction crew building the first city, some properly enthusiastic scientific teams, one bewildered professional hunter, and also the Morgans, which were not men but very close to men, who killed a good many of us and who had us seriously worried that they might be intelligent, which luckily, as the report turned out, they were not. He came at this moment, then, Nielson, a good, raw moment, because Morgan was new and wild and badly needed for its substance and its living room.

"Why did he come? Well, Director Maas said he came to hunt for us free, without pay, had volunteered his services merely to look at Morgans, which on the face of it was ridiculous, since hunters do not do Game Control work for nothing, so there must have been another reason, and another, but nobody knows it, not I, not even Nielson, who thought he came to help a friend. What brought him to Morgan to meet what can only be described as fate? But I see I confuse you. Let it go.

"And what did he look like?

"A matter of record. A Swede, thick all the way down like the bole of a tree. Round stomach as a wind reserve and heavy thighs built up by walking many hundred miles. Strange shape for a woodsman, not slinky at all, more like a big heavy bomb. Blond hair, bullet head, close shaven, and in the Swede blood somewhere something dark, for the eyes evolved coal black. Muscular out of proportion,

232

the kind of man that other men stood near with a sort of tense unconscious caution, a man who when he moved made you inadvertently start to jump back. Yet, for all the steely mean look of him a cheerful man and after all really only a boy, not yet thirty, rosy faced and clean. Only the dark eyes strange in the lighted face, a man to remember and ponder over, if you are the type to ponder, which no doubt you are. But still only a boy, this Nielson, Joe, complete with a great happiness at being alive and a lurking rage at conformity and an as yet untapped determination to go his own way. And eventually a killer. How many is it altogether? Let's see. Something like forty.

"And the events?

"He came to Morgan to hunt and Maas called me and had me fly him out to where the other hunter, Wolke, was, somewhere out across half a continent, and I did. On the plane on the way out he fell asleep instantly like an animal and so I never said a word to him at the beginning, and when he got out at the camp he armed himself and went immediately into the woods, not knowing where Wolke was, not knowing anything about the Morgans except that their danger lay in their ability to sneak up on you and kill you with a rock at fifty feet. But he had no fear of anything sneaking up on him, not on *him,* not of anything in the woods, for he was a professional and hunting is now almost a science, and so off he went. And there it began, although I did not know it then, watching him go off into the trees of Morgan on the way to be hunted simply because he came to help a friend, and moving so quietly even the birds in the trees around him continued to sing."

"Well," the psychologist said stiffly. He was dazed.

"Digest it slowly," George said. "It takes time, but in the end it's worth it. You'll get more than you bargained for."

"Well," the psychologist said again, groping. "You say he didn't come just to hunt?"

"Of course not. We already had the hunter Game Control had sent down, Wolke, and Maas knew that ethically it was not right to let Nielson in, good kind Director Maas, and though he was usually very strict about visitors before a planet was ready, still he let Nielson through, which was unlike him. But then, Nielson was unique. Maybe Maas was just in a hurry to get the job done."

"Wait a minute," the psychologist said. "Simplify it. What do you mean?"

"Well, look at it on the surface. Young hunter comes to Morgan for own reasons. Why? To help a friend. Director gives him permission. But that is unlike Director. Why? Ah! Now we begin to get the point. Now ask me about the Morgans."

The psychologist blinked.

"Well, what about the Morgans?"

George settled back, smiling oddly.

"I'm glad you asked me. Having discovered the planet, you see, one could not help but discover the Morgans, much as we would rather have not. Vicious things they were —long, lean, apelike creatures of great cleverness. They took a dislike to us and killed us whenever they could— which was only natural, as we were doing the same to them. The law concerning dangerous game is that specimens are to be taken and the rest destroyed, so that the whole planet is safe for parks and such. Then the specimens are taken and put on a huge reservation, which is kept exactly as it was when the planet was discovered. That was the way it was to be with the Morgans, but they proved difficult. They managed very quickly to avoid our traps and our poisons, and to kill us with rocks whenever we were incautious. They were indiscriminate. They killed women and children impartially.

"Game Control sent one man down to clear them up. He did very well, captured several and seriously depleted the rest by the hundred, and then one day several apparently ganged up on him and we found him in pieces. His successor was Wolke, but Wolke did not do well at all. He was an amiable, cheerful man, not really a very good hunter, but simply a man who loved the open life and who was very well liked because of his cheerful nature. He had a wife and two children. He took the job with Game Control because he needed the money—he was paid by the head. But the Morgans had already learned a great deal before he came, and what few were left mostly evaded him.

"And there, you see, was the reason Nielson came. Wolke was failing, and if he failed he would not get paid and his reputation would suffer and he would get no more guide jobs and would have to leave the woods. So he wrote for help to the only really good hunter he knew who would understand what it meant to remain a hunter, and who would come.

"Nielson came. His visit was unofficial. Maas let him come, you see, because on the surface he was anxious to have all the Morgans cleaned out and the job completed. But the truth is that he was more than anxious, he was sincerely worried. He used Nielson's visit to get rid of the Morgans as quickly as possible. And now, you see, we are getting to the point. He thought the Morgans were intelligent."

The psychologist's eyes widened.

"Yes," the older man said, smiling oddly, "that is the real point of it, the question no one ever answered. Not really. Not scientifically. The thing was, you see, that the Morgans *couldn't* be intelligent. Morgan was such a beautiful planet, and we needed it so badly, and besides, they showed no sign of intelligence, no culture. They did not band together, they had no tools, no gods. And they did not respond to tests. When we caged them they would not even move, just sat and looked at us and ignored the tests. But they couldn't be intelligent. All that land, you see, all that living room, all those wild, green, ore-rich plains, we would lose all that if they were intelligent. The law says we cannot dispossess an intelligent people, no matter what their cultural status. So Maas was very relieved, we were all relieved, when the psychologist's report came in and said that the Morgans were only animals after all."

The psychologist stared with mounting confusion.

"But what do you mean?"

"I don't know," George said, still smiling, "nobody knows. Or will know. But was there a little fixing, do you think? Did someone in authority realize the simple, practical truth quite early, and send down Word that the Morgans could not be intelligent? And after all, was there really any blame? Here was room and resources, land and prosperity, sunlight for children, here was a home for ten billion people and another stepping-stone to the far stars. Alongside this what are the claims of a few thousand naked beasts?"

"But who was the psychologist! You'll have to verify your charges!"

"I make no charges," George said softly. "I verify nothing. You wanted the story. I tell it as it was. No one can really say if the Morgans were intelligent. But if anyone knew, Maas did, and Wolke did, and later on, certainly, Nielson did. That's what makes it interesting. Picture now

235

the way it might have been down in the forest with Wolke and Nielson.

"If the Morgans were intelligent and Wolke knew it, what happened then must have been interesting. There was Wolke, a nice, decent, genial man, greeting Nielson with open arms, Nielson, the man who had come across light-years to help him. What would Wolke say?

" 'Oh, Joe, dammit,' he would say, 'thanks for—I appreciate—' and he would break off, because there would be no need to say that. Then, perhaps, as they sat together in some sheltered place from which they could not be seen but from which they could see everything clearly, he would tell Nielson about the Morgans. He would say that they had been too smart for him, surely, and other things. He would say that hunting them really should be easy because they had been cleared out of every area except one long dense wood below the great northern mountains. For some reason they never left that area, perhaps because they did not really know any other, and therefore you knew in general where they were. But you could not get close to them, no matter how hard you tried or how softly you moved, and you had to keep a close watch behind you, especially at night. They were not hard to kill, but if you got in a shot you better make it good, because you would not get a second one. This Wolke would say, or something like it, but what then? Talk about the family, the wife, the weather? Talk about the theory he had that all the dinosaurs had disappeared off Earth because once, long ago, someone had hunted them out? Talk about Nielson's latest clients, whose wives he had slept with? Yet clearly, if anyone knew other than Maas, Wolke did. But could he mention it? Which was more important—the wife, the job, or the friend? And after all, in the end, did Nielson really care? Oh, it's all very interesting, and very complicated. And I really don't know what happened. But surely, before long Nielson knew some of it. He learned it in the woods that very same night . . ."

And the old man stopped his musing and went on with the story, telling it now with his eyes closed as he began to lose himself in it, telling it in great detail and realizing now that he would have to tell it all, and not caring.

"That night they decided that they should move out as soon as possible before too many of the Morgans knew that there was another hunter in the woods. But little

Wolke was overjoyed to have Nielson with him here and wanted to celebrate a little, so he went out at dusk and silently killed four partridgelike birds, and they sat on a high knoll munching bones until late in the evening. They had maybe two or three hours to talk and then they moved out.

"Now understand, they were very well equipped, for hunting is a science. They had soft tight clothing which would not scratch on twigs as they moved and a cream which coated their bodies and removed their scent so they could not be smelled. They had lenses for night vision and pills for endurance and chemicals which made their own nostrils sensitive. Each carried two guns—an electron handgun and a rifle. Like most hunters, Nielson preferred a missile-firing rifle to an electron one; he told me that the blaster causes too many fires and too much smoke, and though it cuts a hole right through whatever it hits, even rock, still, it does not have the shock effect, the vital stopping power, of a solid ball. Therefore Nielson had a .300 H. & H. Magnum along with his handgun. But most of all, of course, what Nielson had was that magnificent inborn skill which comes to very few men—certanly not to Wolke—that ability to move quickly and be unseen, to be silent but very, very swift, which Nielson had to an almost unbelievable extent. And so armed they were.

"Wolke had located a group of Morgans in a valley to the north. He briefed Nielson carefully on the terrain and then the two of them moved out together. The way Wolke had chosen to go down into the valley was through a narrow ravine—not through it, really, but along the sides. When they reached the mouth of the ravine they split up, each taking one side, timing themselves to arrive at the end together. It was a fairly cold night in autumn, and very dark, for Morgan had no moon. The stars were clear but unfamiliar, so Nielson had to be very careful about his direction. And so they went down the ravine.

"Now here, you see, we have a clue. Why is it Wolke chose such an obvious, incautious way to go down into the valley? That is very odd. He had been hunting the Morgans for months now with very little success, yet he apparently had so little respect for them, for their cunning, that he chose the worst possible way to go in after them? Creeping over the sides of the ravine over rocks, rifle in hand, separated as they were, what position were they in to fight if they came across Morgans? Cramped and awkward they must have been, should have known they would be, yet that is the way they went in, and that was where the Morgans ambushed them. Maybe Wolke was so emboldened by Nielson's presence that he became overconfident. Or maybe, and this is likely, he did not want Nielson to see that he had so great a respect for the Morgans and therefore took the simplest, quickest way down. At any rate, there is something about it which looks almost *arranged,* and yet I know Wolke was not a man to commit suicide.

"Well, they had been moving down the gorge for maybe half an hour, and they had just crossed the ridge and were on their way down when Nielson became aware of something ahead of him in the woods—something quiet and still but alive, waiting. He did not see it or hear it or smell it, but he knew it was there. Take that as you will, that is the way he told it. It is a sense he had, an electric sensation, and it was his most valuable tool. That night he *knew* the thing was in front of him, did not doubt at all, and so he melted down into an alcove between a rock and a bush and waited without moving. He was sure the thing ahead was large and dangerous, because in the past these were the things his sense had warned him about. He was also sure that it did not know he was there.

"Now just faintly he heard the thing moving in the leaves, shifting its position. He could not hear any breathing but he began to be certain the thing was a Morgan. For a while he thought it was sleeping and was about to move toward it when he heard something else moving up above, another one, and then all at once he realized that there were a great many of them all around him in among the bushes and trees, spread out and waiting. It was possible that they already knew where he was so he began to move. There was nowhere to go but down, and in the bottom of the gorge there was no cover. Nielson stopped by the edge of the bushes, trying now to think his way out, beginning to understand that the position was very bad. He could not be sure whether to warn Wolke, to make a noise, because more of them were probably on the other side of the gorge, or maybe Wolke already knew, and maybe the ones above had not yet spotted him. But then in the next moment it made no difference.

"Suddenly, viciously, out of the blackness across the gorge came a quick whish and a cracking, horrible thump. Then there was a thrashing in the leaves, which was an enormous uproar in the night, and a terrible victorious inhuman scream from above, and Nielson knew that Wolke had been hit. They could kill you with a rock at fifty yards, Nielson knew, and then he heard the ones above him beginning to move down toward *him,* moving without caution or cries, rustling in the bush and leaping toward the place where Wolke lay. Instantly Nielson lay down his rifle and drew his pistol and knife and crouched with both hands ready for close action, tensed and huge and vicious, overwhelmingly ready to kill—but then he heard them running down the gorge and up the other side, seven or eight of them, and they had not known where he was after all. But now they were going to Wolke, who might still be alive, to make sure that he died where he lay.

"And then all this in an instant: knowing he could escape now easily back up the ravine, knowing that there were at least a dozen of them ahead, knowing that Wolke was already probably dead or at the very least would die before he could fight them off and get him back across half a continent to the city, still Nielson leapt out of the spot where he crouched and screamed his own human scream that made the one Morgan who crouched over Wolke leap up in surprise; and then he flew straight up the side of the gorge, roared like a great black engine through bushes and over rocks to the spot where Wolke lay, knife in one hand and pistol in the other, lips drawn back like an ape, enormous body of flying steel running into and over one lone stunned Morgan, bursting through a thicket and snapping off dead tree limbs with his head and shoulders, moving all in one frantic moment to the leafy hollow where Wolke was hit, arriving before the one Morgan there knew what had happened, killing that one on the spot, to whirl then and crouch and wait for the others.

"Then they should have rushed him, of course, or at the very least turned their rocks upon him, but here now again the likely did not happen. In the dark they were none of them sure what had happened. But they had seen the flash of his gun and one or two had seen the huge flying form of him, and they had no idea how many men had really come, so they sank into the bush and waited. Therefore Nielson had time to pull Wolke with him into cover, and also to cool his rage enough to think and let his senses work, to tell him where they were.

"As it turned out, he was very lucky. The Morgans had been upset, because they had learned by this time that their sense of smell was no good in hunting humans. And then

239

Nielson saw one and killed him with a flash from the blaster, which made up the minds of the others. And then also the Morgans were thinking simply of self-preservation, for there were not many of them left, at this point only fifteen or twenty on the whole continent. Therefore most of them left.

"But still two remained, one on the rise above him and another on a level with him across the ravine. These two remained after the others left. Were they more bitter, these two, for private reasons, or simply more stubborn and courageous? Odd that they should stay, but you can see that the Morgans were in this at least unusual. Would two wolves remain if the rest had left?

"Well, there was a long time yet till morning. Nielson moved quickly to stop the flow of blood from Wolke's head, and at the same time watched and listened for the two Morgans. From time to time, with a terrible unseen violence, a sharp rock would rip the air above him, to tear with mortal rage through the leaves around him, to shatter on a boulder or plow its way into a tree. Then the Morgan above, seeing that Nielson was well hidden, began craftily to lob bigger rocks down, heavy jagged rocks, heaving them into the air on a high trajectory like a mortar shell, so that they came down on Nielson and Wolke directly from above. Immediately that was very bad, and so Nielson turned and concentrated his attention uphill, perilously ignoring the one across the way, and when the Morgan above heaved up another rock his long arm was briefly visible, flung out above the cliff like a snake, and Nielson shot it off.

"Then there was only the other one across the way, the last helpless, mad, indomitable savage who still would not move, who waited until the dawn, flinging rocks with a desperate, increasing frenzy. But now Nielson was safe and knew it, and turned his attention to Wolke.

"By that time, however, Wolke was dead. He bled to death at approximately the same time as the Morgan in the rocks above, like the Morgan silently, like the Morgan a creature hunted in the dark.

"And so Nielson passed the night with Wolke soft and sleeping on the ground beside him. You wonder, don't you, what he thought of the Morgans then. And shortly before dawn the last Morgan left, for unlike Nielson he could not slip the night lenses from his eyes and see just as well, or better, in the daylight, and therefore even this last stubborn one saw that he was exposed and had to leave. When he was gone Nielson knew it, but remained where he was until the sun was fully up. Then he picked up little Wolke and set him gently across his shoulders, went down into the gorge and retrieved his rifle from where he had left it, and walked back to the camp.

The sun had lowered and the old man had gone into shadow, so he shifted himself out into the light. The psychologist continued to stare at him without moving.

"If you had known Wolke—" The old man stopped and shrugged, embarrassed, then looked at his watch. There was now about an hour until sundown.

"We had better get on," he said, now somewhat wearily. "Now I will have to tell you about Maas."

"But—"

"All right, I am no storyteller. But you see Maas is the next important thing, not Nielson. Eventually you will learn about Nielson. Don't get the idea—I see you already have it—that Maas is the villain of the piece. No, not any more than that this is the story of a noble wild man betrayed by a city slicker. Maas was a genuinely worthwhile man. For what he did no doubt he suffered, but still, he believed he was right. That's what makes it so difficult to judge, to understand.

"Maas, you see, was a man of substantial family and education, of all the best schools, the best breeding, the best of everything. And he turned out the way men like that rarely do, a really sincere idealist. He believed in Man, in the dignity and future of Man, with something like a small boy's faith. Perhaps he substituted Man for God. At any rate, he made his faith evident in his speeches and his behavior, and men found him an exceptionally good man to work for, even though he was very handsome and suave and clean cut. For cynical men he had a charm. They followed him because of his great desire to conquer all the planets for Man, to reach the farther stars, not because they also believed, but because they would have liked to believe, and at any rate, it was inspiring to be believed *in*. So Maas was a very effective man, a comer. He gained his directorship while quite young, and so came to Morgan, and so set in motion, because of his great faith, the dark damned flow which was to destroy Nielson.

"Yet blame? Where is there blame? Here was a man, Maas, who believed that Man was the purpose of the universe, that he would eventually reach out ever further and eventually, perhaps, to transmute himself into a finer, nobler thing. And then, of course, keeping with this philosophy in mind, you can see how he must have looked upon the Morgans. How easy it would have been for Maas, how right for him in the long run, to overlook a report on the Morgans. Not really falsify, perhaps just not press it, perhaps just approve it when it had not been thorough—for let us remember that the Morgans paid no attention to tests. And then, did it bother him, Maas, that he had done it? Did it weigh with him at all? Where really was the wrong in it? I mean ultimately, from the viewpoint of a thousand years?"

"And Nielson," the psychologist said. "I begin to see. Nielson was at the other extreme. 'I think I could go live with the animals, they are so clean and pure'—that sort of thing?"

"No. Not at all. I told you this was not the story of a noble savage. Exactly what Nielson was I am not sure, but he was not simply a nature lover, nor a man hater either. Even when you know the whole thing you may not be able to classify. Always behind it there is some dark point that eludes you . . . but we had better get on."

"When Nielson came back with dead Wolke over his shoulder, no doubt it was with certain questions in his mind. But of course he could not be sure. And anyway, he could do nothing immediately, for there remained the grave question of Jen Wolke and her two children. Wolke had no insurance, being a professional hunter, and for the same reason had little in the bank. What money she had, Jen Wolke, was barely enough to get her home to Earth. Many of us chipped in, of course, as we had done when the Morgans killed others, and yet in the long run the end was automatically that Nielson had to go back into the woods. Killing the last of the Morgans would complete Wolke's contract and earn a few thousand, and also, perhaps, there was for Nielson some primitive debt of honor besides, yet the end was that he who had come here to help through killing was forced almost, impelled, you see, to go on helping, and at the same time killing, and so forged on to the last inevitable moment.

But he could not go right away. He saw Wolke into the ground—there was not money to send him home—and then for a while he moved in with Jen Wolke, who was a fine woman, tall and soft, with thick black hair, fiery at times but also very affectionate—perhaps a strange wife for Wolke but a good one, and Nielson knew it. And did tongues wag? Oh, yes, indeed. But not to Nielson. There were many very large and ominous men among us, but none to jest with Nielson, or argue with him, and perhaps even many understood. To the woman Nielson was a great help. Although he was not what you might call an overly domesticated and helpful man, still, he was beyond doubt a tower of strength, no matter which way you look at it, and he was very good with the children, what with tales of lions and tigers and so on, and there was much room on his shoulder for crying.

"But in this I ought not be ironic. I don't mean to be. I do it to hide. He was a good, sincere man, and a great help simply with his presence. And I suppose few people had ever really needed him. Later I learned that he was debating with himself whether or not to ask her to marry him. He told me she was a hunter's wife and he was ready now and he needed *her*, was not doing any favors. But I am not sure he believed it, or knew really what he believed. Up until then he had been a man who went his own way.

"And so, as it turned out, he remained.

"Well, then, shortly after Wolke was in the ground Nielson came to ask me for a look at the captured Morgans. I was happy to allow it and went along with him, and oddly enough, we were not at the tank very long before Director Maas came in behind us and stood in the doorway watching.

"Now here is the scene. In the Bio tank were eleven Morgans—seven male, four female. The Bio tank was a huge steel affair with plastic windows, standardized model built to hold any game yet known, with pressure, atmosphere, temperature all carefully controlled from the outside. The windows were one-way—you could see in without the things inside seeing out—and that was Nielson's first real sight of the Morgans.

"Eleven of them sitting in the tank together, close together, not moving, not scratching or picking at themselves, not even sleeping or resting, just sitting upright, all of them, arms folded in various positions and eyes partly closed, statuesque, alien even in a setting of their natural bushes and trees. Occasionally one would stretch slightly and a weird ripple would flip down its body, but otherwise there was no movement at all. And even at rest like that, perhaps

243

because of it, they were distinctly ominous. The least of them was seven feet tall. They weighed an average of two hundred pounds, lean and whiplike with gray fur all over them. Short fur, silvery in the light. Their arms were long, out of proportion and three-jointed, which was the only really fundamental difference between their body structure and ours. Their faces were flat nosed and round, the fur on their heads was no longer or different than the rest of their hair, and of course they had no eyebrows or hairline. But what you noticed most, after the long flowing arms, was the eyes. Set deep in the silvery fur like black rubber balls, no pupil, just wide solid balls. A long time after you left you could see those eyes. A long time.

"When Nielson turned I saw he was smiling. Then he saw Maas and he broke into a grin. Maas smiled too, very nicely, the two stood smiling together, Maas cautious and perhaps even now a little worried, Nielson beginning to understand and also beginning to wonder whether or not this was intentional, and so going directly to the point.

" 'Where do they rate on the intelligence scale?' he said, gesturing at the Morgans and still grinning, and Maas said cheerfully, 'Higher than most animals,' although he should have known Nielson had some professional knowledge of animal intelligence, and then somewhat surprised when Nielson wanted to know the exact figure, but saying, still smiling, that the figure was approximately level with that of a dog. And then, as I recall, Nielson did not say anything, but just looked at him for a long while, wondering now for the first time seriously if someone here was trying to put something over on him, and wondering also at the same time if he should say anything about it, and possibly perhaps unable to keep himself from letting this character know that they might be kidding each other, but they weren't kidding him, because then he said, 'Somebody's been kidding you.' And he turned to go, but Maas was not smiling now and stopped him. 'Why, what do you mean?' Shocked, puzzled, wounded, and now also Nielson was not smiling, and he said, 'They're a hell of a lot smarter than dogs.'

"And Maas said, 'You think there's been a mistake?'

"And Nielson said, 'Can't you tell just by looking at them?' And Maas, recovering himself now, said a bit more suavely, 'No, I confess I cannot. But then, undoubtedly, I don't have your natural sensitivity to animals.'

"And Nielson shrugged, annoyed with himself now for

having brought up the obvious and become involved in it, and glanced at me, wishing for me to say something, but until that moment I had been incurious, had not thought, and was useless.

"So Maas said, 'The man who examined them was quite reputable, Mr. Nielson.'

"To which Nielson said stiffly, 'Don't worry about it. Forget I said anything.' And turned to go, but Maas said, 'But this is a very serious business—' to which Nielson replied, 'Not to me it isn't, just so long as it's legal, that's all,' at which point, with a slight nod at me, he went out the door and away, leaving Maas standing somewhat stunned with one hand out like a man reaching for the keys of a piano.

" 'Well,' he said eventually, 'now what do you make of that?' wondering, no doubt, just how much I really did make of it. And I, fumbling, turned to look in at the Morgans, not doubting Maas at all yet, but doubting Nielson certainly, until I looked in and saw the black rubber eyes, and so began the doubt which has lasted from that moment until this day.

"Maas said then, feeling his way, because actually you know he had not been very bright about this, that he knew there were rumors going round, but had not paid them any attention because everyone knew how reports of animals are exaggerated, how just normal cleverness in an animal often seems remarkable, and besides, there was the psychologist's report, and the psychologist was a reputable man. Testing me, you see, and then looking into my eyes and intelligent enough himself at least to see the vague doubt forming there, so bringing himself to say that it was, after all, the question of our right to an entire planet, 'Man's right,' he said, and therefore we must, of course, have the Morgans reexamined. He said that when the first rocketload of immigrants landed next week perhaps there would be a qualified man aboard, and if not we would send for one. And I agreed, was wholly in favor, still in no way suspecting Maas, my mind occupied now with the last alarming question, which was, namely, that Nielson thought the Morgans were intelligent and yet could apparently easily go on killing them."

"And so we entered upon the last few days, during which I found out all I was ever to find out about Nielson, and during which he also found out a great deal about himself.

I went to him and got him to drink with me—no small feat since he was not a drinker—but he had seen the Mapping Command patch on my shoulder and had some small respect for Mapping Command men, and so came with me to learn a few things about the uncharted region of the Rim, although to end by doing most of the talking himself, under the influence of liquor he ought not hold but seemed, at that time, to accept with relish.

"First I wanted to know why he was willing to kill the Morgans if he thought they were intelligent, for though I am no moralist I still am curious what people think about things like that, and he told me without ceremony. Hell, he said, everything is eaten. Everything alive is sooner or later killed and eaten. The big animals are allowed to grow old first, but the end is the same. The only real difference between man and animal, Nielson said, was that man was eaten after he went into the ground, but the animal rarely got that far.

"So there we sat in the beery afternoon—you begin to see him now, yes, he so very grave and so young, so young, not a fool, but simply young. He had given the matter a great deal of thought, that I could see, for when I asked him if he really believed that he said, Well, partly anyway. The point is: sometimes a man can be a magnificent thing. But so also sometimes can an animal. Not all animals, not all men. But then a great many things can be magnificent in different ways, like a mountain is magnificent, or a waterfall, or a big wind. And if it all has no meaning, if there really is Nobody Above who really gives a damn, if there are really no rules, still, a man can make his own rules and with luck he can get by. 'What bothers me most though,' Nielson said, slightly drunk now and brooding, 'is the goddamn blindness of it. A big wind, you see, is not aware of the ships it wrecks, nor is a tiger aware of the body it eats, but you die all the same, and what bothers me most is that you are eventually killed by something that doesn't give a damn. What I would like is to know that when I die I get it from something that has a good reason for it and knows it's me he's killing.'

"And thus Nielson the philosopher. And if that is all nonsense, well, that was three years ago and I still remember it almost word for word, and I put it in here because you cannot understand him without it. And see, in the end, the strange twist we take. Nielson, the woodsman, becomes the cynic, and Maas, the city man, is the idealist. But again,

246

too simple, too simple. For deep down in Nielson, under the fragile outward layer which reasoned and saw much too much hate and waste and injustice, much deeper down in the region which knew the beauty of a leaf and a stormy sky, down so deep that Nielson himself was not aware of it, was something . . ."

"But I philosophize," George said wearily. "Let me get on with it. Listen carefully now. The sun is going down and we'll kill him soon. I would like you to know before we kill him. Watch how the rest of it happens and tell me then why.

"The rocket came and Nielson went back into the woods. There was no qualified man on the rocket to examine the Morgans so Maas sent for one, yet also let Nielson go kill the few remaining.

"And then, when Nielson was gone a week, a strange thing happened, oh, an odd, unfortunate, annoying thing. Such a time for it to happen too, because Nielson had just sent in several bodies by plane and informed Maas that there were only two left, and that he had them pinned down and would get them certainly by the end of the week. On that same day, in the evening, new atmosphere was given to the eleven Morgans in the tank. Curiously, it turned out that by a rare error someone mistook a tank of chlorine for a tank of oxygen—it was lying in the same rack with all the other oxygen tanks—and this man did not notice and so fed chlorine to the Morgans, who all strangled in a very short time. All eleven. It was not noticed until the next morning, because the Morgans did not move much anyway, but by that time it was much too late and none of them ever moved again. And Maas was greatly shaken when he heard of it, was he not? because racial murder is a very serious thing, and immediately he sent out word to find Nielson before he killed the last two.

"But Nielson was half a continent away.

"That same evening Nielson shot one of them as it came down to the river to drink. He shot it from a perch in a thick thorn bush across the way, in which he had been sitting for almost three days. During all that time he had not moved out of the bush, but sat waiting with diabolical patience while the last two Morgans, undoubtedly in a state of panic now, tried to sense him or get some sign of him. At last they thought he was gone, or at least not in the area, and they came out of hiding to drink at the stream. That was when Nielson got one of them. But the shot was from a long way off, and the Morgan had been careful to drink from a sheltered place, so it was not immediately fatal. The Morgan moved away as quickly as it could, plainly hit. The other seemed to be helping it. Nielson left the thorn bush and began to track them.

"It kept coming into his mind then, as it had kept coming to him during the three days in the thorn bush, that if you thought about this in the right light it was a dirty business. The two Morgans were sticking together. For some reason that bothered him. The unwounded one could easily have gotten away while Nielson trailed the other, could even circle around behind and try to get him from the rear. Yet the two stuck together, making it easy for him. He found himself wishing they would break up.

"They were moving to the north. He wondered where they were heading. He was between them and the only real cover, a marsh to the west. He supposed that they would try to double back. It was already quite murky in the woods, so he slipped his night lenses on, pressing forward silently and cautiously but very quickly, keeping his mind clear of everything but the hunt. He wondered how badly the one was hit, then began finding blood and knew. Pretty bad. And moving like that the Morgan would keep bleeding. Well, by morning he should end it. And then get off this planet for good. Go somewhere else and hunt things with tentacles. Maybe not hunt at all for a while. Maybe marry Jen Wolke. Have a home to go to and someone to talk to at night . . .

"All night long the two Morgans dragged on into the north, with Nielson closing in steadily behind. Early in the morning they began to climb, reaching the first line of low mountains, and then Nielson knew they would try to find a high rocky place where he would have to come at them from below. He quickened his pace, slowly passed them in the night, knowing where they were by little far-off movements. When daylight came he was well ahead of them, up in the high cold country, beginning to feel unnaturally tired now and wondering how in hell the wounded Morgan could keep it up, looking for a good place from which to get them as they passed.

"By eight o'clock he had figured the path they would take. He found a dark narrow place on a ledge between two boulders and wedged himself in. It was very cold and he was not dressed for it. He sat for a long while with his

248

hand tucked in his armpit to keep the trigger finger warm and supple. At last he heard them coming.

"The wounded Morgan was breathing heavily. Nielson heard it a long way off. Then he heard a clatter in the rocks and thought they'd seen him and were trying to run away, so he peered out.

"But the two of them were in the open, perhaps fifty yards away, and they had not seen him. The wounded one had fallen, which was what made the clatter, and lay now on its back while the other bent over, talking to it. Talking to it.

"Quickly, not thinking, making a special effort to bring the rifle to his shoulder slowly, icily, Nielson aimed and sighted and pressed the trigger, but the trigger wouldn't pull. He was suddenly dizzy, swore at himself. He bore down on his hand, on his mind. The gun went off. The kneeling one jerked, then fell across the other one. Although Nielson's hands had been trembling the shot was clean. When he reached them both Morgans were dead.

"He stood for a long while looking down, feeling very odd, very quiet and dazed. The one underneath, which he had wounded the night before, was a female. Nielson felt a cold wind begin to blow in his brain. The female had been with child.

"He sat down on a rock, rested his head in his hands. He sat there for a long while. When it began to snow he put out his hand and watched the flakes melt on his palm.

"The snow began coating the dead Morgans. Eventually they were completely covered and Nielson was able to leave. He did not take them with him. He wanted to go somewhere quickly and take a bath . . ."

"Oh my Lord," the psychologist said.

"Yes," George said. "He came back and they were all dead. All the Morgans. All of them. Racial murder. But even before he knew that he was already damned. He told me all about it on the plane coming in. He did not blame himself, he said. How could you break the rules when there were no rules? He said what he was feeling now was probably something left over from his childhood, something childlike and virtuous they had put in him when he was young but which he knew amounted to nothing and which he would certainly easily get over. And then I had to tell him about the other Morgans, the dead Morgans, the last eleven all dead, and when he heard that he sat with his hands shaking until we got back to the city, and then he left me and went to Maas's office and killed him with his bare hands."

The psychologist bowed his head.

"So he put the blame on Maas. He had to put it somewhere. He knew that Maas and he had done it and in killing Maas unconsciously punished them both, for he made it necessary then, inevitable then, that we should come after him and kill him too. But he could not face his own guilt and his huge sad terrible pride would not let him quit, so he destroyed Maas, really destroyed him, and then went back into the woods. We came after him. He fought back. Maybe he thought that in this way he was for a while at least taking the Morgans' place. Or maybe after the event he was cold and realistic about it and realized there was nothing else to do. But the point was that he could not admit to himself what he had done. It was all his parents' fault, or Maas's, or God's, that such a rage should be in him, but not his own. And yet always, always, always running through the dark trees he knew, *he knew* it was wrong. And so will die knowing, God help him, unclean, unclean, and yet in the end of him somehow magnificent, if wrong before God and man then wrong all the way, all the last bloody way down to the futile tragic last second of his life—heroic, damn it, no matter which way you look at it, taking on a whole planet with no hope of winning, knowing the end is a bullet or a burn, a bullet or a burn . . ."

The two men sat silently in the hot red glare of the dying sun. A little while later there was a single shot from the rocks near them and someone cried exultantly, "Got him!" and there was a scramble down to the river.

George and the psychologist rose and went down, found Nielson lying face down in the water, the blond hair long and dirty and bloody. His back was pink and bare, because when he had come out into the open he had taken his shirt off before going into the water. He was already dead. Even in death he was still very big.

AUTHOR'S AFTERWORD

In the spring of '51 I was a student at Rutgers and I took a course in "creative writing," and I remember clearly that I wrote "All the Way Back" while sitting all night in a small kitchen, my feet propped up on the door of the refrigerator, writing on a notebook in my lap. Wrote with true excitement, wandering around in the new world. I gave it to the professor, an elderly chap named Twiss, and three weeks later he gave it back to me, looking down on me with sad distaste, and he said: "Please don't write this sort of thing. Write *literature.*"

I read the story over and changed a word or two, and mailed it off to *Astounding,* and on May 29, 1951, I came home from class to find a letter in the mailbox from John Campbell, offering the cataclysmic total of $209.70. I flew upstairs that day: a day to remember. Twenty-five years later I chanced into a bookstore in Cape Town, South Africa, picked up a hardback anthology by Brian Aldiss, and saw there, in a book, twenty-five years later, "All the Way Back." That story has given me some pretty fine moments.

At about that time I met a young sf writer, just beginning, and his main advice was: "Write one new story every week. One a week. You want to survive, turn 'em out." And so he did, for a while, turn out one a week. I never could. I had the story only by thinking for a long while, because for a long while there were only fragments, pieces of scenery, blotches of dialogue, and then, one day, the door would open, and I'd wander on in—happily, I must say, happily—and there would be the live world of that story, and I'd be in there till it was over. I've had many ideas, over the years, which are still there, behind the door, which is not yet open. That's the way it has always worked. When the idea is ready, you know it. There come the labor pains. But if it isn't ready, there's no point in sitting at the typewriter. Result: I never made much money, never supported myself writing. Don't think now I ever will. Eh.

Some friends were chatting one day, at school, and happened to mention the difference in tides caused by the moon—tide at the Bay of Fundy being so huge, tide in Maine much higher than Florida, etc. That same day I had been reading about the moons of Jupiter and got to wonder about the tide *there,* and then, with all those moons—a dozen?—what would happen if and when they came conjunct? Boy, what a hell of a tide. So I wandered off and drove the car, thinking, and there was a planet with four large moons, an ocean, and when the moons were conjunct: boom, a monstrous tide, and evolution therefore gave "Grenville's Planet." It turned out to be probably the most popular short sf story I ever wrote. It was reprinted over and over again. And it was an idea that came in, a vision of that watery world, that brought with it, and always has, a fine delighted feeling.

"The Ophans" was the original title, there was no "Void." The world of the lonely robot. Can't explain where it came from, except perhaps my own view of the parable of men, as Nietzsche once put it: God is dead. In this case, he really is. Problem: how do you explain it to that poor metallic thinker at the end? Had to leave that alone. Has no end, I guess. Not much character in it either. But that was only the second story I wrote, and I admit I didn't know much about characterization—or anything else. Certainly not myself.

"Soldier Boy" was fun to write. Truly. That day I slipped into the mind of that Alien I'll always remember. I was the Thing from Outside. Oh, a charming day. Especially charming to nail him at the end. After "The Orphans," this was truly fun.

"The Book" on the other hand . . . This was the only time I ever, in all thirty years of writing, got a little smashed with good Scotch while writing. You may begin to notice, friend, that I write about damaged people. But of all the words I've written in thirty years, I remember first of all these words from that Bible: "seek not redemption, for thou hast not sinned. And let the Gods come unto *thee.*" And so I lived, guiltless. But . . . the Gods never came.

"Wainer." Evolution and genetics, and the equality of man. All my life I go stumbling along with no message and no meaning, and yet always behind each day there is a sensation of pattern, of a path going somewhere, in which I've never been able to disbelieve. Wainer was hope, I guess. Which led to the novel, *The Herald*.

"Citizen Jell." Friend of mine, outraged, told me that one day he saw this on TV, exactly this story, which no one had bought from me or ever even suggested buying. Only thing changed he said, was the ending, where Jell was told to come back to the place where he was *king*. Future, advanced society where he was *king*. Not plagiarism, there, of course, not if he was king. Totally different, if he was king. I never met the guy who stole it. Lucky fella.

"Death of a Hunter." This was the one that was real work. I moved off into that world with Nielson and was there a long time. It began only as a vague idea about following certain professions into the future, and so I followed hunting, and suddenly it was game control on an alien planet, and then the game was intelligent, and the rest was snowy. Very little I wrote has ever moved me as much as being with Nielson when he killed those two in the mountains. I felt, for the first time in my writing life, that maybe I was growing up, and maybe I'd done something truly worth doing, and I mailed it off to H. L. Gold, at *Galaxy*, and he mailed it back with an apology. He said this kind of story wasn't for his readers—too serious, too gloomy. I remember that shook me a bit. I got it back from Campbell, and then *F&SF*, with no comment. I remember thinking, but this may be the best I've ever done. But nobody took it. Finally it sold to *Fantastic Universe*, for—as I recall—$75.

Later that year H. L. Gold was definitely feeling a bit guilty. He wrote me a note offering me $2,000 for any science fiction novel I had in mind, no matter what the idea. But I was beginning to drift away from sf then, and didn't write the novel, because there was none there. I wrote "Come to My Party."

That was the first one based upon something that happened to me. I did fight a guy once who boxed, but couldn't hit, and I nailed him in the fifth round of a six-round fight, and he went down but got up, and I never caught him again, and for the rest of my life have known that he won on the rules, but he would never have won in natural life, in a fight in a bar, and that wounded the pride, I think, for about twenty years, until this story showed up. And so I lived it through to the end it should have had.

"Peeping Tom Patrol" was also based almost exactly on something that happened in my days as a cop, on the St. Pete, Florida, Police Dept. But well, I won't tell you who.

"Opening Up Slowly"—the title was "Romeo and Son," and the editors at *Redbook* changed it, as they often did, wrongly. This story was written after I had the serious motorcycle accident, in '72, that near killed me, and I wrote it and mailed it off to Scott Meredith, who mailed it back saying it was unsalable. I knew that if it was unsalable I was loose in the trees, so I mailed it off to *Redbook* myself, and they accepted it, a new editor there not knowing I'd already had about fifteen stories in Redbook, welcoming me as a new writer. This is truly funny—sometimes. So I let them have it, and it's been reprinted ever since. I saw one copy in Dutch. So I was a bit reassured by this one. And ended Scott Meredith.

"Border Incident" is, in truth, occurring on the border between Syria and Jordan, where I stopped once, just before sunset, years ago, out in No Man's Land. I did stop for quite a while (the novel, "The Broken Peace," covers this same ground.)

"The Dark Angel." The title came from words used, in this situation, by my son, and this was too religious an idea, and nobody would print it at first, and this was the main reason I began to back away from magazines, just as "Death of a Hunter" pushed me out of sf. Even after the Pulitzer I gave this to *Redbook,* and they wanted me to change it by telling the dear reader what was wrong with the father, so the dear reader wouldn't worry too much. Which I thought would ruin the story of the mysterious, terrifying world of a little boy. Also, they wanted the right to change the title, and I thought it was about time to stop that. The title comes also in a poem by Ernest Dowson written around 1880, and is in the public domain, but *Redbook* wouldn't bend, and neither would *Good Housekeeping,* so I said the hell with it and refused to sell it, first time, me now becoming an irascible old man. But I like this very much the way it is, and I no longer need the magazine, and hope somebody else likes it.

"Starface." I was at work on Shakespeare and in the world of play-acting—all the world's a stage—and for many reasons I began to examine the acting around me, which I had never truly understood, and slowly began to realize, from a girl who wanted to be "taken as I am," that I couldn't, or rather, wouldn't take her as she was. And the question of *what* she was, and what she *seemed* to be, became for a while there quite startling. I was on the road up from the Cape of Good Hope, where I'd just been talking to a surgeon who was working on a friend, when this idea occurred to me, that the changing of the face can mean the changing of the man, in a way I had never truly grasped, and it delighted me so much I stopped at a roadside cafe—the Pavillon—off Sea Point, and wrote this in a notebook.

THE BEST AUTHORS.
THEIR BEST STORIES.

Pocket Books presents a continuing series of very special collections.